ONE NIGHT STAND

BETTY SHAFER

Outskirts Press, Inc.
Denver, Colorado

This is a work of fiction. The events and characters described herein are imaginary and are not intended to refer to specific places or living persons. The opinions expressed in this manuscript are solely the opinions of the author and do not represent the opinions or thoughts of the publisher.

Outskirts Press, Inc.
http://www.outskirtspress.com

ISBN: 978-1-4327-2478-8

PRINTED IN THE UNITED STATES OF AMERICA

Acknowledgement

To the many writer friends and teachers who have helped me along the way to finishing this novel, belongs my gratitude forever. Sheila Bender, poet, essayist, Writing It Real in Port Townsend, (writingitreal.com); Jessica Barksdale Inclan, novelist, UCLA instructor (jessicabarksdaleinclan.com); Caroline Leavitt, novelist, essayist, UCLA instructor (carolineleavitt.com), and the Writing It Real instructors Meg Files, novelist and teacher, Jack Heffron, editor and teacher, and poet Susan Rich; each has enriched my writing in some way.

From Quack Lawyers, Quack Doctors, Quack Preachers,
Mad Dogs and yellow fever, good Lord, deliver us.
Farmers Almanac 1809

Prologue

Belle 1946

The Greyhound waiting room is empty except for me and the man behind the counter. He's tall and gangly, like a teenage basketball star. But his voice is deep and gravely.

"Where to, young lady?"

I rise up on my toes and look over his shoulder. I study the blackboard behind him. Scribbled in chalk is the information I need. The next bus leaving is to Los Angeles.

"Los Angeles, please, sir."

I think he's looking at me kind of funny when I pay for the ticket. So I force a smile and say, "I'm going to visit my Granny."

Does he think it's strange that I don't have a suitcase?

"My things were sent ahead," I say. "My Ma doesn't want me to lose them." I pick up my little bag and hitch it onto my shoulder. "She had to go on to work now."

His face becomes more relaxed and he asks, "Name, please?"

"Belle. Belle Carter Williams." He writes it on the ticket.

I take a seat on the far side of the waiting room, under a miner's mural. I think, *maybe my life isn't as hard as the life of those men.* They're emerging from a cave in the side of the mountain, wearing hard hats and carrying lunch pails. It's the look on their faces, though, that makes me pause. Their faces are drawn, weary-looking, as if they've been beaten. I see that look on our neighbor, Mr. Sounder, when he comes home from working the mine. I saw it many times on my Daddy's face, even though he wasn't a miner.

The clerk is looking at me again. I'm afraid he's going to pick up the phone and call the police any minute. But I'm forty miles from home and I don't think they know I'm gone yet. They'll find out that I bought a ticket to Nashville at the Greyhound station in Bear Creek, but not for awhile. The Greyhound window in the drug store only opens when a bus is due and I took the last one of the day.

I'm shaking all over and can't seem to stop. The bench where I sit is hard and my bare legs stick to it. Even in the heat my stomach feels like a block of ice.

The clerk looks at me from across the room, and says, "Are you all right?"

I don't answer. I just get up and go into the rest room. I splash cold water on my face. The roll-out towel is dirty so I dry my face on my shirt. I open the stall door and sit on the toilet and cry, hoping I can't be heard in the waiting room. I don't know what to do but I know that I don't want to go to jail. I just sit there, drying my eyes and reading the handwritten scrawls on the wall "Kilroy was here." "Mary loves Steve forever;" "Josie fucks anyone," followed by a phone number. I take out a pen and write, "Belle was here but not for long."

I get up from the toilet and wash my hands, dry them on my shirt again. I take a seat in the waiting room facing a big window with my back to the clerk. He has turned aside, writing something in his books. Three more people have come into the room. I look around but they don't seem to notice me.

I watch the gray-haired man and woman inspect their tickets; hold them close to their glasses and squint. They remind me of my Granny and Grandpa. I wish I had known them better. I think of how much they loved me and how I just did whatever I wanted without considering them. I want to go to the phone and hear Granny say, "How's my angel?" But I can't; they're dead now.

A man of maybe thirty with a GI haircut and a duffel bag at his side sits in the next row of seats He is gazing out the window and rubbing his hands together as if he's washing them.

A woman comes through the door with a young boy. The boy is blond and blue-eyed. He must be eight or nine years old. He looks around, wide-eyed. They walk to the ticket window and the clerk raises his head from his books. The boy looks so much like my brother when he was a kid that I stare at him. He catches me looking at him and I wave. He waves back. His mother grabs his hand and takes him to a seat.

I was six and my brother was nine when his Aunt Mary came and took him away. I watched as he climbed into the front seat of the old Ford, squeezing his cousin Jack closer to his mother. Ma lifted his box of clothes into the truck bed and sighed. Then she slammed the truck door shut. She said, "Bye now, Jesse. Be good, you hear?"

Jesse turned and rolled down the window. He looked at me, his eyes wet, his left hand in a slow wave. I waved, too, and looked at him. Through my tears he seemed like a blurred snapshot.

The truck pulled away and I ran after it until I could no longer see it in the cloud of dust. I wandered back and sat under the weeping willow tree. Ma came and dragged me into the house. I shut the door to my room and cried for days. Nothing that Ma said could make me stop.

The bus will be here in twenty minutes. I look at the woman with the young boy. She raises her eyes from her book and smiles at the boy. I wish I had a mother like her.

Ma and I haven't talked much lately, except for her telling me I should be nicer to Bart. For my fifteenth birthday six months ago she didn't even have a party for me.

"You're grown up now and parties are for little kids," she said. Her fingers drummed the table as she talked. She's been nervous lately and her headaches come more often. She looked out the window, and then back at me "Why don't you go to Alice's house and spend the day with her?"

I thought she probably wanted me out of the house for her Bible study group. I didn't mind. It gave me the chance to avoid my stepfather.

I did go to Alice's house on my birthday. Then we walked two miles down the path through Bear Holler woods to the cabin my Daddy built. My brother left his Aunt Mary's house and moved into the cabin when he turned eighteen, six months ago. His cousin Jack moved in with him when he came back from the war. Their friend Tennessee was there so much that he finally moved in, too. Then Dave, Jack's buddy from the Army, came to join them. So there were four of them jammed into the cabin. They formed a band called One Night Stand.

I've seen them a lot the last few months. I guess I was trying to make up for all the time Jesse and I were apart. Ma and Bart don't like it but I go anyhow. The guys let me sing with them when they practice. Jesse says that I can join the band when I'm eighteen.

Now it might never happen. Maybe I'll never see him again.

Ma sent Jesse away when our Daddy died. She said, now that he was an orphan, he was better off with his mother's sister. I didn't see why he would be better off. He hardly knew his Aunt Mary. He was with my Ma for seven years and she always said how she was his mother when she married our Daddy. So how come she didn't act like his mother.

Tears spill onto my cheeks, but no one in the station looks at me. The clerk is still bent over his books. The gray-haired couple is deep in conversation. The man is pointing to the miner mural on the far wall. The woman pats his shoulder twice; so tenderly that it makes my throat feel tight. The quiet man is still staring out the window, eyes half shut. The boy is playing with a toy car and his mother is reading her book.

I wipe my face with the sleeve of my shirt. More people are coming through the door and lining up in front of the clerk. A wave of fear crashes over me every time another person comes into the room.

Where I sit, the window is smudged and dirty. I keep looking for the bus. It seems like it will never come. I shift my weight, bracing myself with my hands on the bench seat. Someone has stuck gum under the bench and my fingers pull back in disgust. In the doorway, I see a big man surveying the room with intense dark eyes, and my stomach does a flip-flop. But he goes to the ticket counter and I see that it isn't Black Bart.

Yesterday, my room was really hot. I was changing into my shorts when Bart knocked just once before opening the door.

"You're not wearing those shorts. They're way too skimpy." His voice was so loud it hurt my ears. My fingers were shaking and I could hardly button my shorts.

I looked up. My stepfather's big frame filled the doorway. Every time I saw him my heart thumped in my chest and my breath stopped. Bart had lots of black hair and it was so thick it sat on his head like a hat, no matter how much he tried to slick it down. His eyes were deep-set; cold and dark His lips lay in a thin wide line that looked like it was pasted on his face. He was wearing a black suit and his white Reverend collar

"The Bible says a woman should dress modestly." His bushy black brows frowned and almost met above his nose. "Those shorts are not modest, so change them." He folded his arms across his chest.

"I won't. You're not my father. You can't tell me what to do." I decided right then that he wouldn't bully me anymore.

He hesitated; seemed surprised. "You will. As long as I'm the head of this house you will do as I say." The heavy brows raised and deep lines formed on his forehead.

"Ma will let me wear them." I edged toward the door but he was blocking the way.

I called out, "Ma?"

"Your mother is not here."

I felt my throat closing. We were alone. Usually I manage to get out of the house when Ma is gone but this time she didn't tell me she was leaving.

"Where is she?" I willed my voice not to quiver.

"At Marj's Beauty Shop, getting her hair done. She said about three hours." He sounded smug and confident.

I said, "I have to go. Alice is waiting for me."

He smiled and took hold of my shoulders. His hands felt rough and tight, like a vise. My eyes searched the room for a way out, but he blocked the only exit.

"Come on, Belle, you know I love you." His voice was

soft, the harshness gone. "I want what's best for you. Come, give me a hug." I had avoided him for a long time but I was finally trapped. His hand was rough on my left breast and his lips wet my cheek.

I thought, *maybe it was time to tell Ma about him. Now that I'm older I don't believe that God speaks to him or that God wants us to be together.* But I do still believe that it would break Ma's heart if she knew. We have our differences but she is still my mother. And like she says, blood is thicker than water.

Bart's hands were all over me, groping, on my stomach and pushing into my shorts. I brought my right knee up hard into his balls. He groaned, bent over and grabbed his groin with both hands, letting me go. But he still blocked the door. His eyes looked hard into my face, wide with surprise. What was I thinking; now he'll be angry enough to hit me like he did the first time I tried to stop him. I backed away, sweat dripped into my eyes and I shuddered. My legs felt like they would collapse and throw me onto the ground.

"Hello, where is everyone?" Ma's voice echoed through the parlor. I felt weak with relief. Bart stepped backwards, dropping his arms to his side as if they had touched hot coals. The way was clear so I walked fast out the bedroom door. I lowered my eyes so she couldn't see the fear.

"Marj's boy broke his arm and she couldn't keep our appointment. Now my hair will be a mess all week." Her voice was loud and angry sounding. She fluffed her hair with her fingers.

"Hi, Ma, I'm just on my way to Alice's."

She didn't answer so I looked up. She was staring at Bart who stood in the doorway of my bedroom.

"Nadine, tell Belle she cannot wear those shorts. She has defied me once again." He looked composed, his voice sincere and pleading.

Ma looked at me, mouth open. I turned and glared at Bart. I thought *here's one he can't get out of. She sees that he was in my room.*

Then he walked over to Ma, put his arm around her and kissed her cheek.

"I just closed the window in Belle's room. I know it's hot, but the flies are coming in."

Ma smiled at him, then turned to me. "Belle, the Reverend is right. You need to change your clothes."

I stared at them both for a moment. *God, he's slick.* Silence hung in the air.

"Not likely," I said. I let the front door slam behind me.

Last night I saw Bart at the church dance, sponsoring and preaching. Ma was home with a headache. He looked at me and frowned. I stared back. Alice caught my look; followed my eyes to his face. Then the bastard smiled and waved. He actually smiled. As soon as Alice went to the bathroom, I left the dance.

I wander back into the bathroom. Better go before the bus gets here. The bathroom lights are flickering. I look like someone in an old time movie. My face in the mirror looks tired and drawn, like those miners in the picture. My hair is stringy and dull, the color of river water on a cloudy day.

This morning, Sheriff McMahan came to tell Ma that her husband was dead. My mother married Bart six years ago. When he couldn't hear me I called him Black Bart. Even though I was only nine, I knew there was something wrong with him.

They didn't know I was listening in my bedroom. I heard the Sheriff asking for me. He told Ma that once I said I would kill my stepfather if he didn't leave me alone. This is true; I did say that. Who could blame me if they knew the truth about him? But I'm not going to jail. I'm not.

I return to my seat just as the overhead speakers announce the bus's arrival. It's that time in the evening when the sun has set but it's not yet dark. The lights come on in the waiting room. I stand and turn towards the door. The man behind the counter raises his head and smiles at me. I try to smile back but I just can't. Instead I follow the others outside and climb the bus's metal steps. I feel nauseated when the exhaust fumes hit me. A breeze cools my legs. They're sticky from sitting on the bench.

I hand my ticket to the driver who takes it without looking at me. Then I walk the length of the bus past the seats full of people. I can tell that some of them have been on the bus for a long time. Their eyes are bleary and they look tired. The new arrivals settle into their seats and stow their belongings.

Finally I reach the very back, behind the Negro section, and sit down on the wide empty seat. A Negro woman gets up to give me her seat, closer to the front. I shake my head and she looks at the bus driver, who is adjusting his seat. She sits down again. The lights dim and the bus pulls out of the station.

Black Bart is dead and I killed him.

Part One

The elements that produce the rural sound are vanishing. No one ever again will sound like the performers of the early period. The factors that contributed to the vocal style of performers such as the Carter Family or the Blue Sky Boys were not synthetic commercial creations. These styles were the result of complex and deeply ingrained mores and behavior patterns bred by the rural southern environment.

If one would preserve the rural musical styles he would also preserve the culture that gave rise to them, a society characterized by cultural isolation, racism, poverty, ignorance and religious fundamentalism. It is doubtful whether anyone would seriously suggest a return to such a society despite the simplicity and sentimental attraction such a society might hold.

Bill C. Malone, Country Music Historian

Chapter 1

Bear Holler, Tennessee 1928

Emma Sue was sitting in her favorite chair by the front window when she felt a familiar dull pain in the small of her back. A tiny foot kicked her ribs and she grabbed it through the skin of her belly and pulled it gently from under her rib cage. She shifted her weight to the other side of the chair. She gazed again out the window and up the path that led to the road. She told herself that Josh would be home soon.

A pale winter sun hovered on the horizon, and then dropped behind the willow tree. It cast long shadows on the cabin walls. She watched a small ground squirrel scurry across the frozen dirt. He stopped now and then and raised his twitching nose to the cold evening breeze.

When at last she left the seat by the window, the sun had plummeted below the horizon and darkness shrouded the path and the tree. The air inside was chill and she struck a wooden match to light the kindling in the cook stove. She struck another and lit the kerosene lamp. She set the lamp on the kitchen table and opened the back door. A cool breeze chased her down the path from the kitchen to the well. She carried a wooden bucket that held a little water for priming the pump. Once she stopped and waited for a crushing pain in her pelvis to go away. Then she pumped cold water from deep in the earth and carried the heavy bucket to the stand that sat beside the back door. She was sweating in spite of the cold.

She shuffled from one side of the cabin to the other; from the parlor to the kitchen, then back again. She paused once to take a sip of cool water from the gourd in the water bucket. She was dipping water and scooping coffee into the old enamel coffee pot when she heard the front door open, then a soft whistle. Laughing with relief, she put the coffee pot on the stove and rushed to meet Josh at the front door.

"It's the baby, Josh, he's coming early."

Josh let out a whoop and tossed his battered hat to the ceiling.

"Josh," she said, "go get Aunt Ellie. I don't think we have much time."

He kissed her cheek, retrieved his hat from the ground, and started across the hills in a dead run to fetch the mid-wife.

When Josh decided to build himself a cabin, long before he married Emma Sue, he thought long and hard about where it should be. He knew he wanted to be close to the river, but not so close that he would worry about his future children falling into it. He wanted to look out his window and see trees, and fields of grass. And he certainly didn't want to be in Bear Creek town.

Bear Creek's population was only 3,000 but that was too crowded for Josh. Still, he reasoned, he needed to be close enough that shopping would be fairly easy when he needed a new pair of overalls or staples like flour and sugar. What if his future wife needed some dry goods to make a dress? There wouldn't be enough money for a train trip but there was a dry goods store in Bear Creek.

So he chose the small community of Bear Holler, population maybe 500 souls. He built his home with three small bedrooms to accommodate the children that would come. It took much longer to build than a one room cabin, which would have been more than adequate for him. But Josh liked to look ahead, and plan for the future.

Bear Holler was so small that you could drive your buggy down the main dirt road and pass the whole town before the horses broke into a trot. And, it was only two miles from Bear Creek. He thought Bear Holler was perfect.

He first saw Emma Sue at the church dance on a Saturday night. He knew the Scroggins lived down the road from his cabin, but he'd not seen Emmy before. She dropped out of school early, while Josh managed to finish grade school and even a year of high school. He vaguely remembered her as a gawky ten year old and he, seven years her senior, had not found her memorable. But at fifteen she had blossomed into a shy, winsome, pretty girl. He couldn't take his eyes off her. They danced every dance together, under her father's frowning stare.

Two weeks later he managed to take her away from her chores long enough to show her his cabin. He thinks it was the cabin that sold her on marrying him. Her Daddy gave his permission for her to marry when he learned she was with child. There was no doubt in the years that followed, that Emma Sue loved Josh. And he loved her beyond all reason.

Josh raced across frozen fields of brown dirt patched

with snow, through the woods with trees barren of their leaves, over desolate hills aching for the summer sun.

He thought of Emma Sue's face, more beautiful than ever since being with child. He thought of how her hair, soft as corn silk, brushed his cheek when she bent to kiss him. He thought of the touch of her hand, how it still thrilled him. How all he could think about while he worked the fields was how soon he could come home to her.

Last night Emmy reached for his hand and pressed it on her swollen belly to feel the baby move. He marveled once again at the feel of the human being they had created together.

"He's so impatient, Josh. If I sit where it's not comfortable for him, he really lets me have it. This one knows what he wants."

"How do you know it's a boy?" Josh teased.

"I just know. He's special, Josh, he hasn't quit moving since the quickening. Anxious to get here, he is, like he doesn't want to be cooped up for long."

"Well, if it's a girl I bet you keep her anyhow." He rubbed her belly.

"It isn't a girl. It's a boy; I know it." Her face flushed and her voice was soft in the southern way. "Josh, let's have a girl next. Right away. I'll be thirty next week, you know, and we need to finish up a family before I get too old."

He smiled and ruffled her hair, then smoothed it from her face. "Maybe we better wait awhile. It's a lot of work for you."

"I don't mind. I really don't, Josh. I want a little girl. I want to make her dresses and comb her hair into pigtails. And I can teach her to cook and sew. You can show her how to milk the cows, and ride horses. And you can teach her to play music. And she'll have a big brother to look after her. I even know her name. We'll call her Belle."

Emma Sue dropped slowly onto the soft feather bed and fell into a light sleep. The lamp burning on the kitchen table cast an eerie glow into the bedroom. Water simmered in the coffee pot but the untended fire was nearly out. She lay half asleep, half awake, thinking and dreaming.

The night she became pregnant she laid longer than usual in Josh's arms. She felt especially close to him that night. Their lovemaking had been surprising, unplanned, in a bed of sweet-smelling hay under a round white moon. Earlier Josh and Emma wandered through their woods and fields, talking and laughing. They planned which crops to plant the following year. At dusk they paused to watch catfish swimming along the river banks.

Then they walked slowly toward the cabin. A mound of fresh raked hay stood near the cabin door. Like two children cut loose from their chores, they ran and jumped into it. Emma threw a handful of grass down the back of Josh's shirt; he picked her up and threw her into the pile. She, spitting out hay, grabbed his leg and wrestled him back to the ground. Soon they were kissing and hugging.

Lying quietly on the soft hay, Josh snoring beside her, Emma knew as some women do when they are caught that she was pregnant. She rose up on one elbow and told herself she was lucky to have a strong man like Josh to look after her. She brushed his dark hair with her hand and he stirred, opened his eyes and she thought how she loved the way he looked at her with those deep-set warm brown eyes.

Her eyes flew open with a start and she cried out in pain as a crushing force pushed the baby towards her pelvis. How long had she been asleep? She rose up on one elbow to look at the ticking clock on the dresser. Only 7:30. Josh had left 20 minutes ago, it was 30 minutes to where Aunt Ellie lived, she reckoned, maybe less the way Josh was running, and another 45 minutes back. Aunt Ellie wasn't as fast as Josh. She pushed away the thought that they might not be back in time. But deep down she knew. She would have her baby alone.

She fell back onto the bed. She thought of Josh. He was a good man and she loved him. She married him when she was fifteen. They had three boys, one every year. Two died at birth and one caught pneumonia at age seven months and died within a week.

At age 29, thinking she would never have another child, she was pregnant again.

She drifted off again and dreamed of a large white figure with thin arms and flowing robes holding a baby in front of her, offering and then withdrawing the tiny figure. An even larger, dark and fearsome giant with green eyes chased the white figure back and forth, hissing at her. No, it was the coffee pot hissing and sputtering on the stove.

She awakened to the pain in her pelvis, sharp and insistent and much more intense. She thought she should go move the coffee pot from the stove. But then if the fire light was fading and nearly out, maybe it was okay to leave it. A stronger pain yet forced her back onto the bed.

Josh and Aunt Ellie heard the baby's angry cries as they rounded the willow tree. Damn, Josh thought, we're too late. She must be scared to death. The heavy aroma of burned coffee permeated the air and the room was getting cold. The fire burned low, nearly out. Aunt Ellie grabbed the lamp from the kitchen table and headed for the bedroom, leaving Josh to feel around the kitchen for another. She pulled the heavy curtain closed behind her. Josh took the coffee pot off the stove with a towel after lighting another lamp. He rinsed out the pot and drew fresh water inside and then put it back on the stove. He rekindled the fire and the room began to warm. He wanted to see his wife, hold her, but he knew that he, the husband, was barred from the birthing room until his wife and baby were tended to.

Aunt Ellie opened the curtain at last, cradling Josh's new son in a blanket he had warmed by the stove. She sat down in a chair close to Josh and lifted the blanket so he could see.

Josh thought he was handsome. He had a smattering of blond curly hair topping a face much like his mother's. His perfectly formed nose topped a rosebud mouth that still seemed masculine. White membrane clung to his face but his head was round, not cone-shaped like so many newborns. It was the result of his quick entry into the world. Josh touched his cheek with cold fingers. The baby squirmed and opened his eyes. Josh smiled.

Then he looked at Aunt Ellie and his smile froze at something he saw there. She wouldn't meet his eyes. She rocked the child in her arms and squeezed her eyes shut.

"What's wrong?" his voice was shaking. "Aunt Ellie, what's wrong? Is there something wrong with the baby?"

"He's a healthy boy, Josh," she replied, looking at him. "He's got all his fingers and toes. Weighs at least seven pounds, I'll wager. And he's strong, got broad shoulders too. He'll be a big help to you on the farm."

Josh laughed softly, his dark eyes sparking in the glow of the lamp.

"Emma Sue says he's not going to be a farmer. She's crazy on the subject. But you know what? Sometimes I think she's got a gift for seeing the future. "She knew when her brother was going to die, even though he was healthy as a horse." He looked at his son. "She picked out his name already…Jesse."

But Aunt Ellie sat quietly, watching the baby close his eyes again. "Josh, I have to tell you…" Her voice broke. She carried the child to the cradle and laid him down.

"Emma Sue," Josh whispered. The midwife raised her eyes to his and he knew. He grabbed her shoulders with strong hands and shook her. "Is Emma Sue all right?"

She shook her head. Josh ran into the bedroom where his wife lay cold and still. Her pale face reflected how much blood she lost. He took her hand and rubbed it in his, but it stayed cold. "Emmy, Emmy," he moaned, "Wake up, wake up."

His wails echoed through the cabin; for how long he didn't know. When he was still at last, Aunt Ellie came into the room.

"I should have stayed with her," he said. He brushed a lock of hair from Emma Sue's forehead.

"There's nothing you could have done, Josh. Nothing. The afterbirth came first, that was the problem. It caused her to bleed too much." She put a warm hand on his shoulder. "I don't think there was anything that I could have done, either. It's not your fault."

"I should have been here."

Josh sat, silent now, by Emma's side, listening to the tick-tock of the clock on the dresser. When she began to blue and the bedroom was numbingly cold, he stood and stumbled into the parlor to look again at his son.

Jesse was asleep in the cradle that Josh had made for him. Only yesterday he had brought it from the storehouse and Emma Sue washed it with soap and water and oiled it until it shone. He thought *if it wasn't for you, child, Emma Sue would still be here. What will I do with you, without her? What will you do without a mother?*

Josh thought of her smile, her dark blonde hair the color of winter wheat, the blue eyes that pulled him into her whenever he looked at her face. She couldn't be gone, she couldn't. They still had to have their girl; Belle.

What kind of a God would take a good woman away? He remembered how Emma gave the last of her egg money to a beggar who showed up at their door on a cold December morning. She sat the ragged man down to the kitchen table, as if he didn't smell, and served him eggs and bacon, grits and biscuits.

Josh pushed the front door open and staggered into the winter night. He pressed his forehead to the willow tree, raised his fist and hit the frozen bark as hard as he could. Then he watched his blood drip onto the ground at his feet.

The next night, Josh and his two brothers hammered a casket of pine wood. They lined it with Emma Sue's favorite quilt. It sat in the parlor on wooden horses brought in from the shed. Josh's mother, Martha Williams, Nadine Potts, and Aunt Ellie washed Emma Sue, brushed her hair and draped her body in a pale blue dress, the one she wore when she said her vows to Josh. Finally, Josh and his brothers laid her gently into the casket. Neighbors came, and said how peaceful she looked. They silently placed fragrant herbs and pine boughs inside the casket. They patted Josh's arm or hugged him, murmuring words of consolation. He couldn't answer.

Emma Sue grew up a Scroggins. They had a broke-back farm down the road from Josh's cabin. She had worked the fields since she was six years old. She added cow milking at age seven. Her day started at four in the morning when she rousted the chickens from their nest to gather eggs. It ended at dark when the last cow was milked. When her baby sister Anna May was born Emma Sue took care of her while their mother and her sister Mary worked the fields along side her brother and father. She never finished grade school or traveled out of the county where she was born.

Martha Williams and her friend Nadine Potts came to cook and clean. Nadine welcomed the guests and comforted mourners. She dabbed her eyes with a handkerchief. She fixed a plate of food for Josh and watched while he pushed the food around with his fork. She urged him to eat, but he couldn't. She fixed bottles of goat milk for Jesse, testing the temperature on the inside of her wrist before she fed him.

The preacher came, and all the Scroggins were there, too. Emma Sue's father Luke, bent and coughing, could only stare at the coffin with watery eyes. Mary and Anna May and the rest of the clan sang gospel songs and brought food from their kitchens. Mary Scroggins milked the cows, and the goat. She fed the chickens and the chestnut mare.

They buried Emma Sue early Friday morning. They loaded the casket in the back of the pickup truck and drove it the quarter-mile to the cemetery. The ground was cold and hard. They hauled hot water and dumped it there so the men could dig six feet down.

Josh shoveled the first scoop of hard cold dirt onto the closed casket. Then he fell to his knees and clawed the frozen ground until his fingers bled.

Bear Holler 1930

Jesse was almost two years old before Josh could bring himself to empty Emma Sue's clothes from their bedroom closet. But the cabin was small and Jesse was growing, He needed more room.

He took her hairbrush from the dresser where it sat for those two years. He laid it on top of the clothing ready to take to the church charity bin. Then he noticed that it still had strands of baby fine hair enmeshed in the bristles. He picked it up and inspected it, turned it over and over. Then he put it in the top dresser drawer under his shirts.

It was supper time when he finally came out of the bedroom. He could smell fresh baked bread and his stomach rumbled with hunger.

Martha Williams sat at the kitchen table drinking a cup of tea when he came in. Josh's Ma and Aunt Mary, Emma Sue's sister, took turns coming in to watch Jesse when Josh was in the field working.

Josh looked at the empty chair where Emma Sue last sat. He stared out the window where the lamp light shone on the front porch and the willow tree. New snow was starting to fall and it sparkled as it settled on the porch railing.

Jesse ran to him and grabbed one of his legs, riding it as Josh walked across the floor. He picked him up and tossed him onto the settee. Then he tickled him until he begged for Josh to stop.

"Supper will be ready in a few minutes. Josh, take Jesse and go wash up."

"Okay, Ma. What's cooking?"

"Beans and hog jowl; it just sounded good to me on this cold day."

"It sounds good to me, too." He washed his hands in the kitchen sink.

Martha Williams was not the kind of woman to hold back her opinions and tonight was no exception. She watched her son grow thin and sallow, worried about the bags under his eyes that showed lack of sleep. She noticed the depression that still dragged Josh's footsteps. He missed his wife, no doubt, but there was nothing to do but buck up and go on. She'd said it before and she would say it again; he needed to get married.

"Tomorrow is St. Valentine's Day, Josh. Be careful of

the first woman you see because that will be your new wife." She laughed at the frowning face he made.

"Seriously, Jesse needs a mother. And you've been moping around way too long."

"Not yet, Ma. I just can't think about that now."

Martha carried food from the stove to the table. She put fresh baked bread in front of Josh to slice up and fetched butter from the ice box.

"Well, you'd better start thinking about it sometime soon. That boy needs a mother. Jesse," she shouted, "come to supper."

The next morning, Nadine Potts happened to be strolling down the path that led to a clearing in the woods. She stopped when she saw Josh swinging his axe across a felled tree trunk. His denim shirt was soaked with sweat and his breath made the air steam around his face. Dark curly hair fell into his eyes giving him, she thought, a little-boy look. Nadine stopped in the clearing long enough to smile and say, "Hello, Josh."

He raised dark eyes to her face and lingered there for a second or two Then he grunted a "Hi" and swung his axe again. She continued walking through the woods to Martha's house. A smile lingered on her face.

Nadine settled in the chair at Martha Williams' kitchen table for her daily visit and cup of coffee. They had grown close since Emma Sue died. Martha missed her daughter-in-law and she enjoyed Nadine's company. Nadine reminded Martha of herself when she was her age, though by then she had been married for fifteen years and had three boys.

Nadine at thirty hadn't married yet. She was not a beautiful woman, but had a certain prettiness about her. The gossip was that her bad disposition had kept her from catching a husband. It was whispered that she would die an old maid. But Martha thought the gossip was wrong. Nadine had always been sweet and kind to her. She brought something with her every day; a batch of fresh-baked cookies, or a spray of wildflowers.

Martha also noticed how considerate Nadine could be. She hung her heavy wool coat on the peg by the door after wiping her boots carefully on the porch mat. Then she removed her boots so as not to muddy up Martha's immaculate kitchen floor. And she talked with Jesse, smiling at him and even reading a story to him now and then.

Nadine laid her package on the kitchen table and untied the string. The sweet smell of yeast and cinnamon and sugar permeated the room. The two women ate the rolls with fresh coffee Martha had made.

"I just saw Josh chopping wood in the clearing." Nadine dipped the corner of her roll into her coffee mug.

Martha raised her eyes to Nadine's. "Was he the first man you saw today?"

"Yes; he was. Be sure to save a cinnamon roll for him, won't you, Martha?"

Martha smiled at Nadine and their lips curled around the edge of the big white coffee mugs.

Nadine carried her empty cup to the sink and rinsed it out.

"I'll be on my way, Martha. I'm opening up the bank this morning."

"See you later, Nadine. I'll be sure to tell Josh you left a cinnamon roll for him and Jesse."

On a Sunday afternoon in May, wearing a new white shirt and his only suit and tie, Josh sat on a bench in the church courtyard, his back stiff and his feet on the ground.

The sermon had been long and dreary, the suit was feeling hot and he longed to loosen his tie and take off the jacket.

It was not the first time he had been to a box lunch. He tried to get out of it, but Ma insisted that he come with her. It was easier to go than to fight with his mother.

He held a ticket with the number seven handwritten on its backside. Since seven was his lucky number, he went over his limit a bit and bid fifty cents. After all, it was for the benefit of the church.

He looked up to see Nadine Potts walking toward him, smiling. She reached out one hand to show him her own ticket with the number seven emblazoned on it. There was a huge basket swinging from her other arm. She wore a soft yellow summer dress without sleeves. Her hair, a little redder than he remembered, suited her pale green eyes. He was surprised at how pretty she looked that day. He wondered why he hadn't noticed before how sweetly she smiled.

He hadn't seen her looking over his shoulder when he pulled the number seven out of the box. And it would be years before Marcie Pratt told him how much Nadine had paid her for Marcie's number seven ticket.

Josh jumped to his feet and took the basket from Nadine. They found a place on the grass under a tree. He spread the blanket he had carried from his old Ford pickup under the tree. She draped her checkered cloth in the center of the blanket and spread the food before them. They ate fried chicken and corn on the cob and Cole slaw and warm biscuits soaked in butter. They washed it down with lemonade, and then leaned against the trunk of the tree and talked. They talked about the weather, and Jesse, and Nadine's job at the bank. Josh said he was worried about his Ma, who was looking kind of peaked these days.

"Josh, do you think your Ma is getting worn out looking after Jesse? He's at the age where he keeps her running after him. She seems a lot more tired lately." She smoothed her dress with both hands, pulling back a little on the skirt and letting it climb from mid-calf to her knees. "And your Pa is so busy in the fields that he doesn't have time to help her."

Josh watched her dress smoothing with interest. "Yeah, I suppose so. I keep telling her I should hire someone to take care of him, but she says Jesse shouldn't have to put up with strangers when he has family to look after him."

"Well, I have some time on weekends when I'm off from the bank. I'd be willing to take Jesse for awhile on Saturdays so she can rest."

"That's a lot for me to ask, Nadine. I would have to pay you something, though I can't afford too much." He moved closer to her,

"No, I wouldn't hear of it. Not having any children yet, I would enjoy having the chance to spend time with him. I could give him some Bible lessons, too. And Jesse is used to me. I'd be glad to help Martha. She's my friend." She raised her eyes to his. "I would like to help you, too, Josh." Her cheeks blushed pink.

Josh looked around and saw that most of the others were gone. He put his arm around Nadine's waist and kissed her cheek, then her mouth. An almost forgotten longing coursed through his body and he held her tighter, kissed her harder. Maybe Ma was right, maybe it wasn't fair to Jesse not having a mother. Besides, his bed had grown colder lately. He didn't mind before, but he thought that maybe it was time to open the shutters in the musty cabin and let the sunshine in.

Three months later Josh married Nadine in the same church garden where he first kissed her. His Ma smiled with tears rolling down her cheeks. His father patted his shoulder and shook his hand. Nadine didn't have any family still alive, but the rest of Bear Holler was there, including Sheriff McMahan. Even the Scroggins family was there, saying they were glad that Josh had found someone now that Emma Sue had been in the grave for more than two years. Jesse stood with his Daddy, a somber frown on his face.

The honeymoon was spent in the cabin, as was Josh's first honeymoon. Jesse was sent to his grandparents for a week. Nadine swept and cleaned while Josh worked his fields. She tried, she would say later, to make that place into a home. But it never felt like home to her.

Bear Holler 1931

"Josh," Nadine called from the kitchen when she heard the cabin door open. "You've got to do something with Jesse." He could hear the rattle of pans on the stove. He was hungry having missed dinner at noon while he was in town.

Josh looked at Jesse, playing in the front of the cabin. He was rolling a homemade wooden car back and forth in the dirt. His cousin Jack crashed his truck into Jesse's car and they both laughed.

"I'm coming, Nadine." What now, he wondered.

She stood in front of the stove, sweat dripping from her chin onto her apron. "I tried to set Jesse down for Bible lessons but he kept squirming and giggling until I gave up and sent him outside." She wiped her face with her sleeve. "He's just growing up to be a heathen, Josh, on the road to hell. It's all your fault. You're his father and you need to get tough with him. A good caning wouldn't hurt and it might get his attention."

"I won't hit him, Nadine. He's only three. There's better ways to teach him." He pulled out a kitchen chair and sat." I'll have a talk with him, okay?" The boys' shouts drifted into the kitchen.

"Spare the rod and spoil the child." She slammed a pot onto the stove. "It's downright neglectful not to discipline him." She turned and pointed a big spoon at him. "And that Jack. He's two years older and a bad influence on Jesse. He just runs wild. Mary doesn't discipline him at all."

She suddenly weaved from side to side, eyes half closed. Josh thought she might fall down. He rushed to her side and put his arms around her.

"Come sit down. I'll get you a glass of water. It's just too hot in here." He walked her to a chair.

She took the water and drank it down, then jumped up and ran outside. Josh followed.

"Nadine, what's wrong?"

She was sitting on a stump, retching, with her head between her legs. He knelt down beside her. When she was finished he wiped her face with his handkerchief.

"What's wrong," he said again.

"I'm pregnant, Josh. I missed two of my monthlies."

He didn't know what he was feeling at first. Happy? Scared? Did he want another child?

"That's good, isn't it?" he said finally.

"I'm not sure at my age, Josh. It's okay if it's a girl. But what if it's another boy? I don't think I could take it."

"Aw, boys are all right, too, aren't they?"

"I want a girl, and that's what I'll pray for. God will grant me that, I know. I'm a good Christian woman."

She stood and smoothed her hair. The weather was unseasonably hot for the end of May. She put a hand on Josh's arm and smiled at him.

Josh thought of his last night with Emma Sue. "If it's a girl, let's call her Belle. I've always wanted a girl named Belle."

"No, her name will be Annemarie after my auntie, God rest her soul. And if it's a boy we'll call him Walter, after my Granddaddy." Her face was set. "But I'm sure that God will give me a girl."

"We can talk about it later. Right now, let's get you into bed for awhile. I'll finish supper." He took her elbow and lifted her from the stump walking her toward the cabin door.

Nadine's voice became hard again. "No, I'm fine now. Josh. I'll finish supper." She bit her lip. "But you'd better talk to Jesse. He needs to stop opposing me. I'm his mother now."

"I will. Okay, I will."

"I'm leaving, Josh. I tidied up and did the wash. There are plenty of clean diapers on the dresser." Aunt Ellie called him from the parlor. "Nadine is in the bedroom with the baby. Anything else you need before I go?"

"No, I'm okay for now. Thanks, Aunt Ellie, for everything." He stood in the doorway of the kitchen; taking off his boots. "I'll be getting the rest of your money to you next week. I've got a bunch of winter squash in the root cellar I can take to market this weekend.

"That would be fine, Josh. I'll see you tomorrow, then."

Josh wondered how much longer Aunt Ellie would be working as a midwife. Every year, it seemed, she was having more trouble getting around. It took her longer to climb the steps these days. She took them one at a time, placing both feet on each one and holding onto the rail all the while. He watched as she dropped her heavy frame down step to step and finally onto the path to the road.

She was teaching one of the Scroggins women, Julie May, to take her place. But Aunt Ellie would be missed. She had delivered 223 babies in Bear Holler and Bear Creek, including Nadine and Josh's girl.

Josh lifted the bedroom curtain and stepped inside. He paused for a moment, watching Nadine lying in bed with their daughter in her arms. The baby was nursing, eyes closed and sucking hard. Nadine gazed at her with a smile on her face. Josh realized that he hadn't seen her smile like that since the day they married. And here she was, looking quite beautiful and content after two days of hard labor. He thought that maybe he did love her after all. He pushed into the room and lay down beside her on the bed, careful not to jiggle the mattress.

He reached over Nadine and stroked Belle's cheek. That's what he called her when Nadine couldn't hear. She was a beautiful baby with a mop of light brown hair, blue eyes, and skin the color of cream

"Careful now, Josh, you're going to wake her up," Nadine said, pushing his hand away from the baby's face. She turned to her side away from him, gently laying her baby onto the bed beside her.

Josh stroked Nadine's back, his face in her hair. She smelled like pine and talcum. He felt a surge of love and admiration for his wife. She had given him the daughter he always wanted. He would teach Belle how to sing, and play the guitar. He would show her how to break a horse, how to ride. He would teach her and Jesse about plants, and animals, and how to run a farm. And Nadine would sew clothes for her and brush her hair. But she would still be Daddy's girl.

"Stop it, Josh. You're pushing me into Annemarie." Nadine gave her shoulder a little shake, her elbow jabbing into his chest.

He slowly got up from the bed. Nadine called out after him. "That Jack needs to go on home. He's been here two days now."

"Okay, Nadine." Josh answered, and went outside to toss a ball back and forth with the boys.

The next week, early on a Monday morning, Josh saddled the chestnut mare. Nadine came out on the porch and stood watching him with her hands on her hips.

"Josh," she said.

He hitched the saddle tight before looking up at her. His hands were cold. A light blanket of snow covered the ground and his breath made little puffs of steam in the air.Nadine was wrapped in a flannel robe. The steam from her breath made her face look distant.

"Now be sure that you spell this exactly right. Annemarie Christiana Williams. Look it over good before they take the paper. And make sure you get the date right. I know how careless you can be."

"Yeah, I've got it in my pocket, just the way you wrote it." He patted his overall pocket.

"And hurry back, too; don't dawdle in town. If you're thinking of stopping at Bear Creek Tavern just get that out of your mind." She tapped her foot on the porch planks. "Don't think that I've forgotten how you stayed there all afternoon last month playing music while I was worried sick at home. Worried sick and pregnant, and those two boys running me ragged."

"Okay, Nadine. I got it. I'll be back soon. Just get some rest. I took the boys over to Granny so you don't have to worry about them."

"Humph." She went inside, slamming the door behind her. He mounted up and walked the mare slowly down the path to the road, ducking under the weeping willow tree.

The County Court House was a handsome building that sat in the middle of the town square. It held all the important records for the residents of Bear Creek and Bear Holler; every marriage, birth and death. Three years ago he had recorded Jesse's birth and Emma Sue's death.

He tied the mare to a rail in front of the courthouse. He talked to her and stroked her nose. It felt soft as velvet. Emma Sue had loved Molly, rode her often just for fun. He could see them galloping across the wheat field; Molly stretched full length and Emmy's hair flying in the wind behind her. When Molly's colt was born Emma Sue was right there, brushing her with her hands and whispering words of encouragement. He remembered how gently she stroked the mare's shank.

He remembered too, how loving her touch was, how she smoothed his hair from his face before she patted his cheek.

This baby should have been theirs; his and Emma Sue's. If there was a God, He would not be this cruel. And who knew if there was a God at all. The Preacher couldn't explain it to him. Neither could his Ma.

He stroked Molly's neck. She whinnied and nodded her head, as if giving him permission to go on. Then he lumbered up the courthouse steps, very slowly, stopping at the landing to gaze down the street. Two wagons were hitched in front of the dry goods store. Three horses were tied at the post of the Bear Creek Tavern across the street from the courthouse. He could hear the faint whine of a steel guitar and the lilting notes of a fiddle. Shouts and laughter drifted from the front door.

Josh stood in front of the barred window waiting for the clerk to look up at him

"Can I help you, Sir?" He was a squat man with thick rimmed glasses.

"Yes. I want to register a birth. A girl..."

Josh pulled out the paper Nadine had given him and read it. Annemarie Christiana Williams. It didn't even sound right.

"Date of birth?"

"December 1, 1931." He double-checked the note in his hand.

"What is her name, sir?" The clerk pushed his glasses back on his nose.

Josh hesitated. Then he slowly crumpled the paper in his fist. "Her name is Belle; Belle Carter Williams."

Josh loved the Carter family. He listened to Mother Maybelle Carter until he got her guitar riffs just right. He played Carter family records over and over until he could pick at the strings and bring forth a full, multilayered sound just like Mother Maybelle. That's how he would teach Jesse to play. He would teach Jack, too, if he wanted to learn. And Belle. He would teach her how to play and sing, too.

It took him months to figure out, just from listening to the records, how Mother Maybelle played her guitar. After countless tries he finally got it. She played it just like she played the banjo. She used her thumb pick to play melody on the bass and middle string and with her fingers filled out the rhythm on the other strings. He was elated when he finally mastered "Wildwood Flower."

Belle Carter Williams. It sounded just right.

The winter sun had filtered through the clouds and was melting the snow. The sun felt good on his back. He untied Molly and patted her neck. Then he walked her across the street to the water trough. He broke a thin layer of ice and watched as she drank. He dipped his handkerchief and wiped his mouth with icy water.

Josh looked at his guitar, its strap slung across the saddle horn. He had slipped it onto the saddle after Nadine went back into the cabin. The guitar was battered with nicks and dents and the wood was dulled. The bridge was worn. The strings could use replacing. And yet the tone was true, full and resonant, pleasing to the ear. He unwound the strap from the saddle horn and draped it onto his shoulder.

He tied Molly to the rail in front of Bear Creek Tavern. Then he pushed the door open and let the music out.

.

In the days and weeks after Josh handed Nadine the birth certificate with Belle's name on it, she still called her Annemarie. If she said the name in Josh's presence, he would only glare at her until she cringed. So gradually, she stopped calling her anything except "the baby" and eventually, "the girl."

But as Belle grew, she had to call her something when it was time for dinner, or when she wanted her to do something. So she relented and called her "Belle." But every time she called her name, she remembered what her husband had done.

Bear Holler 1936

On her birthday when she was five, her Daddy found Belle under the willow tree. She was sitting cross-legged, her back against the rough bark of the tree trunk. She often sat for hours in that secret hiding place just watching the sun spots dance across the ground as the low-hanging boughs brushed the dirt. Sometimes she would just sit and think. Her new puppy, she named him Red, lay on the grass beside her. His tail slowly swept back and forth as she talked to him. But now, the winter air was cold and the grass dried and frozen. She sat on a blanket she had carried from her bed, careful that her Ma didn't see.

Sometimes she made up songs and wrote the words in the dirt with her finger. Then she would stand, as if she was before an audience. She would smooth her dress, stand taller yet, and sing the words she had written to the music in her head. She sang as her Daddy had taught her; at the top of her voice, as if she was calling someone in to dinner.

Often she took her peanut butter and jelly sandwich and milk to sit under the tree and eat. Nadine didn't seem to mind and even looked relieved to see her leave the kitchen. Sometimes Jesse would find her there and plop down beside her, pulling at her sleeve and pinching her nose until she had to pay attention to him. Most of the time, though, he was at Jack's house.

Josh lifted the branches and stepped inside, letting in a ray of sun. He thought of the night Emmy died, how he had struck the tree in anger and grief. Belle squinted, unable to see who it was in the shadow of the tree branches. By the time Josh sat down beside her, she could see again. Her eyes grew wide at the sight of a shiny new guitar

So that was what Daddy had been doing in the work shed every night. That's why Belle was forbidden to join him there. That was why the light from the kerosene lamp was still burning in the shed's window when she went to bed at night. He was making a guitar for Belle, just like he had for Jesse when he was five.

Belle took the guitar in her hands and turned it over and over, gently, admiring the polished wood. She could see her reflection in the smooth finish. She strummed the catgut strings slowly.

"This here's a C chord. Just drag your fingers across the strings." Josh showed her which strings to hold down at the neck.

It had a sweet sound. It was too big for her small frame,

but Josh told her that she would soon grow into it.

"Show me another chord, Daddy."

"Okay, now here's a G. Put your fingers like this. Now, here's an F chord. Learn these three chords and you can play lots of songs."

Belle played C and G and F chords until her fingers were raw. The sun fell behind the hills, and Nadine's shrill voice called her to supper. It was then she realized that her Daddy had left her alone under the tree and she felt chilled. She waited until Nadine called again. The anger and irritation in her voice moved her to get up and stretch her aching legs. She carefully wiped her guitar with the tail of her shirt, and then sucked her sore fingers.

When she carried the guitar to her room, her Daddy was there, putting up a hook for the guitar. Josh stooped to hug the exhausted girl, and Belle threw her arms around him, holding tight. Daddy's attention was rare and she didn't want to let him go. She thought of all the times her Daddy stared vacantly into space. Those times, even if Belle tugged on his sleeve and called to him, Josh didn't seem to know that she was there.

"Thanks, Daddy. When I'm famous I'll still play this guitar to remember where I started."

Josh laughed. "Jesse's Mamma always said that he would be famous. In her dreams, thousands of people were at his feet. I think if she was here today, she would say that's true for you, too."

From then on every night, right after supper, Jesse and Belle, and Jack if he was there, waited for a signal from Josh that it was time to get their guitars. Josh hitched his chair closer to the fire and strummed his mandolin, or pulled the bow across his fiddle, or maybe just drummed his thighs with the flat of his hands while Belle, Jesse and Jack plunked away on their guitars.

Sometimes Belle laid her guitar down after playing a couple of numbers. The boys were better at playing than she was; they were older. Then she danced and sang to the music. She twirled across the floor, her skirt billowing around her, and sang at the top of her voice.

Nadine sat in Emma's old rocking chair by the window reading her Bible. Every once in a while she looked towards the sitting room and scowled at the noise. As soon as the clock chimed eight, she grabbed Belle's arm and took her off to bed.

Sometimes Josh didn't signal for them to get their guitars. Instead, he sat on the porch swing with Red at his feet. Those nights, the melancholy tones of his harmonica drifted across the night. Josh didn't have to say that he wanted to be left alone. They all knew it. Even Nadine stayed away from the porch.

When she couldn't play with her Daddy and Jesse, Belle sat alone in her room practicing all the chords that Josh taught her. Jesse did the same. But Jack, he learned with ease, as if he was meant to play the guitar. He played all the riffs and variations of those chords, until hundreds were stored in his quick mind. Jesse's voice became more strong and sure. And Belle sang with joy, dancing as if she were on a stage looking down at her audience.

Bear Creek 1938
Belle

I was six when my Daddy died. I was in my bedroom, playing with my dolls. The little table Daddy made for me was set for a party with Janie and Sarah. They sat in their little chairs, staring straight ahead. I liked Janie best because she was always smiling. I had just lifted the teapot to pour when I heard the shot.

Ma screamed. I heard footsteps in the hallway, running. It was Jack and Jesse. I went running after them. Ma was still screaming. When I got to the shed, Jack and Jesse were trying to lift her from the ground. When she saw me, she got up and blocked the door to the shed with her body. But I could see around her legs.

Daddy was on the floor of the woodshed. I could see a hole in his forehead. There was blood spattered all over the back wall and pieces of white stuff spread all around. A chair lay on its side next to him. His legs were sprawled out and one arm was on his chest. I couldn't see his other arm.

But Daddy's eyes were open and staring straight ahead. The hole in his forehead was hardly bleeding at all. His head was turned slightly, towards me.

"Oh, Lord. Oh, God. Dear God." Ma fell to the ground again and we tried to help her up. "He's dead. Done killed himself." Ma had a thick mountain accent and when she was stressed it could be hard to understand her.

"He's alive," I cried, "he's looking at me!"

A flock of chickens gathered around us. The rooster walked through and they all parted to let him by. I looked at Daddy again, watching to see if he moved but he didn't.

He couldn't be dead, could he?

"Oh, God, oh, no, he's dead. He's dead."

Jack was trying to help her up but she fell to the ground again, her skirt above her knees and legs splayed.

Jesse looked at me, then at Daddy, then back to me. "He's dead, Belle. I can see he's dead." His voice sounded like he was choking.

"Why, why, dear God?" Ma was wailing. "Why would he kill himself?"

My legs gave out from under me and I sat down in the middle of the chickens. They went running every which way. I put my hands over my face.

I think I know why he killed himself. It was Ma's nagging that did it. Just that very morning, Ma was yelling at Daddy. It was her fault he killed himself. She was always nagging at him for something. And he was always trying to pacify her by making promises.

Most evenings after supper he spent with me and Jack and Jesse, teaching us music. Ma acted like she was mad the whole time we were singing and playing. He put a phonograph record on the turntable, cranked it up, and we tried to play and sing along with Bob Wills or The Carter Family. We were getting pretty good, too, especially Jack. He was a natural with the guitar.

Jesse was the performer, the singer, the show off. He liked it when I sang with him.

Ma didn't like that Jack was at the cabin so much. But he and Jesse were like brothers. Ma hated the music. She said it was the devil's tool. She read her Bible all the time we played, saying she was offsetting the evil we were doing. Then she would close her eyes and say that she was praying for our souls.

Ma was mad at Daddy this morning. He had been promising to fix the gate to the chicken coop for weeks now. Every time Ma went to gather eggs, she had to lay down her basket and lift the gate open with both hands. Then with her basket full of chicken eggs, she had to do the same thing coming out, this time while the rooster pecked at her heels.

Daddy would just go through the pen and into his work shed. He didn't look like he was bothered by shaking the gate open himself.

"I'll fix it tomorrow, I promise. I meant to get to it today, but just couldn't get myself going" he said. His head was in his hands, elbows on the kitchen table.

"The road to hell is paved with good intentions." She yelled at him. "I'm not gathering any more eggs until it's done, you hear?"

He raised his head and looked at her. Then he slapped the table and got up from his chair and walked out the front door.

She might as well have pulled the trigger herself, I thought. And I vowed I'd tell her so, after she calmed down some. But I couldn't talk; my throat felt sore and tears blurred my eyesight. I couldn't stand up.

All four of us sat on the grass in front of the woodshed, like a flock of those silly chickens. We cried and wailed until our tears were all used up. Then we went inside. Jack walked to the neighbor's to get a ride to town and fetch the Sheriff. He came right away.

Nadine kept watch over the coffin in the parlor. Aunt Ellie sat on the couch beside her, patting her arm and talking. Jesse and Belle wandered into the room, stole glances at their Daddy's face, then averted their eyes.

"Can I go outside, Ma?" Jesse begged.

"Me, too, Ma?" Belle said.

Nadine stared straight ahead, not answering. Ellie said, "Go ahead."

Nadine turned to look at the children as they ran out the door. "Ellie, they should stay here."

"Now, Nadine, they're young. They can't sit here all day like two stones. That doesn't mean they didn't love their Daddy."

Neighbors and friends left at dusk after cleaning the kitchen, milking the cows, and feeding the chickens. The Scroggins' were there, as they had been the day after Emma Sue died. Other neighbors from around the Holler showed up all day, coming and going. They brought food and bouquets of fresh picked spring flowers. Sheriff McMahan stayed until every else was gone, except Aunt Ellie.

Later, Ellie reached over and patted Nadine's arm. "I'll keep watch tonight, Nadine. You go on to bed."

"Oh, Aunt Ellie, I didn't know I would miss him so much." Sorrow washed over her again, as it had all day. "I want to sit here a while longer."

"Sure. You just do whatever you want to do. I'll be helping the children to bed while you stay here, all right?" Ellie stood and called the children inside. "He was a good man, Nadine."

Jesse and Belle kissed Nadine's cheek, and then followed Ellie to their beds. Ellie sat at Belle's bedside until, exhausted, Belle drifted off to sleep.

Ellie settled onto the sofa next to Nadine. "I'll be sitting right here, keeping watch all night. You go on to bed whenever you want."

"Thanks, Ellie." Nadine tucked her legs under her. "You know, when we married, I thought Josh was my last chance. Honestly, I think I married him because no one else had ever asked me. But now, after all these years, I've become quite fond of him." She dabbed at her eyes with her handkerchief.

"There, there. Of course you cared for him. Anyone can see that."

Nadine stood and walked to the casket, looking down at her husband. She thought *I didn't know that I would end up liking you so much. But you've left me with a mess, haven't you? Took the coward's way out, you did. That really galls me, Josh. What will I do with these kids anyhow? Who's going to take care of me? It's not like you didn't have a choice. You decided to leave me, and your kids.*

Nadine turned to Aunt Ellie and frowned. Then she walked to the bedroom, lifted the curtain, and dropped it behind her.

Not quite a month after Josh died, Nadine sent Jesse to live with his Aunt Mary, Emma Sue's sister. Mary said she wanted him and Nadine didn't argue. Actually, she felt relieved of the responsibility. Boys were dirty little mongrels in her opinion, especially Jesse and Jack. Jesse was always at Jack's house anyhow, or Jack was at Jesse's house, under Nadine's feet. Now that Josh was gone and she was on her own, she only wanted to raise her daughter and live in peace. She found it a relief not to listen to the caterwauling from the parlor every night.

Nadine rented a small house in Bear Creek for her and Belle. She had never liked the cabin, where Josh had insisted they live. There were constant reminders of Emma Sue there. Josh still kept her hairbrush in his drawer, for God's sake. The cabin was small and cramped with the four of them. She had to struggle endlessly to keep it clean and tidy. She missed her coworkers at the bank in Bear Creek. She thought she might even go back to work part time.

Nadine's grandmother was left a widow without any funds at the age of 42. So, heeding her grandmother's advice, Nadine bought a life insurance policy on Josh when they married. He never knew. She didn't think it was necessary for him to know. She didn't know why at the time, but she had insisted that it covered death by suicide. The money would allow Nadine to take care of Belle without working. She could read her Bible and go to church all she wanted. And, she never again had to listen to that awful music in her parlor.

It worried her though, that Belle missed Jesse so much. She often asked to go to the house where he was staying and visit, but Nadine always said no. She had heard that Mary let Jesse and Jack run wild. Her neighbor Jessica told her she saw them hanging around the back door of the bars in Bear Holler and Bear Creek, listening to music.

Not that Jessica was a friend. Nadine didn't approve of her going to bars and picking up men. But she thought she might get her to change her ways. And she liked hearing the gossip they exchanged over coffee, though she would have denied it if anyone had asked.

She missed the gossip sessions with Martha Williams. She lived too far away from the Williams farm to get there every day like she used to before having Belle, before moving to Bear Creek.

Every Sunday and twice during the week, Belle was dressed up and trundled to church. Nadine showed everyone how well she was raising her child. She wanted them all to notice how clean and well-behaved Belle was. If Belle squirmed or her attention strayed, Nadine grabbed her arm and squeezed until Belle stopped squirming and paid attention to Reverend Barker.

Nadine sat next to Belle, her gingham dress buttoned to her neck, her skirt well below her knees, and her shoes freshly polished. A conservative hat sat on her neatly combed hair. Her eyes never left the preacher as he delivered his sermon. She bowed her head devoutly for each prayer and sang well with every hymn. She was determined to prove to the Reverend, to the congregation, and to Jesus that she was worth saving.

Bear Creek 1940

Nadine stared at the poster on the church bulletin board. The following weekend, the Reverend Bartholomew Hollister would be speaking at the Baptist tent revival meeting just outside Nashville.

Nadine's neighbor Jessica reluctantly agreed to go with her. Nadine made it clear to Belle that she was expected to go, too. She was balking at the suggestion but Nadine had already decided that she wasn't going to get out of it. The girl was becoming hard to handle at age nine. She was often sullen and defiant. Nadine longed for Belle's baby days when she looked up at Nadine and smiled at her. She wondered sometimes, if she shouldn't go to court and try to change her name to Annemarie. To Nadine the name Belle seemed better suited to a harlot.

The Reverend Hollister was a "fire and brimstone" preacher, it was said. He could cleanse Nadine of her sins, she believed, and even save Belle and Jessica if they were willing. Edna Brumley had seen him one year ago at the same tent meeting. She told Nadine how charismatic he was, how he seemed to be touched by God. She said she believed that God was talking to him when he stood on the stage, gazing up toward Heaven. When he described Hell, it sent shivers up her spine. Edna swore that she saw a halo of light around the Reverend's head.

The first time Nadine saw the inside of a revival tent she was no more than seven. Still the memory of it warmed her. She sat squashed between Aunt Sheila and her Ma on a hard folding chair, but she didn't mind. She could smell Aunt Sheila's lilac toilet water. She could hear the hallelujahs of the crowd. And the preacher laid his hand on her head, saying she was saved. It was exciting; the crowds, the air of anticipation, and home-made cookies and cake for after. Now, she had the chance to recapture that cleansing feeling when the Reverend had laid hands on her.

If only she could have convinced Josh to go to the revivals, or at least to church on Sunday. It might have saved him. She wondered if her friends were right when they said that Josh was an atheist.

"Please, Josh. Just come along. It won't hurt you to give me this much." She begged him often to take her. She wanted him to be saved. But he never did. She was sure that he died a sinner, taking his own life.

She pushed that from her mind. Soon she would hear the famous Reverend Bartholomew Hollister preach the Holy Gospel. And she would be cleansed of her sins.

The Reverend stared at his reflection in the full length mirror, and then bent to flick a piece of lint from his black trousers. He examined his manicured nails. He reached for the black jacket that George had brushed and pressed just minutes ago and shrugged it onto broad shoulders. Smoothing the lapels over a white clerical collar he gazed into the mirror, turning slowly from side to side. He picked up a smaller mirror, turned and checked the back of his hair. After brushing a stray lock into place with his hand, he put the mirror back on the table, smiled at his image and listened. He could hear George warming up the crowd.

"I feel the Lord here tonight…" George intoned in a strong loud voice.

"Hallelujah," the crowd roared.

The Reverend gave the mirror another cursory glance, picked up the worn black Bible and lifted the curtain to the stage.

"...the Reverend Bartholomew Hollister!"

The crowd jumped to its feet as one, stomping and clapping. George's timing, as usual, was impeccable.

Smiling and beaming amid deafening applause, the Reverend strode to the podium. Bright stage lights blinded him for the moment, but he quickly adjusted his eyes. The crowd continued its shouts of hallelujah and clapping, stomping their feet on the dusty floor. He raised his arms and made the sign of the cross in benediction.

His dark brown eyes found Belle in the front row and stopped there, observing her pout as she sat in the chair. There's a stubborn one, he guessed. His eyes moved slowly to Nadine who stood with flushed cheeks, bright eyes and a broad smile. This woman is eager, willing. She'll be coming up for benediction. His eyes held Nadine's gaze. She wavered slightly, then grasped her chair back with one hand and eased herself into the seat.

Reverend Hollister paced the stage. The crowd waited. He paced the opposite direction, looking up once in a while at the audience. They waited.

Suddenly, his baritone voice boomed through the silence. "Why are you here?" he shouted.

Every eye followed his walk. Then he stopped. "Why are you here?" he repeated, even louder.

The people looked at each other, confusion written on their faces. The room was silent except for an occasional murmur.

"Never mind, I know why." The Reverend paused, eyes scanning the room. "It's because you're all sinners. The devil has you in his spell. And you don't know what to do. So you come here. You think I'm going to save you, don't you?" He paced again, then stopped, turned and stared out at the audience. "Well, I'm not going to save you. I can't save you. Only you can save yourselves."

Murmurs rippled through the worshippers. Feet shuffled.

"You're all going to hell, if you don't repent. The devil is waiting for you. He's rubbing his hands together in anticipation of capturing so many souls. He thinks he has you all in the palms of his hands. Does he?" The crowd boos and cries "no, no".

"Jesus said, 'What comes out of a man, that defiles a man, for from within, out of the heart of men, proceed evil thoughts, adulteries, fornications, murders, thefts, covetousness, wickedness, deceit, lewdness, an evil eye, blasphemy, pride, foolishness. All these evil things come from within and defile man.' Mark 7:20-23."

He slammed his fist into his other hand time after time to emphasize each and every evil influence in the world. "Drugs, divorce, women painted like whores, the devil sees it all. So does God and he wants you to repent. He wants your soul. He loves you."

His baritone voice filled every corner of the tent, even drifted outside where more people stood. Then abruptly he stopped. It was so quiet that even the air didn't move.

"If you would be saved, come forward now." The crowd again rose to its feet. "Come forward and be saved. Pledge your money, your resources, and your time to the Lord. Come forward, and bring the donation that you can afford; not a cent more. Do not take the food from your children's mouths. Do not bring your mortgage payment. Be generous to your God and bring whatever you can afford. Come forward to meet your Lord"

Belle

I didn't want to go to the prayer meeting, but Ma said that if I didn't go and do something for my wayward soul I couldn't go to the Labor Day picnic on Sunday. So there I was coming down the aisle of the tent, with snotty-nosed boys running in and out, bumping into me. The air was muggy and hot inside and I was sweating. Everyone was saying howdy to each other and mopping their foreheads.

Ladies fanned themselves with the free fans they got at the door.

The voices swelled up and down and I couldn't wait for the whole thing to start so it would be over. My hair was all wet and I could hardly breathe.

Ma was just dragging me along. Other than making sure I was there, she ignored me. I don't know why she even bothered to bring me. Sometimes, it seemed as if I was just something for her to show off to people.

"Oh, yes, I have a daughter, pretty as a picture she is. And a sweeter little girl you would never meet," she would say to folks in the store. "You should hear her recite her Bible verses at church. Never forgets a single word."

But I sensed that she was losing her concentration, forgetting things. Even when we lived at the cabin, she would forget to milk one of the cows and we didn't realize it until we heard it bellow in the middle of the night. She would put the butter in the oven and then, when she started a fire in the cook stove we would smell it burning. Sometimes she stared into her mirror for a long time and seemed to forget I was in the room. I would have to say, "Ma, I'm hungry," before she would remember to fix me a sandwich.

I wondered why Ma had to go to the tent meeting. When I asked, she said it was to be cleansed of her sins. What kind of sins was she feeling guilty about? She just stared at me when I asked. Maybe she was asking forgiveness because she nagged my Daddy to death.

Maybe it was because she sent Jesse away after Daddy died. I wasn't sure, but if she didn't feel guilty, she should have. She was always saying how she was his mother and bossing him around. As soon as Daddy was gone though, she said he would be better off with his Aunt Mary. Besides, she said, he really didn't like her anyhow. I missed him a lot. I guess it was a double whammy when I lost my

Daddy and then my brother, too, except he wasn't dead, of course.

I felt sorry for my brother. He was an orphan after Daddy died. At least I had my Ma. Jesse wrote to me while we were growing up and I answered him every time. I didn't ever want to lose track of him. His letters were short and funny. He slipped them to me in school which was about the only time I ever saw him.

Once he wrote, "Hey, Dippy-Do, how's the music coming along?"

I wrote back, "There's no one to teach me any more. Are you guys playing your guitars?"

He wrote back, "Yeah. And we are really good."

Once Jesse wrote, "You sure are ugly, but I'll help you find a husband even if you are too ugly."

"I'm not as ugly as you, butt face," I sent a letter back.

Sometimes he gave me pictures that he took with his birthday Brownie. There was one with Jesse making rabbit ears over Jack's head. Another one was Jesse swinging on a rope over the river. One of my favorites was Jesse holding up a garter snake he caught. When Jack and Jesse started high school though, I hardly saw them at all any more and the letters stopped. Ma said they hung out in Nashville in the bars, playing music.

Once I wrote and asked if Jesse missed Daddy. He wrote back that he did, and that he kept busy so that he didn't think about him. As for me, I cried every night, remembering how he always said he loved us when he tucked us in to bed. My Ma sat in the rocker, reading her Bible. She called out from the other room, *goodnight and go to sleep now.* Then Daddy kissed me on the forehead and said, "Sis, you sleep tight. Don't let the bedbugs bite." I thought that was funny because we never had any bedbugs. Living in the woods like we did, there were plenty of other kinds of bugs, like beetles and ants, but we never had any bedbugs, whatever they are.

The usher at the prayer meeting led us down to the front row, of all places. The chairs were still being opened up and placed in front of the previous first row. A fat lady in that row gave us a dirty look, as if it was our fault that they sat us in front of her.

I plopped down and crossed my arms over my chest. Ma said, stop that scowling and pouting or you aren't going anywhere for a month.

Jessica sat on Ma's other side. She smiled at me, and then looked all around the room. I saw her wave at one of the men in the seat across from us. He waved back and nodded. I thought Jessica looked like a model. She wore a blue sundress and white high heels with little satin bows. Her hair was bunched up on top of her head. Sometimes she invited me to her house and gave me cookies and milk. Then she put makeup on my face, and opened her jewelry drawer so I could pick out what I wanted to wear. Before I went home, though, she made me wash off the makeup so Ma wouldn't be mad at her.

The loudspeaker squawked. The man on the stage announced "the Reverend Bartholomew Hollister" and Ma was on her feet with the rest of the crowd. She was clapping and hollering and craning her neck to see what he looked like. He was walking fast and the spotlight was following him. He was smiling as he walked out on the stage. He blinked his eyes, like he wasn't used to all that light and attention and all the hallelujahs raining down on him.

I have to admit he was pretty impressive. He walked back and forth across the stage, shouting how we were all going to Hell if we didn't change our evil ways. When he wanted to make a point he'd slam a fist into his other hand, talking about the influence of the world today. His voice boomed like explosions, and then he'd stop and look at the crowd. He used a sweet voice, so soft that you could see the crowd bend forward so as not to miss a word.

"Will you be born again, cleansed of all sin, in the light and grace of Jesus Christ our Savior?" It was almost a whisper. Everyone leaned forward again.

"If you will, then come forward and let the Lord touch you tonight. He reaches out through my hands and He waits here for you. Give Him your heart. Give Him your soul. Tell Him that you love Him. Commit yourself now, before everyone, and give your life to the eternal love of your Lord." By now he was talking loud again.

I still remember what he said, almost word for word. For a minute or two I wanted to let the Lord reach me, too. But while I was off guard like that, Ma got up, grabbed my arm and pulled me to the front of the crowd. We jostled with all the other folks rushing to the stage, but we were first.

The Reverend came down from the podium and went to Ma. He put his hand on her head. Ma was kneeling down already, and she pulled me down beside her so hard it scraped my knees. The Reverend put his other hand on my head. It felt rough and cold, even in that hot room. I got a chill when his hand slipped down to the back of my neck.

"The Lord has given me a special message for you. Please come to see me after the meeting. God bless you both." I looked up then, and he was smiling down at me.

Six months later, my Ma married the preacher. It turned out that was his message from God; that he was supposed to save us. It was never clear to me, what he was going to save us from. When I asked Ma, she just waved her hand at me.

I guessed that you had to be a Minister before God talked to you. I never heard anyone else say that God talked to them.

There was something weird about the Reverend. He ignored me when Ma was around unless she wanted him to back up whatever she was saying. But as soon as she wasn't looking, he was watching me all the time. I felt his eyes follow me as I crossed the room. If I was at the table doing my homework he sat across from me. If I looked up, I saw that he had a little smile on his face. I called him Black Bart behind his back.

"You sure are growing up fast, little one," he would say, and put his arm around me or pat my head.

Or he said, "Come sit on my lap and I'll read you a story." Once I couldn't get out of it and his hand was on my knee all the time he was reading. I finally learned to avoid him by making some excuse to run out the door.

"I have to go. I hear Alice calling me." I could hear him laughing as I ran down the sidewalk to the street.

He was smart. He never did any of that when Ma was around. He acted like I wasn't even there. The only time he took any notice when Ma was there, was when I did something he didn't like. He would deliver his speech like a sermon from the pulpit, and then send me to my room.

"Are you going to tell your mother?" Alice said one day, when I told her about Bart. I said I was kind of scared of him.

"What would I tell her? He didn't really do anything. And Ma knows I don't like him because that's obvious."

"Well, I think you should just tell him to stop bothering you." She said. Then we went into her mother's room and played with her jewelry and forget all about Bart.

The Reverend came to my room one night. I was just

falling off to sleep. He sat down on the edge of my bed. It was about six months after Ma married him.

"Are you all right? I thought I heard you cry." His hand was on my hip.

"No, I'm fine. I wasn't crying. Where's Ma?"

"She took some chicken soup over to Mrs. Daugherty. It seems she's down with the flu." He looked at me with that little smile that was always on his face. My heart was pounding like a herd of horse's hooves. Mrs. Daugherty lived way across town. I tried to get up but he pushed me down and kept talking, telling me how special I was and how he wanted to make me happy. But I didn't feel happy and I told him I wanted to get up and to please, please stop and I'd be good. I cried but he frowned and told me to stop. His voice was so harsh that it scared me.

His hand felt rough going up and down my leg. I thought I was in a nightmare and closed my eyes. I prayed that when I opened them I would wake up and he would be gone. Dear God, please help me. Let me wake up right now. Please, please God, bring my Ma home. But when I opened my eyes nothing had changed. He was in the bed with me.

I closed my eyes again and thought of how it was when my Daddy was alive and we still lived in the cabin. I thought of the cows in the field where I walked every morning, how I herded them into the barn for milking. They grazed and chewed and looked at me with big brown eyes. I loved them. I had to watch out for the cow pies or my shoes would be ruined. In the summer there were wildflowers sprinkled all over the fields; purple and yellow and white ones. In the winter, the ground was hard and sometimes there was snow and I had to wear boots. The cows knew when it was milking time. They walked straight into their stalls as soon as I opened the barn doors. They were soft and warm and they nuzzled my hand when I reached out to them.

When it was over Bart said, "Now this is our secret, Belle. If your Ma knew she would think I didn't love her and it would break her heart. I do love her but I love you more. I know you don't want to break your mother's heart." I just kept on crying, but quietly so he wouldn't yell at me again. "The Bible says to honor your mother and your father. I'm your father now, you know, and I love you like a father. You do know that, don't you? And when God speaks to me, He tells me to love you. We can't disobey God, can we?"

I couldn't answer; I just looked down at my hands. They were still shaking. There were spots of blood on my sheet. I covered them with my leg. My mother would see them tomorrow. She always washed the sheets on Monday, and she would know there was something wrong. But what if I told her and it did break her heart?

"Belle, Jesus said, 'Honor your father and your mother, and he who curses father or mother, let him be put to death.' I'll be angry with you if you don't keep our secret. Promise?"

I nodded my head without looking up.

After Bart went to bed I washed the bloody spots out of the sheet with a wet rag. Then I wrapped myself tight in the blanket, really tight. It was a long time before I went to sleep.

Chapter 2

Bear Creek 1943

Jesse read Belle's letter again. He leaned on his knees sitting on the front porch steps. Later, he would share the letter with Jack and Auntie but for now he wanted to ponder it alone. He folded it and put it in his shirt pocket.

He didn't like the sound of it. Belle was only twelve but her letters were angry, defiant. She wrote how her life was the worst, and how she hated school. She said she couldn't wait to get out on her own and maybe she'd get pregnant as soon as she was thirteen or fourteen so she could get married.

If he wrote and asked if she was all right, she always said, just fine. But she didn't sound fine. He thought, living with Nadine and Bart would make anyone cranky, so maybe he was fussing over nothing.

If he could only see her once in awhile, he could reassure himself that she was really doing okay. But Nadine wouldn't let him in her house, and she wouldn't let Belle come to his house. He thought Nadine was influenced by the preacher and his holier-than-thou attitude.

When Belle and Jesse were younger they met sometimes at school, passing in the hall between classes or rarely, meeting when they had the same lunch hour. And they passed notes back and forth. He missed those notes. Since he was in high school in Bear Creek and she still went to Bear Holler Elementary, he never saw her.

He missed the way they teased each other and played music together. He remembered how she twirled across the floor dancing and singing. He thought of how much fun they had when they played music with their Daddy. She had jumped up and down and laughed when he said, yes, she could join his band when she was grown up. Then her face would cloud when he said, "Only if you stop being ugly." Right away, he mussed her hair and laughed, "I'm just kidding, dummy!" Then the smile returned.

Last Saturday Jesse and Jack were walking around the square in Bear Creek and ran smack into the Reverend, Nadine, and Belle walking the other way. Belle came over to the boys and hugged them, her face sad. Nadine looked away, but Bart frowned at them and called Belle, saying they were late for an appointment. It was three days later that Belle's letter was in the post office box that Aunt Mary kept.

His Auntie opened the screen door and said, "Jesse, did Jack say when he'd be home? Supper's almost ready."

Jesse turned to look at her. "Don't know, Auntie."

Mary Scroggins Dolmen, Emma Sue's sister, was in her early fifties. Her skin, rough as cowhide, spoke of the hard work it was to run a farm. She wore her graying hair into a tight bun which she let down at night, letting it flow to her waist over her long flannel gown. She bore just a vague resemblance to her dead sister. She was an older and heavier version of the slight soft-voiced Emma Sue.

Shortly after her son Jack was born, her husband ran off with a dancer from Ringling Brothers Circus and never came back. She never remarried and didn't bother to get a divorce. She learned how to farm her forty acres, hiring help when she needed it at planting and harvest time.

She told everyone that she liked raising Jesse, and that he was like her own child. And both Jack and Jesse were good at helping on the farm. As they got older they wouldn't let her do much of the work, saying she had plenty to do taking care of the house and cooking. Hard-working teenagers ate a lot, so she spent many hours in the kitchen, cooking and canning.

Jesse squinted at the truck and trail of dust on the road to the house "Here comes Jack now, Auntie." Jesse stood and stretched his legs.

Jack parked the old truck close to the porch and climbed the stairs. "What's for supper? I'm hungry."

"You're always hungry." Mary teased. "A real bottom-less pit."

"Okay, keep it up. You'll miss me when I'm gone."

"And where do you think you'll be going, at seven-teen?"

"I joined up today, Ma." He opened the screen to go in-side.

"Wait a minute. What did you say?" Her hands were on her hips.

"I said, I joined up. I'll be eighteen in three months and I'll be drafted then anyhow. This way, I can choose where I'll be." He pulled papers out of his pocket. "I just need you to sign here."

"That will be a cold day in hell." She followed him in-side. "You can just wait until they draft you, which they probably won't ever do anyhow. You're my only son, and I need you to work the farm. They don't draft only sons, especially if they're needed on the farm."

"You've got Jesse to help. He's fifteen and strong as an ox. All my friends are going, too, Ma. I can't just sit it out."

"Jack, please, I don't want you going off and getting killed." She brought pork chops, mashed potatoes, green beans and biscuits to the table and sat down.

She bowed her head. "Jesus, thank you for all we have."

"Amen" they echoed.

"We sure are lucky we raise our own meat. So many people are doing without. I'm just sorry we missed out on the sugar the other day. I've had a craving for a nice piece of cake." Mary said.

"I'm almost starting to like that damn coffee with the chicory in it." Jesse said.

"If I go now, Ma," Jack downed half a glass of milk, "I'm practically guaranteed to play in the band and entertain troops. I probably won't see battle, anyhow."

"This war won't end anytime soon, Jack. And you don't know where they'll send you." Mary forked mashed potatoes into her mouth.

Jesse stopped eating and looked at Jack. "Buddy, I hate to see you go but I understand. I'd be going too, if I could."

"Jesse, you're no help. Now stop encouraging him. This subject is closed as far as I'm concerned."

Two days later Jack handed Jesse the keys to the Ford pickup. "It needs tires real bad, Jesse, so see if you can't trade off some meat coupons for tires. And take good care of Ma for me. Don't stop playing music now, just because I'm gone."

"I won't. You take care of yourself and write, Jack."

They shook hands. "I guess I'll be driving before I get any license. Auntie doesn't drive much." He bit his lower lip. "She's not going to be very happy when she comes back and finds you gone."

"Yeah, I know. Well, I'll write her as soon as I can."

Jack threw his bag and guitar case into the bed of his friend's truck, climbed into the front, and they drove off down the road. Jack, leaning out the window and waving, looked back until Jesse couldn't see them any more.

Jesse hadn't felt so sad and lonely since he sat next to Jack and Auntie and rode away from Daddy's cabin six years ago, leaving Belle behind. Maybe he shouldn't have helped Jack forge Mary's signature.

Chapter 3

Bear Creek, 1943
Belle

It was a game, a horrible game; Black Bart trying to be alone with me and me trying to escape like some wild deer being hunted down. Ma said she wished we could get along, and couldn't I see that he was trying, so why didn't I try harder? But all I could think of was, what if something happened to Ma, or what if she left and I was stuck with Black Bart?

I told her I would try harder so she would leave me alone.

When I came home from school yesterday Ma was staring at me like she'd never seen me before.

"What's wrong, Ma? Are you okay?" I stopped in the doorway, school books under one arm. "You look strange."

"I'm fine. It's just that, I hadn't realized how grown up you're becoming. You certainly look older than twelve. I think you're just growing up way too fast."

"Well, if you tell me how to slow it down, I will." I frowned at her. I reached back and shut the door behind me. Her eyes followed me to my room.

"How was school?"

"It's hokey. I'm tired of it. Okay if I go to the park and play ball with the kids?"

"I guess so, for an hour until dinner."

I was feeling moody and irritable. Maybe I was ready to start my monthlies. Ma had that embarrassing talk with me a year ago. I reached in the back of my closet and pulled out the booklet she gave me. At the time, I just tossed it aside, but I'm thinking now I'd better read it. I laid it on my bed and stripped off my school clothes.

"You and Your Growing-Up Years," the front cover said. I figured I'd look through it later tonight. It would give me an excuse to go to my room and shut the door.

I looked at my body in the dresser mirror. I rubbed my breasts, trying to make them grow faster. Right now they were just little buds. My friend Alice had more than I did. We compared them just the other day. It was embarrassing that mine were so small compared to hers.

I wadded up some toilet paper and stuffed it into my bra. Yes, that looked better. I pulled on some shorts and a shirt. Then I brushed my hair. It was curly and just went every which way like it had a mind of its own.

"You be sure to be back in an hour, you hear?" Ma said when I opened my door.

"That's too soon, Ma. We'll just be getting started. Can't I eat late?"

"You know the Reverend likes to have his family at the table at supper time." She stared at my chest.

"What about what I like, for a change?" I said.

Ma sighed. She looked tired. She dropped her head into

her hand, signaling another headache. I was out the door and running down the sidewalk before she had time to lift her head from her hand.

I compromised and came back in an hour and a half. The game broke up a little early anyhow. Ma was still sitting in the same chair with a wet cloth on her forehead.

She got up and took some chicken from the ice box. I wondered why Black Bart wouldn't buy her an electric refrigerator. Almost everyone else in town had one. The ice man said he was about to go out of business. It wasn't like Bart didn't have the money, I was sure of that. He made me help him count and stack the offering money after church every Sunday. Then on Monday he carried it to the bank and put it in his account.

He came through the door and hung his hat on the rack. "Where's your Ma?" He stared at my chest. I had forgotten to take the toilet paper out of my bra.

Ma came out of the kitchen and smiled at him. "We'll be eating in a few minutes, Bart."

"Nadine, what does your daughter have stuck on her chest?"

"What do you mean, dear?" She looked again at my chest.

"Just this. Her chest has puffed out considerably since I saw her this morning. Belle, empty out whatever you have stuffed into your underclothes." He folded his arms and frowned.

"I don't know what you're talking about." I felt my face flush.

"Then I'll show you." He grabbed my arm. "You can take out that stuffing or your mother will do it for you."

Ma looked at me, mouth open. "Please, honey, do as you're told."

I shook my arm loose and turned around, my back to them. I took the toilet paper out of my bra and threw it on the floor.

"Jezebel! Pick that up right now." The Reverend's face flushed red. He grabbed my arm again. "And don't let me see any of that evil nonsense again."

I bent down and picked up the paper, then went to my room. I heard Bart say, "Why does she have to aggravate me all the time?" Ma didn't say anything. "She needs belting, and if this continues I'll see that she gets another one. The Bible is clear. 'Spare the rod and spoil the child.'"

I heard my Ma whisper. "That's what I've always said, Bart. But let me talk to her, okay?"

The next day Ma found me on the front porch swing, crying. Ma came out to the porch, a half glass of lightening in her hand. She's drinking it a lot more nowadays, but she manages to hide it from the Reverend. I guess she knows that I would never tell.

"What's wrong, Belle? Stop that bawling, now." Ma put a hand on one hip. "Tell me what's going on."

"I got a letter from Jesse today. He said that Jack lied about his age and joined the Army." I sobbed. He's going to go to war and get killed."

"Oh, stop it, Belle. He won't get killed. All the men are going. And he's almost eighteen, isn't he?"

I sniffled and drew myself up. "Yes, but I don't want him to go." My head hurt.

"Well, just get over it. He'll be fine." She stalked into the kitchen. "Come on, help me with supper. And tomorrow, we need to weed the Victory garden."

In the kitchen, Ma swallowed the last of the clear liquid in her glass and reached into the cupboard for the bottle of white lightening. She poured half a glass full, and then looked up to see that I was watching her.

"Get a move on, Belle. The Reverend will be home soon and expect his supper to be ready." Ma slammed a skillet onto the stove. She reached in her pocket for a Sen-Sen. Sen-Sens can cover up any breath.

I put my school books in my room and came back to the kitchen. I felt dry and wilted.

"What are we having?" My voice sounded dull. I wanted to go to my room and be alone. I wanted to think about Jack being in the Army.

"Beans and the last of the bacon. And cornbread." She looked at Belle as she swallowed the rest of the liquid from her glass. "And perk up now, before Bart gets home."

Chapter 4

Bear Creek 1943
Belle

World War II began to invade Bear Creek. As shortages grew, and everything from cigarettes to gas to tires was shipped overseas to the fighting men, those who lived in remote areas became more aware, more concerned. The young men were drafted or volunteered. There were only the women and children and old men left to work the farms and the factories. Reality slinked into their lives like a thief in the dark of night.

In almost every window there hung a flag with at least one star; blue if a young man or woman was in the service; gold if he or she had been killed. As the stars grew more plentiful the pain grew, too. More and more stars went from blue to gold.

But the nation as a whole pooled resources and banded together. It was like that in Bear Creek and Bear Holler, too. One gave his neighbor a tire coupon; the car owner gave his benefactor a ride to town when he needed it. An-

other traded his dead child's shoe ration for a meat coupon. Still another collected scrap metal and grease to donate for the war effort. Movie stars made appearances across the nation, even in Bear Creek, asking everyone to buy more War Bonds.

Then cars stopped running. No new ones were made and there were few parts for the old ones. Tires and gasoline were rationed. Horses became more and more valuable. Farmers fared best; they had horses, they raised their own meat and grew their own vegetables, picked apples and peaches from their orchards.

No new houses were built and housing costs soared until the government placed ceilings on rent. It became more difficult for many people to find a place to live.

Every Sunday, the nation as a whole turned their radios on and gathered around, heads bent, eyes intent. President Roosevelt's soothing voice asked for more sacrifices, more patience. They listened faithfully to his Fireside Chats, nodding to his pleadings. The nation, he said, would survive.

Everyone knew that the Japanese bombed Pearl Harbor, of course, and that we were at war with Germany and Italy as well. Still it seemed so far away in the beginning that it didn't have much to do with us. At the movies, I went to the lobby for popcorn waiting for the Movietone newsreel about the war to be over so the movie could start.

At first, the war seemed distant to me. When Jack left for the Army, though, it became more real. In the beginning everyone thought we would win and it would be over soon. But now it looked like we might even lose. The adults started to talk about what might that be like? What if we were occupied by the enemies?

Every time Ma heard about a shipment of meat coming

into the corner grocery, she woke me up at dawn to stand in the line with her. When we got there this morning, it was early light. The line at Johnson's market was already wound around the corner half a block. As we waited, Ma leafed through her ration book to see what she might be able to buy.

"Maybe some coffee and sugar will be on the shelf behind the cash register" She closed her ration book and took out the books for Bart and me. "I have enough coupons for one pound of each. What I wouldn't give for a pound of coffee."

"I'm so grateful that Bart bought our house, Belle. We'll never have to worry about a place to live" The line moved forward. "At least, he said he bought it, but I haven't seen the papers. They're locked in his desk. That's all right with me, that he has the worries of money management. It isn't women's work anyhow."

"How come the Reverend didn't go to war?" I asked. It was something I wondered about for a long time, even wished for.

"It's his feet. He has flat feet so they made him 4F. Not that it's any of your business, Belle. Curiosity killed the cat, you know."

I didn't know what that had to do with anything, but I didn't say so. I was tired of fighting with her all the time.

Ma and I planted a Victory Garden. She remembered how to raise corn and green beans, lettuce and tomatoes, potatoes and turnips. If she didn't live in town, she said, she would have chickens and a cow for milk.

The market doors creaked open and the line slowly filed into the store. Ma looked behind the counter and saw that there was no coffee. She sighed and asked for a pound of sugar, handing her coupon book and money to the clerk.

"The Reverend likes sugar with his tea." she said.

Chapter 5

Bear Holler 1946

Three years after Jack went to war, Jesse drove Auntie to pick him up at the bus station.

They watched him climb down the steps, looking very tired. Jack was still wearing his uniform though he had a medical discharge in his pocket. He said they called it shell-shock. His eyes, Jesse couldn't describe. He couldn't tell what was different, but they had a scared look to them, like he was watching a Frankenstein movie. After shaking Jesse's hand and hugging his Ma, Jack picked up his duffel bag and walked toward the dusty old Ford. Jesse climbed into the driver's seat. "We've got just enough gas to get home, Jack. There are still lots of shortages."

When Mary asked, Jack said he couldn't remember a lot of what happened to him. On the ride home, he talked about what he could recall.

He remembered arriving at boot camp. The squat barracks, the barren fields, and the stoop-shouldered men in jeans and overalls. He remembered the relentless rain, how it dripped from the brim of his hat, splattered the toes of his work boots and soaked his guitar case.

A short ugly man with Sergeants stripes on his sleeve walked back and forth in front of the men, yelling about rules and telling everyone to stand at attention. He hoped that the loud-mouthed little guy would stop talking sometime soon so as he could get his guitar out of the rain. Hell, he could hardly understand what he was saying, what with the rain and the man's funny Northern accent.

He saw copies of his own figure in different sizes, shapes and colors. The gruff sergeant stopped talking finally. The men were shuttled in rapid succession through the barber shop, the clothing issue room, and then to the barracks. There were white men only; no Negroes or Asians. They were kept apart, in separate divisions, as if they might contaminate the white men.

Jack said they broke the promise they made to him at recruiting. They didn't have him entertaining the troops at all. They sent him to the front lines in Italy right away.

What he couldn't remember, he said, was what happened to land him in the hospital. The psychiatrists shot him full of sodium pentothal but the memory didn't come back. Maybe it was just as well, he pondered, and changed the subject.

"How have you been, Ma?" he asked.

Mary kept leaning forward and patting his shoulder.

"I've been just fine. I prayed every night for you, son, for the Lord to keep you safe. Remember when you built a radio so you could listen to the Grand Ole Opry? And then you built one for me, too. And every week I listen to music, and to President Roosevelt's Fireside Chats. I don't know what I'd do without my radio."

Then Jack told her that he was moving into Josh's old

cabin, if that was all right with Jesse.

"Why don't you stay at home with me instead of going to that musty old cabin? It's been sitting there empty for years now."

"I'll move in with you, Jack." Jesse said. "I'll keep you company."

"Oh, Lord, I'll be all alone then." Mary covered her face with both hands.

Jack smiled at her and promised to visit every day and help out at the farm. "I won't be a half-mile away, Ma, and if you need me, just holler. But I've got to be alone for awhile. And my buddy Dave is coming next week to stay with me. That wouldn't work out too well at your house"

Then he turned to Jesse. "I don't want to put you off Jesse, but give me a week before you move in. I just want to be alone for awhile, okay?"

Mary talked about how they had to do without sugar and coffee and shoes and gas. It was all rationed. Lucky they raised their own animals or they wouldn't have meat or butter, either, she said. Most people were stuck with using that new-fangled oleo margarine. They had to mash it up and put yellow food coloring in it so they could pretend it was butter.

Later, as Jesse and Jack sat on Mary's front porch steps drinking beer, Jack told Jesse that he just couldn't sympathize with the hardships at home after what he had seen in those three years of war. His eyes looked haunted, private.

They spent the next week cleaning up the cabin, while Mary fawned over Jack, cooking him his favorite meals every night.

Jesse moved into the cabin with Jack a week later as planned. Two days later, Dave showed up. Then Tennessee, a kid they went to high school with, gradually moved his stuff in, too. First his drum set, then his clothes bit by bit.

Jack didn't talk much about the Army after that. It was like he wanted to forget it, put it all behind him. But his sleep was short and restless. Sometimes he couldn't sleep at all. When Jesse asked, he told him that mangled bodies still showed up in his nightmares when he drifted off.

He said he felt better when the guys were around. It was kind of like old times for Jack and Jesse, too, playing music at the cabin. Jesse thought of his Daddy a lot. And he could almost see Nadine sitting in his Ma's old rocking chair and shooting dirty looks at them.

It seemed to Jesse like Jack's depression would go away for awhile when they drank beer and jammed, maybe smoked a little marijuana. It was a habit Jack and Dave picked up in the service, and Jesse and Tennessee joined in with enthusiasm.

Jack said he wanted to form a band. The guys were all for it, and couldn't wait to start playing at the local taverns. They practiced together, or turned on the Grand Ole Opry and drank beer on the front porch. Jack and Dave had their severance pay and there was no rent to pay. Tennie and Jesse just sponged off them for the time being.

They all agreed that Jack should be their manager. He was the oldest and was good at figures, at organization.

Soon they had their first job at the Dew Drop Inn on the other side of Nashville, Friday and Saturday night. All four jammed into the pickup, three in front and Tennessee in back with the drums and guitars. The jobs kept coming in after that. The money wasn't great, but there weren't too many expenses, either. Jesse thought it was a good time.

What made it even better was that Belle came to the cabin almost every day. At fifteen she was already a beauty, but moody with a short fuse. Jesse tried to understand her, though he didn't know why she was so unhappy. Maybe it was her mother. Nadine had always been difficult, and he knew that Belle didn't like her stepfather, either. She called him Black Bart and looked disgusted whenever his name came up. Jesse asked her several times what he had done to her and she always said *nothing.*

Jesse heard things around town; how Bart held a revival meeting twice a year and people came from the next county to see him. He raised a lot of money, it was said. He bought the house that Nadine and Belle had moved to when Josh died. People noticed that the Reverend wore an immaculate black suit that was always pressed, his leather shoes were shined, and a fine fedora hat with a colorful band imported from Haiti sat on his head. He visited the barber in town for shaves and haircuts. His nails were manicured. Every Sunday, the church he built on the hill just outside of town was full of worshippers who sang and shouted Hallelujah and filled the donation baskets with coins.

But Nadine and Belle, it was whispered, wore the same ordinary clothes year after year, and sat on worn out furniture in their house. Bessie Clackton, who worked at the county offices, told Jesse that the house was in Bart's name alone.

"Don't you think that's rather strange, Jesse?"

"Well, I guess it's his business, his and Nadine's." Jesse didn't care much what happened to Nadine. But he did care about Belle.

Belle told him that Nadine hardly left the house anymore, that she was drinking a lot.

She said that her Ma was quiet, which wasn't at all like her. And almost every day she suffered a bad headache.

In six months Reverend Bart Bartholomew would be dead. The gossips in town would say that Belle killed him.

Chapter 6

Belle

I ran away not long after Jack came home from the war. He moved into Daddy's old cabin and next thing I knew, Jesse moved in, too. I was over there a lot, cooking dinner for them almost every night. Ma didn't like it but I went anyhow, sneaking out right after school before Bart got home. Bart didn't like it either, but by now I was big enough to defend myself from him and he pretty much stopped bothering me. If he said anything, I'd just give him a cold threatening look and he backed down. He seemed to know that I wasn't afraid of him any more and acted like he was worried that I might tell on him.

Anyhow, Jack brought his buddy Dave back with him and he, Jesse, Tennessee and Dave were living in Daddy's cabin. I liked Dave; even though he drank a lot. I think it was his eyes that made him seem younger than twenty-three. They were half-shut most of the time like he was day-dreaming. He wore his dark brown hair in a ducktail, all greased down so it looked almost black. And he could play the bass so good that my mouth would just hang open listening to him.

Jack's old radio was always playing country music and we sang along with it. Sometimes I sang while the guys practiced. I pretended I was on stage in front of the band, and the audience was clapping and then some agent would come up and offer us a big contract. Dave said he thought I sounded like Keely Smith.

Tennessee left his drums set up in the parlor. When he sat down on the stool behind the drums, snapped the top off a bottle of beer, picked up the drumsticks and started tapping out a beat, the rest of the guys would jump in right away. Jack played lead guitar. He was the best I thought. Then Jesse would pick up his guitar and strum along, singing in his powerful true voice. Dave would pick deep notes on the stand-up bass, grinning and winking at me.

I looked at the smile on Jesse's face and thought; this is the best time of my life.

Sometimes, Jesse asked me why I didn't like Bart. "Does he hit you?"

"Not any more," I said. "But he's strict, all right. When I was younger he would take a belt to me but he hasn't done that for a long time now."

"Well then, what's going on, Belle?"

"Nothing. Nothing at all, Jesse. I just don't like the man, and I get tired of Ma's nagging."

He looked at me sideways.

"You're looking kind of funny. What's wrong?" He asked again, watching my face.

"Nothing, really. I just had that blamed nightmare again last night."

"What nightmare? Tell me." He lit a Lucky and blew smoke through his nose.

"Well, okay." I said. At least it would distract him and stop the questions.

I'm asleep in my own bed. I'm awakened by a noise, I'm not sure what it is or where it's coming from, but it scares me, whatever it is. A thin beam of light shines right in my eyes, like it was directed to my eyes. Then the beam widens until I'm blinded and suddenly I feel a hand on my leg. I open my mouth to scream but nothing will come out. I concentrate on screaming but still nothing will come out of my mouth. It's like I'm paralyzed.

Now the hand is moving slowly down my leg, to my foot. I'm relieved that it is going to leave me, I think. But instead it starts back up my leg, very slowly, up my calf, then behind my knee where it should tickle but it doesn't. It pauses there while the light is still shining in my eyes. I move my head to try to get out of the light so I can see the hand, or whose hand it is, but the light follows me wherever I turn.

The hand has started moving again, slowly, so slowly that it's hardly noticeable, from behind my knee to the inside of my thigh. It feels almost gentle until it reaches the inside of my thigh, higher and higher, and suddenly the gentleness is gone and there is an urgency, a roughness that wasn't there before and I try again to scream but the scream is silent. I'm still paralyzed, can't move except for my head and my head is turning frantically from side to side, wanting to escape that light, that hand.

And one more time I try to scream and this time it works. I scream and scream, and that's when I wake up.

"If I only knew when it was coming I wouldn't go to

sleep that night. I'm afraid the time will come when the dream keeps going and I can't ever scream or wake up." I never told anyone about this dream, except Jesse.

Jesse stared at me for a long time. Then he ruffled my hair and said, "If you ever want to talk about anything, I'm here."

I said, "Okay," but I never did. Sometimes I wanted to, and came close to telling him, but I was too scared of what might happen if I did. Maybe he wouldn't believe me either. The Sheriff didn't. Maybe Bart would talk Ma into sending me away. Or it could kill my mother if she knew. She seemed more fragile every day.

I was in my bedroom reading with my door shut, like I always do when I'm home so Ma won't bother me. I heard a knock on the front door. It was pretty early in the morning so I opened my bedroom door just a crack to see who it was. It kind of scared me when I saw Horace McMann, because he usually only showed up when there was trouble. His Sheriff's uniform was dirty at the knees and he was all sweaty. His belly was hanging over his belt like always. His hair which is streaked with gray and was normally combed nice and slick, was all messed up and sticking up every which way.

I couldn't really hear what he was saying to Ma, but she let out a loud holler and her legs collapsed from under her. Horace caught her and half carried her to the couch, where she lay down crying her heart out. He was breathing hard from the effort. I thought it must be about Bart.

Last night Ma was fit to be tied about Bart. When I got home from the church dance she was crying and dabbing at her eyes with a handkerchief.

"I know he likes to walk late at night, and I know he

has his preaching duties to perform, but damn it all," and here she put her hand over her mouth like she was trying to stop any more bad words from escaping, "he has a family here. He doesn't have to stay at the dance until the last song is sung. I've got half a mind to go over there myself, except for this headache that came up from hell itself."

Her hand was supporting her head when she got up from the chair. She stumbled to the kitchen and wet a washcloth with cold water. She put it on her forehead and went to lie down on her bed. I took her some aspirin and then I went on to bed, too.

Sheriff McMann pulled up a chair beside Ma and was talking to her in a low voice. I could hear a word now and then like, *found in the woods dead* and *coroner.*

Then his voice became louder and more official sounding. "Where's Belle? She was seen in Bear Holler last night and it was close to where the body was found this morning."

That's when I got really scared. I remember seeing the Witherspoon twins because I was surprised those two old ladies were out so late at night. I didn't run across anyone else. Where I live, no one thinks twice about walking around at night. Most often no one gets murdered. In fact, this was the first murder I had ever heard of in my lifetime. Ma was crying hard again and she didn't answer Horace's question. He was patting her arm while he looked around the room, but I ducked and he couldn't see me anyhow through that little crack.

I was glad that I hadn't gone out there right away. See, once Bart slapped me hard on the face when I tried to stop him from having his way with me. I was about twelve then. The next day I went to Sheriff McMann and told him what happened. He asked did I have any marks on me and I had to say no because the red was gone by then. He stared at the ceiling and wiped the sweat from his face with his hand, then looked at me.

"Are you sure he wanted to get familiar with you? He is a preacher, you know, always trying to comfort someone. Maybe you were just scared, not used to him, missing your Daddy and all." Bart was the only Minister in the holler and Horace isn't generally one to rock any boats.

"I was scared all right but he keeps doing these things to me." I was crying and wiping my eyes with my sleeve.

"You got to be careful, Belle, about misinterpreting things and causing some innocent person grief." He laid a heavy hand on my shoulder.

"I don't want to cause any trouble. I just want him to stop." I was sobbing. I couldn't talk any more, so I just left his office.

Anyhow, he never did anything about it so I just went back home. I never did tell Ma and I guess he didn't either

Ma was still hollering now and then, crying in between, and Sheriff McMahan was looking all around the room and shuffling his feet around. I didn't take the time to pack up anything. I just grabbed the baby-sitting money I had in a cigar box under my bed, $33.45, and my favorite necklace that was a pink heart, made out of some kind of stone. I stuffed a few clothes into a small overnight bag. Then I pulled a chair over to the window, climbed through it and ran into the woods.

When I came out the other side, I hitched a ride into town on the back of Bernie Mathews' truck. I climbed in the back when he was stopped at the crossroad. He was hauling a big load of tomatoes and the boxes covered up the back window. He didn't even know I was there, thank God because I can't be sure he wouldn't have ratted on me later. Once in town, I took the first Greyhound bus that showed up and never looked back

When Belle didn't shown up at the cabin for three days Jesse drove the pickup into Bear Creek He waited for the Greyhound Bus window to open at Bear Creek Drug Store.

"Hiya, Jesse. What can I do for you?" The window creaked open.

"Hello Hiram." He took off his hat.

Hiram swung the wooden window around and locked it to the wall.

"Did you sell a ticket to Belle about two, three days ago?" Jesse asked.

"Sure did. She went on into Nashville. Said she was going to visit her friend there. She acted kind of nervous." He lowered his voice. "I hear the Reverend was killed the other day. Maybe she was broke up about it."

"Yeah, maybe. When Belle didn't come see me for three days, I figured something was wrong and I came into town looking for her. Her Ma told me that Bart was dead and Belle ran off."

"Ran off? Damn, I didn't know that. She didn't have anything to do with it, did she?" He scratched his head.

"I don't really know, Hiram. She never said anything to me. And Nadine, well, you know how Nadine is. She all but slammed the door in my face." He put his hat back on his head. "The Sheriff came out to the cabin yesterday afternoon looking for her. I told him I hadn't seen her since the night of the dance. He said he just wanted her for questioning."

"He was here, too, Jesse. He was going to put out a nation-wide APB. He also told me he just wanted her for questioning."

Jesse turned to leave. "Well, thanks, Hiram." He turned back. "She didn't say what friend she was visiting, did she?"

"I think she said Ronnie or Bonnie…" He frowned.

"Bonnie Jones? Married Aaron Hawkins?"

"That sounds like it. Yeah, that's it." He raised one eyebrow. "I didn't think to tell the Sheriff about that." He smiled.

"Bonnie was in Belle's class, until she got pregnant and married Aaron. They moved to Nashville last month. Thanks, Hiram, that might help. See you around." Jesse shook his hand. "If you think of anything else, let me know, okay?"

"Sure, Jesse. Take care now, you hear?"

Jesse got Bonnie's address from her mother in Bear Creek and drove to Nashville.

Bonnie opened the front door when he knocked, leaving the screen between them. She balanced a baby on one hip. No, she hadn't seen Belle at all.

"Bonnie, Sheriff McMahan said you told him that Belle called you and said that she killed Bart. Is that true?"

"Well, I wouldn't have said it if it wasn't true, Jesse." She shifted the child from one hip to the other.

"Did she say where she was when she called?"

"Nope."

"Did she say why she killed him?"

"Nope." The baby started fussing. She jiggled her on one arm.

"What's your baby's name?"

"Louise Janet, after my Ma."

"That's pretty, Bonnie. How old is she?" He shuffled his feet. She could ask him in, he thought, instead of leaving him stand out in the sun.

"She's going on a year now." Jesse figured in his head. Her baby should be four months older than that, if she was pregnant when she said she was. He let it lie.

"I don't get it. Do you know why Belle called you?"

"Darned if I know, Jesse. Maybe she wanted to brag a little."

"Didn't she sound scared?"

"Nope."

"Bonnie, if you hear from her again, would you let me know? Write to General Delivery at Bear Creek."

"Okay." She shifted the baby again to her other hip and took the paper he handed her."Jesse, you know Belle was always kind of moody. And she never did like the Reverend."

"I know. I couldn't ever figure out why, except he was really strict with her. She probably missed our father, too."

Bonnie sniffed. "Well, I've got to feed the baby."

"Okay. Thanks." He turned to leave. "You've got a pretty girl there."

"Thanks, Jesse." Bonnie backed away from the screen and closed the door.

Jesse doubted that Belle knew anyone in Nashville except Bonnie. So he checked the bars, thinking she might be looking for him there. He showed her picture to everyone he talked to. It was the last one he took of her, sitting on the cabin's front porch swing. She wore cuffed up Levis and one of Daddy's old white shirts. She looked serious, almost angry.

No one he showed the picture to had seen her.

He checked out the railroad station. She hadn't bought a ticket there, at least not under her own name. Then, at the Greyhound bus station the clerk remembered her. A ticket to Los Angeles. Maybe he should go there. But where would he start looking?

He made some phone calls; to the Los Angeles YWCA, to some hotels close to the bus station downtown. But she didn't have any money, did she? *Damn,* he thought, *just when we got to know each other again, and we were all having a good time at the cabin together. I'm worried, but she's a smart girl. She'll find help."*

Jesse tried to visualize her hitting Bart with a rock on the back of his head. Bart would have been bending over or she couldn't have reached that high. And why would she do that, anyhow? She didn't like him. That much was clear. But did she hate him enough to kill him? Maybe Bart was trying to punish her one time too many. Jesse saw her glaring at him at the dance. It was possible, wasn't it, that she didn't do it and was just running scared?

Back at the cabin, Jesse snapped the cap from a bottle of beer and sat down on the front porch steps. Jack came up the path, went to the ice box for a beer and sat down beside him.

"Any luck?" Jack asked.

"Naw. No one has seen her in Nashville. Bonnie said she called her from somewhere, she didn't know where, but she never came to her house. She told Bonnie she finally killed the son-of-a-bitch."

"That's hard to believe. But then, why would she say that if it wasn't true?"

"Yeah. But I know one thing: Belle wouldn't have done it unless she had a good reason."

"I'd say so." Jack finished his beer and got up. "Want another, Jesse?

"Sure." He turned and looked up at his cousin. "Jack, can you see how Belle could hit Bart in the head when he was taller than her? And bigger? She would have to catch him bending over."

"You're right about that. He was a big man."

Jack returned with two bottles of beer.

Jesse stared down the path to the dirt road in front of the cabin.

"I was just thinking about the day I left here, after

Daddy died. I'll never forget the look on Belle's face as we drove away." He rubbed his eyes.

"Yeah, I remember that she ran after the truck for awhile."

"We've got to find her, Jack, but I don't know where to go from here."

"Let's just wait on it for awhile, Jesse. Maybe she'll write."

It turned out Jack was right. Two weeks later, there was a letter at the post office addressed to Jesse Williams, General Delivery, Bear Creek, Tennessee in block printing. Jesse knew right away it was from Belle. There was no return address. The postmark was Santa Monica, California.

Dear Jesse and all you guys. I want to let you know that I'm all right. I can't say where I am because I don't want to put that knowledge on you. But I'm fine. I made some friends here and they're helping me out. I'm looking for work as a waitress. I think I can do that after I cooked and washed dishes all the time at your place! Ha, ha. So don't worry about me, okay? I wish I could find out how Bart died. But I can't let you write to me. Someday you might have a phone and I can call you. I'll keep checking.

Love always, Belle

P.S. I'm getting a good tan.

"Jack, look here. It's from Belle." He took a chair at the table where the guys were eating supper.

Jack took the letter and read it. "If she doesn't know how Bart was killed, then she couldn't have done it, could she?"

"I don't know. I just don't know. She could be putting it there just in case the letter got into the wrong hands." Jesse handed the letter to Dave, then to Tennessee.

"Hell, I don't think Belle could have done it. I don't care what that girl in Nashville said." Tennie threw the letter on the table in front of them.

"Then why did she run?" Dave said. He pushed his plate away.

"Maybe she was scared when the Sheriff came looking for her." Jack said.

"All I know is I won't stop looking for her." Jesse got up from the table and stretched.

Jack stood, too. "I got us another gig in Nashville for this weekend. It's at Jackson Tavern. And, guys, let's get a lot of practice in till then, okay? I contacted Gus Harper from Harper Agency and he promised he'd stop in to hear us. If he signs us up, we'll be playing regular, I bet."

"Damn, Jack, that's good news. We sure do need the work." Jesse punched Jack on the shoulder. "Good job, buddy."

He picked up Belle's letter and tucked it in his shirt pocket.

Part Two

Part of being a true country singer is being able to put your heart and your soul into the music and make you identify with what it says. You get the feeling he's singing those words to you and that he understands your story. They do it for the love of the music, despite the pay check at the end of the shift.

Bill C. Malone, Country Music Historian

Chapter 7

Belle

When the Greyhound dropped me off in downtown Los Angeles, the only money I had left was $3.19. I walked out onto the street and saw a bus headed for Santa Monica. That's what it said on the sign above the driver's window. The lady sitting next to me on the Greyhound had told me there was a beach in Santa Monica, so I jumped on the bus. I always wanted to see the ocean.

I wandered up and down the beach for awhile. I took off my shoes and felt the sand soft and warm between my toes. I waded into the water and looked at how far it went. You couldn't see any land on the horizon. And the palm trees; I never saw anything like them, except in magazines. The sun was warm on my back. It was all so beautiful I thought I was in a dream. I stretched out on the sand and fell asleep for awhile.

I wondered what the people were like that lived there.

They were going about their business like where they lived was nothing unusual. They were pushing baby strollers, drinking coffee in the outdoor cafes, riding bicycles on the concrete path. Do you get used to all this when you see it every day?

I walked onto the pier and watched children riding a merry-go-round. I gazed at the horizon again, just as the sun touched down on it. The red and orange fanned out to cover the whole sky. It put me in mind of the sunsets back home, when the sky turned all blue and pink and red. Maybe I could be safe here.

Home was so far away.

My stomach was growling. It reminded me that I hadn't eaten since yesterday. I wandered into Dean's Café at Muscle Beach by the Santa Monica pier. I checked my money and the sign above the counter. There was enough for some French Fries. I took them out back to the open air patio. It was late and the sun was set, but the air was still hot. I moved to a spot under a tree.

I was dunking a fry into ketchup when six guys in swim suits came through and sat at a big table next to me. They were all drinking beer and pretty soon, one of them brought me a beer and sat down at my table. I really appreciated the beer because my nerves were on edge. After awhile the rest of the guys left, but he didn't. Instead, he brought me another beer.

We stayed on the patio where the bartender couldn't see us. We talked for a long time. His name was Marty and he was muscular and tan and nice looking; clean cut. This is where all the bodybuilders hang out, he said. They worked out at Muscle Beach, which was right beside the pier.

"You should see how it is on the weekend," he said. "People are everywhere watching us do our acrobatics."

"Wow, I'd love to see that," I said. My French fries were gone and the beer was making me a little dizzy.

"Want a hamburger? I'm going to have one and I'll order you one, too."

"Sure." I thought I'd better take it, who knows when I could eat again. I hoped he meant that he would pay for it, because I couldn't.

He soon returned with two hamburgers and another beer for himself.

"So where do you live? Do you go to school?" He wiped catsup drips off the side of his mouth.

I told Marty I was eighteen and out of high school. I was hitchhiking around the country, thinking about college maybe.

"You sure are an adventurous girl,' he said. "You don't see too many women with enough guts to hitchhike. What made you think of doing that?"

"I just got sick and tired of hanging around a small town. You know, I wanted to see the country and money is tight, so the best way to travel is to hitchhike."

"Don't you think it's a little dangerous though?"

"Naw. I'm a good judge of character. I can tell right off if someone is up to no good. Besides, sometimes I take the bus. It all depends." I tried not to eat too fast. "You see servicemen hitchhiking all the time. No one seems to have any trouble."

He looked at me with a little half smile. "What do you do for clothes?"

I only paused for a few seconds before answering. "Good question. I'm not sure what I'll do since mine got stolen. I was waiting in this bus station in Nashville and then I had to go to the bathroom." I crossed my fingers. That means the lie is okay, that I didn't really mean it. "There wasn't anyone else in the waiting room, so I left my bag there. When I came back, it was gone. And these clothes are getting rank, I'd say. I'm lucky that I had one change of clothes in this bag."

"So what are you going to do now?" He took another bite of hamburger.

"Get some work real fast, because the last of my money was in that bag, too. I can waitress and tips would give me money right away." I finished the second beer.

"I'm kind of worried about you. How about staying on my couch, then I won't have to worry and we'll both get a good night's sleep." He finished his burger and took a long swig of beer.

I studied his face. Could I trust him? If anything went wrong, I couldn't call the police. It would be better to sleep on a park bench or maybe in the sand down close to the water where I could hear the waves. But I wasn't sure if that was safe, either.

Marty smiled at me. It was like he was reading my mind. "Look; you told me you were a good judge of character. If that's true, you know that you don't have to worry about me. I promise."

An hour later, we walked up a side street two blocks from the beach to Marty's small apartment. I told him right off that I wouldn't go to bed with him and if that was what he had planned, forget it, and I'd just keep on traveling. He said it was okay, he respected that, and I shouldn't worry at all.

The first night Marty fixed me a bed on his couch. I was so tired I slept like a baby. He bought me my meals, too. He said that he never cooked anything but he knew all the local places to get a cheap meal. He bought me a bathing suit and some shorts and tops and a pair of Levi's. He acted like it was fun, helping me pick out clothes. And I kept thinking, I'd better look for a job tomorrow so I can pay him back. But one day drifted into another and I kept saying, *tomorrow*, to myself. And Marty never pushed me.

Marty had a really fine body, being a weight lifter and all. He sure did love his own image though. Every time he passed a mirror he studied his body, maybe stopped to flex his muscles and pose a bit. I can't say that his face was that good looking, but he wasn't ugly either. He had a nice smile, and light brown eyes and light brown hair that matched his eyes almost exactly. His hair was bleached by the sun and I could see streaks of gold when we sat on the sand and talked.

We walked down to the beach from his place the next morning. His buddies were already there working out on the rings and building pyramids with their bodies. The two girl bodybuilders, being smaller, climbed up on the top of the pyramid. Then we all went for a swim after playing some volleyball.

I did lay out in the sun a lot which Marty said wasn't good for me, but I liked looking in the mirror at my tan body. He made me wear sunglasses because I'd get squint lines around my eyes if I didn't, he said. It really did make me look more grown up. Pretty soon I was getting in good shape, from eating better like Marty and swimming a lot. I wanted him to show me some weight lifting but he said it wasn't good for girls; it made them look like men.

The fifth night at Marty's place, I said my muscles were sore from swimming. Marty said, lay down here on the massage table, I'll give you a rubdown. He went to school to learn how to do massage. That's how he made extra money when he wasn't competing in body building contests.

He knew his business, too. He told me to lie down on my stomach and I did. He went slow and easy, warming up the oil in his hands before he rubbed all my muscles. It wasn't too long before I was really relaxed. His touch was strong but gentle and it really felt nice. His hands lingered on my buttocks, and then moved down my thighs. I was tingling; a good kind of feeling though. It wasn't at all the same as when Bart touched me. Soon he turned me onto my back and he kissed me full on the mouth and then his mouth was all over my body until I was almost begging him to put it in. His arms were strong, his whole body hard and muscular.

"Are you sure you're eighteen?" He stopped and looked at me. "I'm not into cradle-snatching. I don't want any trouble."

"Marty," I said. *Don't stop now*! "I wouldn't lie about that." I had my fingers crossed but I don't know if that counts.

I slept in his bed from then on. We had sex two or three times a day sometimes. Marty didn't like to use condoms and he said he couldn't get me pregnant anyhow because he's been fixed, so what was the point?

I felt a little guilty about liking the sex because the Bible says not to do that until you're married. But what about Bart having sex with me, and he was a Minister. I worried that I could get something, like those movies they showed us in high school about syphilis and gonorrhea and stuff and getting pregnant. Marty said he didn't have anything, so it was okay. He said the Bible was all in how you interpreted it anyhow. I respected that he was honest, and being a lot older than me he was probably wiser. Marty was 32 but he said he never got married and he didn't have any kids. I didn't tell him about Bart. He thought he was the first with me and in a way, he was.

Six weeks later, just when I was all settled into the beach life, a truant officer by the name of John Atkinson came around while I was eating lunch at Dean's. He wanted to see my identification. Well, I didn't have any, except my student body card from Bear Creek High School, which I definitely didn't want anyone to see. I tore it up the first chance I got.

"Mr. Atkinson, I don't carry my Drivers License to the beach, but I'm eighteen and out of school. I just got to Los Angeles recently." It took every ounce of concentration to keep from giving myself away, I was so scared.

"Where are you from?" He took out a notepad.

"Indianapolis. I'm working at Shay's Café on Second Street, evening shift." That's where Marty and I ate all the time and it was the first thing I could think of.

"Where do you live?" He licked the pencil lead.

"101 Beach Avenue. I can get my roommate to verify that for you if you like." I hoped I didn't have to call Marty from the beach where he was working out on the rings.

"Sir, I can bring my ID with me tomorrow. I'm here every day. You can ask Georgia." I pointed to the waitress behind the counter

Mr. Atkinson said, "I guess that would be all right. I'll see you tomorrow, then. Right here, at noon, okay?"

"Sure. I'll be here."

I felt so weak I could hardly move by the time Mr. Atkinson left Dean's Cafe. I sat there for a good long while before I went to lie in the sun.

I know I've always looked older than my age, and I know how to put on the airs of someone older. I learned early on that men can be swayed by a pretty face. I know I'm pretty, though I'm not the most gorgeous girl in the world. I have light blue eyes which people tell me are my best feature, and long wavy light brown hair, which I make lighter by putting lemon juice on it when I wash it. Marty says my body is well proportioned though I'd rather be thinner like Marlene Dietrich.

The next morning, as soon as Marty went to the gym for his workout, I took some money from his drawer and packed up the things he bought me. I can say for myself, that I left an I.O.U. for the $50 and a note saying thanks for everything. I wrote down his address and when I started making money in Alaska, I sent him what I owed, plus a ring made from gold nuggets. He never wrote back. But maybe that was because I was moving around so much that his letter never caught up with me. Or maybe I didn't put a return address on the envelope.

I took a bus to the main highway going north, route 99. If I had to leave the beach then I wanted to see San Francisco. And I wanted to put some distance between me and the truant officer before he put two and two together and talked with the police. I didn't want to leave Marty, and I didn't want to leave the beach.

I really missed my brother and the guys. I even missed my mother, now that she wasn't around to nag me. Damn that Bart. It seemed to me he was reaching out from the grave to make my life miserable. I thought it would be easier when I was rid of him.

Chapter 8

Belle 1946

Every time a big truck went by, I stuck my thumb out because I thought a truck driver would be safe to ride with. You never know who might be in a car. That was when the Johnsons rolled to a stop in front of me and my little red bag, the new one that I just bought at the Five and Dime. They were driving a pickup truck and pulling the most beautiful trailer you ever saw in your life. Both of them had gray hair and smiled at me. They reminded me of my Grandma and Grandpa, God rest their souls.

The Grandma, her name was Minnie, talked to me all the way to San Francisco. Her husband, Arthur, drove and every once in a while he looked over at me and smiled. Minnie said they were going to visit their son and grand-children in San Francisco. The children liked to sleep with them in their trailer, which they parked at the beach.

Arthur pulled the trailer into the Sears parking lot so

Minnie could buy some things for the children. I told them to go ahead; I was going to take a nap if that was all right. They said, sure it was. I climbed into the trailer and lay down on the couch there. I fell asleep right away.

Next thing I knew, Arthur was beside me and running his hand up and down my arm.

"You sure are sweet, Belle. I'd like to give you some money to get by, okay? Come give me a little kiss."

It turned out the old grandpa was a real lech. I had to fight him off. I bailed out of their trailer right in the Sears parking lot in San Francisco while grandma was inside shopping. It was like my Granny used to say: "You can't always tell a book by its cover."

I found a park and slept on a bench under a tree that night. It was cold and raining some and all I had on was shorts and a sweat shirt that Marty had bought me. We needed one for cool nights at the beach. And all I could think about was those grandchildren that liked to sleep in the trailer with Minnie and Arthur.

The next day I headed on up to Alaska and never had any more trouble with hitchhiking. I rode with a nice young couple in their truck all the way up the road to Anchorage. We broke down five times, what with all the potholes and mud on the road. It was fun, though, because they were laid back and easy to get along with. They acted like they believed my story, whether they did or not.

It was raining the day we pulled into Anchorage. Joy and Bill, that was their names, took me to a restaurant and bought me a nice lunch. Then I excused myself to go make a phone call. I crossed my fingers and said, "I'll let my friends know that I'm in town."

"Belle, are you going to be all right?" Joy said.

"Sure, why not? I'm fine. My friends will come pick

me up as soon as they get off work. You go on, now."

"I don't feel right leaving you here like this." Bill laid a dollar bill on the table for a tip.

"Don't you worry one little bit. I have money, and my friends are very reliable. If you don't leave now, you're not going to make your sister's wedding in Fairbanks on time. You said so, yourself."

Bill paid the cashier, and then they both turned to look at me one more time. I waved and smiled and they went out the front door.

I looked around. Then I picked up the dollar from the table, tucked it in my pocket, and went to the rest room.

Washed up and clean clothes in place, I came back into the restaurant and asked for the manager. The cashier motioned me into the bar. I took a seat at a table there and soon a middle-aged balding man pulled up a chair opposite me.

"I understand you're looking for a waitress job."

"Yes, sir, I am."

"Are you experienced?"

"Yes, sir." I really was, considering how much waiting I'd done on Ma and Bart and Jesse and the guys.

"Please, call me Vernon. What's your name?"

"Belle. Belle Jones." I had thought this out already so I didn't hesitate.

He raised his eyebrows. "Where did you work last?"

Vernon lit a cigarette and offered me one. I shook my head.

"Well, I just got into town from Los Angeles. I worked at Shay's Café there, and also at Dean's, by the Santa Monica Pier. I'm a good worker, Vernon, and I really need a job." I wasn't sure that it was right to beg, but I was feeling kind of desperate. I spent the $50 I took from Marty on food and a bag for my clothes, so I didn't even have enough money for a hotel. I figured that I would be sleeping on a park bench tonight. It was late September and it was getting really cold even in the afternoon. It wasn't anything like California or Tennessee for that matter.

Vernon looked me up and down. He took another drag on his cigarette and smiled. "You can start tomorrow, 10:00 AM till 6:00 PM. Margie will train you into our system. And Belle, don't be late. I don't like it when employees show up late."

"Oh, no, sir, I won't. Thank you, Vernon."

I went to find Margie and get a uniform, like he told me to. She was a rough-looking redhead with an acne-scarred face. But she was friendly and she had a nice smile. I guessed she was in her thirties.

"It's hard to find good help up here. I'm sure you'll do just fine," she said. "How old are you, Belle?"

"I'm nineteen. I know, I've been told I don't look it."

"Not to worry. I'll bet Vernon didn't even ask, did he?" She searched through a stack of green uniforms, looking at the back label for my size.

She was right. He didn't.

"Where are you staying?" I felt like her eyes were looking right inside me.

"I just got into town, so I'll stay in a hotel until I get a paycheck and can find a place." I looked over the green uniform she handed me. It was pretty ugly; it had big white cuffs and a wide collar.

"You can bunk on my couch if you want. Save your money. Hotels are expensive. You'll need lots of money in this town."

"Really? Oh, thanks Margie. That would be great." I was near ecstatic that I wouldn't be sleeping on a park bench.

I was almost sorry that I took her tip money.

Margie lived in a small apartment close to the restaurant. It was full of plants, and orange curtains with beads on them, and astrology stuff. I found out she was a huge fan of astrology; even planned her life around it. I leafed through some of her books. Maybe it did make sense, the stars directing your life.

It seemed to me that nothing people do makes any difference in their life. It's just whatever happens, how the stars and planets are aligning in the skies. We had some talks about this and I began to think she was right. It was all about fate. We had no control over our destiny, so why worry about anything. It wasn't the way I was raised, but I was beginning to think that no one was in control. Take my life; I didn't want Ma to marry Bart but I didn't have any say in it. I didn't mean to kill him but it happened just the same.

Margie's boyfriend Gordon stayed overnight on the weekends. Late at night, stretched out on her couch, I tried to block out the sounds from the bedroom. I put wads of toilet paper in my ears. It didn't work. I couldn't go to sleep until they did. I thought of Marty and how sweet and gentle he was. I guess I missed him.

I wanted to move out when I got my first paycheck, but I needed to buy a heavy coat, and cap, and gloves. There was snow on the ground and the air was like ice. The tips at the restaurant were okay, and I was learning fast. But food was expensive and so were apartments. I needed to save a little more. Margie wanted me to stay on and she wouldn't let me pay any rent.

"You eat at the restaurant most of the time, and it doesn't cost me a dime when you sleep on my couch. You stay as long as you want, okay?"

When none of us was working, we played monopoly or

poker and drank beer. Bob Ryan, one of the bus boys, came over and played with us. Gordon always brought a bag of pot. He would make a big ceremony out of rolling a joint and passing it around. When it came to me, I just passed it on. It was all I could handle to drink alcohol.

I liked Bob all right and sometimes we went to a movie together. But he never made a move on me, and I didn't care if he did or not, to tell the truth.

It was pretty comfortable at Margie's and we got along fine. We drifted along like this for several months; working, playing board games, drinking and smoking with Gordon and Bob. I saved enough money to find my own place next payday. Sleeping on Margie's couch was getting old. But deep down, I was afraid of being alone and wasn't looking forward to moving.

One Saturday night I was curled up on the couch reading a book. I was alone because Margie had picked up an overtime evening shift. There was a knock on the door. I ignored it. Gordon knew that Margie was working and I wasn't in the mood to see Bob.

The knock came even louder and more insistent. Finally I opened the door a crack, thinking there might be some emergency.

"Hi, there, Belle."

It was Gordon. He was a good-looking guy, a blond with dreamy brown eyes. I probably would have dated him if he wasn't Margie's boyfriend.

"Hi, Gordon. Margie's at work, you know."

"Oh, damn, I forgot." He slapped his forehead. "Can I use the bathroom?"

"Sure." I opened the door all the way.

When he came out of the bathroom, he sat down on the chair across from me. I was reading but laid my book down.

"How about a drink? I could sure use one. We could talk awhile, if you don't mind." He stood and walked into the kitchen and pulled out a bottle of whiskey from the cupboard. I didn't think anything of it because he always made him self at home and he bought most of the booze anyhow.

Still I was feeling a little uneasy at this point. You know, that little warning sign that pops into your head when you least expect it. Since you don't expect it, you tend to push it aside. But I still said okay, I'd have a drink.

"Whiskey and Coke all right with you?"

"Sure." Maybe he did just want a drink and some small talk.

When he came out of the kitchen he sat down on the couch next to me, putting our drinks on the coffee table in front of us. I thanked him and said it was mixed just right. It was nice, sitting here like this, in good company. Gordon could be a lot of fun. I told myself, he wouldn't be here if he thought Margie wouldn't like it, would he?

"Do you like being a bartender, Gordon?"

"Yes, I do. I sure meet some interesting people. And the tips are fantastic. Just last week this older woman flirted with me all evening and I flirted back a little bit. At midnight she laid a $100 tip on the bar and said she'd see me the next night." He laughed. "The next night, I had to talk one of the waitresses into sliding onto the seat next to this woman and telling her to leave her husband alone." I laughed.

We talked awhile, and then turned on the radio. Gordon fixed us another drink, then another. When the news was over, he turned on some soft music and sat down beside me again. Next thing I knew, he had his arms around me and was kissing me. And I was kissing him back.

He drew back and looked into my eyes. "Belle, I guess

you know I liked you ever since I first met you."

"Wait, Gordon. What about Margie?" My hand on his chest, I pushed him back.

"It's okay. We aren't exclusive, you know."

He had one hand on my breast and with the other, pushed up my skirt.

I can't say why it all seemed okay. Maybe it was because I was missing Marty. Maybe it was the drinks. Or maybe I just wanted someone to put his arms around me and make love to me. I wanted to be held, that's for sure.

His pants were off and my skirt was almost around my neck when I heard a key in the lock. I'll never forget the look on Margie's face.

"It was quiet so I came…"

She was across the room in a second or two.

She grabbed my hair and pulled hard. "Bitch! Bitch! This is how you repay me?"

I tried to get free but she wouldn't let go. Gordon who was stark naked, grabbed her from behind, lassoing her arms and torso. I jumped up and pulled down my skirt. I wasn't sure what to do next.

Margie turned and slapped Gordon, hard. He reeled back, looking surprised. He grabbed his pants and pulled them on, hopping on one foot then the other. Then he headed for the door. "I'll call you tomorrow, Marge." I thought, *thanks for deserting me*.

Margie yelled after him. "Coward. Don't bother. And you," she whirled around and looked at me. "I'm going to knock the living shit out of you." She slapped my face, hard and pushed me down on the couch.

I struggled to find my voice. "I didn't mean to…"

She cut me off. "Probably not. I know what a womanizer he is. But I want your ass out of here first thing in the morning." She looked drained.

She went into her bedroom and slammed the door. I stared at her door for the longest time, relieved that it was over.

I slept in fits all night. I kept expecting Margie to come barreling out of the bedroom and make good her pledge to knock the shit out of me. I was ashamed and I knew I deserved it. But I still didn't want another confrontation.

I was out the door at dawn. I had a stash of money and some warm clothes. I hailed a taxi, tossed my bag inside, and checked into a motel on the other side of town.

A week or so later, I was almost out of money again. There was no way I could go back to work at the restaurant and face Margie. The motel wasn't anything fancy, but like everything else in town it wasn't cheap, either. It was lonely there and I missed Margie. I realized what a good friend she had been, and what a rotten friend I was.

I was coasting, trying to get up the nerve to look for Gordon. I didn't know anyone else in town, except Bob. I didn't know where he lived and I couldn't go to the restaurant. Gordon had told me he worked at a strip joint but I didn't know which one. In fact, once he tried to talk me into stripping, saying I had a nice body and was pretty enough. At that time, I told him I wasn't interested.

But now, looking another waitress job in the eye, stripping was beginning to sound better. Waitressing is hard work and the money isn't that good. The tips vary a lot. I didn't think I could get by in Anchorage on my own, just working in a restaurant. I didn't know if I could do stripping or not, but it was worth a try. The money is good, I'm told. Since the war, there have been lots of servicemen stationed in Alaska. They fill up the bars and strip joints almost every night and on payday you could hardly get in the door.

I made the rounds. The joints were all close together, essentially in the same place around the end of Fourth Avenue. I looked in every one until I found Gordon behind the bar at the Anchorage All-Girl Revue. I didn't much like him for leaving me to Margie's mercy but right now I needed him.

"Well, this is a surprise. Hello, Belle." He wiped the bar in front of me.

"Hi, Gordon. I'm glad to see that you're still in one piece."

"Same here. Do you want a Coke?" He lowered his voice and bent forward. "I'll put a little jolt in it."

"Okay. But what I really want is a job. I couldn't go back to Artie's and my money's running out. Are you still with Margie?"

He put a napkin under the drink. I took a sip. It was strong.

He hooted. "She won't have anything to do with me."

"Who could blame her?" I dropped my chin in my hand. "What would I need to do to get a job stripping, Gordon?" I looked up at him.

"Well, first, you need some identification that says you're twenty-one. I can help you with that. Then, you should spend a week just watching the girls work. Eight hours a day, just like it's your job, until you get all the moves down just right." He poured me another drink. I was getting light-headed.

"After that, you come in and I'll introduce you to Mr. Sobel. He'll ask you to show him your stuff. By the way, you'll need your own costume." Gordon poured him self a drink. "If Mr. Sobel likes what he sees, then you're in."

I sighed. "Okay, ID is no problem. But I don't have another week living at the motel. I don't have enough money to pay for any of this. I'll have to drink if I'm sitting here every night. And I can't imagine what a costume would cost."

"Be right back." Gordon fixed drinks for a couple down the bar.

When he returned he said, "Look here, Belle. I've been thinking about your dilemma and I really want to help. I feel responsible for you being out on the street. And, I caused you to lose a good friend in Marge." He frowned. "So did I for that matter."

He leaned on the bar toward me. "Here's my idea. You stay at my place for awhile. I'll spot you the money you need for drinks and for a costume. You're right; they're expensive if you get a good one, even if they don't have much material in them. Use what money you have for food. When you're on your feet, you can pay me back. How does that sound?"

I thought about it for less than five seconds. "Okay."

Gordon smiled. "I'll pick you up tomorrow afternoon and we'll get that ID." I gave him my address and went back to the motel

That night, I wrote another letter to Jesse without a return address on the envelope. Then I waited until I found someone traveling to the States and asked them to mail it for me from Seattle. I called information again but there was no phone listed for Jesse Williams in Bear Holler, or Bear Creek, or Nashville.

I watched the girls do their stuff every night for a week. During the day I practiced the moves I'd seen the night before. If Gordon was home, he sat on the couch and watched, making a suggestion here and there. He knew their moves almost as well as they did, so he was a good coach.

"Don't drop your bra right away. When you take it off,

hold it across your breasts for a minute before you drop it. And look at the audience, not off to the side like that. Concentrate on one person at a time and look right into their eyes."

I'd do as he said, and he'd clap and say, "Yeah, that's it! You've got it."

I slept with Gordon. I figured, why not? Margie was through with him anyhow. But he wasn't all that good in bed.

I got into the routine of drinking three straight shots of tequila before I could make myself go on the stage. And I drank a lot more during the night to keep from throwing up when men tucked dollar bills into my G string.

It's a habit I picked up in Alaska; drinking a lot.

My life was going pretty good, if you considered that I made enough money to buy some really nice clothes and jewelry. I got my hair done twice a week, and manicures and pedicures whenever I wanted to. I managed to save almost $1300 and planned to buy a car. I moved out on my own and had lots of boyfriends who bought me presents. Of course, the bad thing about it was what I had to do to get them.

I felt safe in Anchorage. Alaska wasn't even a state, though it was an American territory. It was really far from Tennessee. Sometimes I forgot that I might still be wanted. I didn't shake any more when I saw a policeman.

I didn't think anyone was still looking for me, but I couldn't be absolutely sure.

I often thought of how far I was from Jesse, and Ma, and the woods in Bear Holler. And Daddy. I still thought of Daddy and how he died. Sometimes I remembered Black Bart. I remembered what he did to me and wondered what made him do those things. Sometimes I thought he was just a troubled person. I even wondered what it was like to be him, to have to stalk little kids. What made him do that? Did it bother him at all to be a monster?

But most often, I cursed him and had no pity for him. He deserved what he got. No need for me to feel guilty about it.

Seven more years of stripping and a nice hunk of cash in my drawer I decided to leave Alaska. When I got up in the morning I could see bags under my eyes. My hair was dull and stringy, no matter what I put on it. My skin was pale and sallow. I was looking older than 24, I thought. And I was tired of the rain, the snow, the short two months of summer that was nothing but a tease. I wanted a change. But I didn't know what kind of change, so I just kept doing the same thing every day.

Chapter 9

Las Vegas 1955

Jesse gazed out the window at the neon lights down Las Vegas Boulevard. He was beginning to like this town a lot, he reflected. It still had some of the small town atmosphere when you got away from the boulevard. And there sure wasn't anything to keep him in Bear Holler any more.

It was a good gig here at the Country Door. Gus had done a good job of keeping One Night Stand working all the time and the money was decent, if not extravagant.

Jesse hadn't been back to Bear Holler since Aunt Mary died a year ago. She was the only mother he had ever known. His Auntie took him in without question and raised him like her own, right along with Jack. He imagined his mother would be like her if she had lived. Mary was a good woman and let him grow up without restrictions, criticism, or resentment. Now that she was gone, his father and mother long dead and Belle gone, too, there was nothing to hold him in Bear Holler. He and Jack laid Mary to rest and sold her farm, paid off her mortgage, and bought an old school bus. Soon after, the band left for Las Vegas.

Only Nadine stayed in Bear Creek and Jesse had nothing to do with her since she sent him away when he was nine. When he tried to see her, to see if she had heard from Belle, she refused to answer the phone or the door.

His Daddy's cabin sat empty. He didn't want to sell it, or even rent it out. As long as it was there, he felt like he always had some place to call home. If he ever found Belle, or if she finally came home, it would always be there for her, too. He didn't want to think about whether she might spend the rest of her life in jail if she came back.

Belle. It had been nine years since she disappeared but he still showed her picture to everyone he met, asking if they had seen her. He wasn't a religious man and never went to church. Still every night he asked God to help him find her. He wondered if she was alive or dead, if she was all right or was sold into some white slavery market that he read about. Women and girls were stolen and slipped over the border into Mexico, the news said. Then they were shipped to the Orient where they were kept drugged and made into prostitutes. *It would be better is she was dead,* he thought, *than kidnapped.*

Thc last letter he received from her was mailed from Seattle just before they went on the road. That was almost four years ago. How could he even look for her in a city that size? And she could have sent it from another city with someone else mailing it for her. She wrote that she would never let him know where she was at any time. She didn't want him to get in any trouble. He never told the Sheriff about her letters. They were always short and said that she was all right, but not much more. Nothing about where she was, or what she was doing, who she was with.

Dusk and the neon lights on the Boulevard were brighter yet. Jesse got up and switched on a light. He heard a key turn in the lock and looked up to see Jack.

"Hey," Jack threw his key on the dresser. "I'm going to shower and get ready. Are you all set?" He paused to look at his cousin. "Are you okay? You look pretty grim."

"Yeah, I'm ready. I've just been sitting here thinking about Belle." Jesse sat down again, rubbing his eyes. "I was wondering what she looks like now, and what she's doing."

"Well, I'm sure she's fine, wherever she is. She's always been a smart girl, and resourceful. Who knows, Jesse, she might just show up someday back in Bear Creek."

"And if she does, we won't be there." He ran a comb through his hair. "She won't know how to find us."

"Someone would tell her, don't you think?" Jack turned on the shower. "Jesse, Maybe it's time to let this go."

"Maybe you're right." Jesse checked the mirror. He picked up his Stetson and placed it square on his head, then cocked it slightly and pulled the brim lower. "See you downstairs." He closed the door behind him.

"Country music fans, I promised you a surprise and by Jesus jumped-up Christ you're gonna get it."

The little fat man at center stage mopped his bald head with a yellow-stained handkerchief. Tennessee poked Jesse in the ribs with his elbow, rousing him from a drunken doze.

"Where the fuck are we," Jesse groaned, sitting up in his seat. He wanted to be back at the hotel, sleeping off the beer he had been drinking all afternoon.

"Hear that, Jesse? They're gonna play some country." Tennessee's accent was thick when he was drinking.

"Oh, shit." Jesse stared at Tennessee in disbelief and slumped back into his chair.

Dave drained his glass. “Hell, Tennie, we got a show in less than an hour. Let’s get out of here.”

“We just got here and I want to finish my beer. Besides, we’re only a few minutes away and we can do that show with our hands behind our back.” Tennie leaned back in his chair.

“Tennie,” Jack said, “Come on, let’s go. His southern drawl was almost as thick as Tennessee’s.

But Tennessee’s eyes were already riveted on the fat man weaving in front of the faded red velvet curtain.

An hour earlier Jesse, Jack, Tennessee and Dave stopped at the Palomino to check out the club. They spent their free time visiting other clubs, even though One Night Stand was rated the top country group playing in Vegas.

Jesse wanted to stop for another reason. He had shown Belle’s picture around to all the employees at the Hotel where they were staying, like he did everywhere they went. One of the front desk clerk’s had stared at the picture and said, “That looks just like a waitress at the Palomino Club. I was there last week. But she said her name was Carla, not Belle.”

“She might have changed her name. In fact, I think she would have.” Jesse thanked him, and shook his hand. He was excited; it was the first time anyone had recognized her.

He brought the guys to the Palomino to check out Carla and, though there definitely was a resemblance, Jesse knew right away that it wasn’t her. Carla was heavier and had dark hair and brown eyes. He was ready to go after they saw her, but Tennessee was hooked into the music and stage show.

Jesse was worried and he wanted to talk to Jack alone. They had been playing at the Country Door for three weeks and they hadn’t been paid. A phone call to Gus Harper, their agent, that morning had put Jesse in a bad mood. Gus said there was no money yet from the club and he wasn't getting any response from their payroll department. Jesse stopped in and had a talk with Susan in Accounting. She let him know that the money had been sent to Gus almost a week ago. Jesse had a sick feeling in his stomach that he hadn't yet shared with the group. He'd have a talk with Jack when they got back to the hotel and Dave and Tennessee weren't around.

Patsy Montana's voice shouted through two large speakers, one on each side of the stage "I want to be a cowboy's sweetheart…." The worn tape dragged a little.

"Hey, that's Patsy Montana!" Tennie said. "Did you know she was the first female country singer to sell a million records?"

Jesse shook his head slowly. "Tennie, you are a case for sure."

On stage, the fat man's pudgy hand pointed toward a faded stain near the center of the curtain.

"And here she is, Ladies and Gentlemen, the little girl who put the cunt in country; Dallas Starr." Loud applause and hoots from the crowd drowned their conversation.

Creaking and jerking, the heavy curtains inched their way to each side of the stage. A lone spotlight in search of Dallas Starr threaded the smoke-filled room. It found her, still as a statue, mounted on a western saddle thrown across a wooden sawhorse. Her slender body was draped in short shorts and a scant white leather bra. There were tiny strips of sequined leather that heaved up and down on her full breasts. She wore a huge white cowboy hat pulled low on her forehead. Light brown curls fell almost to her waist.

Slowly, she began to rub the saddle horn in front of her with her gloved hands, gradually gaining speed and keeping time with the music. Her bottom slid back and forth in the saddle. The room was suddenly still. Tennessee's mouth hung open and his eyes widened. Patsy sang on and Dallas doubled the tempo to the pounding beat of the bass guitar.

She stopped suddenly, the music done. She threw one leg very slowly over the saddle and planted two gold boots firmly on the floor. The church-quiet air filled with heavy breathing. The smell of smoke and stale beer hung in the air.

"Howdy, cowboys." She stamped a slender foot. "Wanna ride?"

Shouts, whistles, and a Texas whoop echoed throughout the room.

"Yeah, Dallas, right on."

"Do it again, honey." Heavy feet pounded the floor.

"Them are happy trails, Dallas."

Jesse shook his head. "Jack," he leaned toward his cousin. "Doesn't she look familiar? Maybe I've seen her in a show somewhere else."

Dallas pushed her Stetson back with a white gloved hand and grinned at the crowd.Jesse felt a curious chill shake his body.

"It's Belle," Jesse whispered.

"What? I can't hear you." Jack stared at Jesse.

"It's Belle," now a shout, "Goddam; it's Belle. Look at her! I'm sure of it. I'd know that face anywhere."

"You 're right. Come on, let's go!"

Jesse and Jack jumped to their feet and broke out running to the stage as if by silent agreement. The music had started again "I want to learn to rope and ride…" Jesse, running fast, watched as Dallas, or Belle, swayed and bumped in time with the music. She slowly peeled off one glove and dropped it onto the lap of a gray-haired man in the front row. She took off the other glove and twirled it in the air above her head. "I want to be a cowboy's sweetheart," the tape played on and Belle unfastened her bra. She held it across her breasts before slowly dropping it to the floor. Pink-nippled breasts bounced slightly as she stepped across the stage, swaying to the music. Shouts of encouragement echoed throughout the room.

Jesse and Jack were up the stage steps and running past the fat man. He grasped the edge of the red curtain with both hands, pudgy legs running in place. Jesse and Jack stood on each side of Belle. Again the room was quiet, the audience watching with interest this new twist to the show.

Belle pulled away from the men; eyes wide, mouth open. "What the hell?"

"Belle, it's me, Jesse. And Jack's on the other side of you." He whispered, avoiding the microphone over their heads.

"Oh, God!" she let them grab her arms.

Jack pulled the Stetson off Belle's head and pressed it across her bare breasts. She grasped the hat with both hands. Jack and Jesse propelled her across the stage. They ran down the steps on the other side of the stage and headed for the front door. Close behind, Dave and Tennessee were rushing toward the door. They were just in front of the little fat man, who had lumbered down the other side of the stage. The bartender suddenly appeared with a baseball bat and joined the chase.

Jack, Jesse and Belle stood outside watching the barroom door. Tennie stopped, blocking the door. "What's going on, anyhow?" Tennie shouted.

"Tell you later, come on," Jesse shouted back, wondering why Tennessee was standing in the doorway.

"Excuse me, sir," Tennie said, turning to the red-faced fat man who had somehow outrun the bartender. "I would like to make an inquiry about the next show. What time does it start?"

"Outta my way," the fat man growled.

Jack and Jesse moved Belle to their bus parked in the lot near the front door. They hesitated, watching the door. Then they climbed on the bus and Jack started the engine. He backed up a bit and waited for Dave and Tennessee.

"Sir, would you let my friends through, right behind you?" Tennie said, still blocking the door. Dave dropped to his hands and knees behind the fat man

Jesse laughed. This was a move he knew, one that they practiced whenever they ended up in a bar fight. The fat man turned his head to look behind him for just a second. Tennie shoved him hard; knocking him across Dave's back and square into the bartender and his baseball bat.

Dave and Tennessee dashed side by side to the idling bus and climbed up the steps. The laughing and clapping of the crowd could be heard through the open door. Jack closed the bus door, put it in gear and pulled out onto Las Vegas Boulevard just as the bartender and the fat man got up and ran towards the bus. Jesse watched them shake their fists as the bus drove away.

"Hell," Jack said, "we ought to send them a bill for that show."

Back at their hotel room, Jesse and Jack and Belle cried, hugging and wiping their eyes. They were quiet then, just looking at each other.

Belle hugged Dave and Tennie.

"Damn, I'm so happy to see all of you. I can't believe you're still together after all these years."

"Little sister, do you know how long I've been looking for you?" Jesse put his arm around her.

"I couldn't write any more, Jesse. I was afraid they'd find me."

"You could have called me. We got a phone two years ago."

"I guess I gave up after trying for a few years to find a phone number for you. The information operators must have gotten sick of hearing from me."

Jack patted her hand. "We found you now and that's the main thing."

"But the problem is what do we do now? I don't want to get caught after all these years." Belle wiped her eyes with the back of her hand. "And I don't want you guys to get in trouble, either."

"Damn, Belle, it's been more than nine years. No one even talks about the murder anymore. I bet they aren't even looking for you now." Jesse sat down on the bed beside her. "Sheriff McMahan told me once that it was near impossible that they would find you, given the fragmented communication system between agencies. Hell, even between local counties and cities, not much gets through."

"I sure hope that's true." She draped her arm around his shoulders.

She had to ask. "Jesse, what did Bart die from?" She could feel her body start to shake.

"Someone hit him on the head with a rock. He had a skull fracture and a piece of bone went through his brain." Jesse turned to face her. "Belle, you didn't know how he died?"

Belle sobbed. "I wasn't sure. I just thought…" she was shaking all over now.

Jesse put his arms around her and waited for the crying to stop. He thought, *if she didn't know how Bart died, how could she have done this?*

"Belle, how'd you get work when you were so young?" Jesse had been working on losing the southern accent but when he was excited, it slipped right back into his speech

"I just lied about my age. And you can get any kind of identification if you're willing to pay," she said.

She was conscious of how she must look to them; thick makeup, false eyelashes, and a well developed body covered now by a huge shirt from Jesse's dresser drawer.

"We worried a lot about you. Belle, I've got to say I was shook up seeing you on that stage with your clothes coming off. What the hell were you thinking, girl?" Jack stood with his hands on his hips and stared at her.

"Jack, that was good money. And I have to eat, don't I?"

"Seems to me like you could figure something else to do." He poured some water into a glass and brought it to her. He sat down on the floor next to the bed.

"Well, what else could I do? I had to take whatever I could get in the way of work" She felt a lump in her throat.

"I know, honey. I didn't mean to criticize." Jack leaned his elbows onto his knees, sitting cross-legged on the floor.

"Fellows," Dave interrupted, "I know we've got a lot of catching up to do. But right now we're due on stage." He was back from his room and dressed in jeans, western shirt, boots and Stetson.

"Belle, you stay here and keep a low profile, okay? No phone calls. If anyone knocks at the door, don't answer it. If the phone rings, let it ring." Jesse combed his hair and checked it out in the mirror. "I don't know if that manager will cause any trouble. I doubt it. Still, just in case…"

"All right, Jesse." Belle stretched out on the bed. "I think I'll catch a nap."

Jesse turned his back, dropped his jeans, and pulled on a pair of white pants embroidered around the pockets with bright red sequins and black thread.

"Belle, how did you find out Bart was dead?"

"The sheriff came to tell Ma and I was listening in my bedroom."

"I don't think that anyone would have blamed you except that you ran." Jack looked up at her and frowned.

Belle scrunched her eyes closed, then looked at Jack. "Well, there were two ladies passed me on the way out of the church dance; you know the Witherspoon twins."

"Oh, yeah, Margaret and Florence. Did they say anything to you?"

"Nope, just 'nice night isn't it?'" After years away from the south, Belle's voice was soft with very little drawl.

"Must have been them that started the hunt for you."

"Yeah, that and the Sheriff. He came to the house to tell Ma that Bart was dead and he was asking about me. I knew from what he was saying that he suspected I was the one who killed him. That's when I ran."

No one spoke for a few minutes.

Belle sat up straight. "You seen Ma?"

"She doesn't answer her phone, or her door, but so far as we know she's still living on Hickory Street," Jesse said.

"Yeah," Jack said, "Ever since the murder she's never come out of her house. She calls out for groceries and stuff she needs and has it delivered. It seems like she's still broken up about the whole thing. We tried to see her the last time we were in town, just to ask if she ever heard anything from you."

"Who found Bart?" Belle propped two pillows behind her back, then leaned forward hugging her knees.

"A hunter found him, early the next morning. Someone bashed his head in and left him under a tree in Bear Holler."

Belle was silent once again. Jesse looked at her face, pale and tense. He wanted to ask her if she killed Bart but he was afraid of what the answer might be. She stared at her hands for a long time.

"The Sheriff was eyeing the both of us I can tell you.

We had a run in with Bart once." Jesse said. "We were deer hunting out by the Witherspoons when we ran into him, walking in the woods. He said we shouldn't be shooting God's animals and we told him to go to hell. We almost came to blows over the whole thing. He called us heathens and said we were going to hell, just like Belle. Jack wanted to punch him out, but I convinced him not to, and we walked away. I never cared much for the asshole. I could see why you didn't like him, Belle."

She lowered her head, silent.

Jesse said, "Yeah, Sheriff McMahan would have nailed us except we had an airtight alibi. We were still at the church dance until it shut down, and then we went to Homer Carter's house with a gang of people. The Sheriff actually seemed disappointed that he couldn't arrest us."

Belle looked at Jack. She could see him standing up to Bart. When they were younger, Jack was the scrappy one who took care of her, protected her; chased off bullies who teased her. Many times, back at the cabin when her Daddy was still alive, Jack watched over her and Jesse when her Ma was off visiting friends or down with one of her headaches. Now, he looked much as he did when she last saw him nine years ago. Thick, caramel-brown, almost black hair falling onto his forehead; brown eyes so dark they looked black. His ruddy brown skin was acne-scarred. His build was that of a short stocky farm horse; solid, reliable, used to hard work. When she was young, he seemed more like a brother to her, instead of Jesse's cousin.

She remembered when he was ten some boy called him "nigger" and Jack hit him in the face so hard he broke his nose. Even now, as he talked with her, it seemed as though he was still protecting her. It made her feel safe.

"Jack, are you guys still playing country?" Belle asked.

"You bet. And that's what we'll keep on doing." He

glanced at Jesse.

"I've been trying to talk him into some changes," Jesse sighed. "But he's such a stubborn son-of-a-bitch I can't budge him."

Belle thought Jesse looked like his mother, Emma Sue. He had dark blond hair and eyes as blue as a cloudless sky on a summer day. Belle and Jesse found Emma Sue's picture one day when they were playing in the attic. Jesse stared at it as if he had never seen it before.

Jesse was the one who played hide and seek with her, hid her favorite book, and short-sheeted her bed. When it came to music, though, he was always dead serious. He was three years older than Belle. He seemed much younger than Jack although Jack was only two years older than Jesse.

Belle sat up and reached for a cigarette, accepted a light from Tennessee and took a drag. She watched the smoke drift in front of her face.

"Thanks, Tennie. It's nice to see that you haven't changed a bit. Same little boy grin. Still all arms and legs." She'd known him almost all her life.

His face flushed. "I'm glad we found you, Belle. I was sure worried when you disappeared." Belle always thought he had a crush on her when they were in school together.

Jesse slipped into a white satin western shirt. "When did you come to Las Vegas, Belle?"

"Just a couple of weeks ago. I got tired of the cold in Alaska and headed for sunshine. The only ride I could get was to Las Vegas." Belle caught a glimpse of herself in the dresser mirror and tried to pat down her hair. "I've been staying in a motel downtown."

"We'll go pick up your clothes tomorrow. You can stay here, in our room." He buttoned his shirt. "You were in Alaska? Damn, girl, you sure did get around."

"Let's go," Dave was standing at the door. "Tennessee is already headed downstairs. See you later, Belle." He gave her a smile and a wink. "It's good to see you again." His eyes looked tired to her. She always liked Dave. To her, Dave was a dark, romantic and mysterious older man; black hair, emerald-green brooding eyes.

Those months that she spent hanging out and singing with the guys in the cabin back in Bear Hollow were always some of her best memories. She didn't want to let them go now.

Belle closed her eyes, really happy for the first time in years. She thought of her Daddy and Jesse and Jack, and how they played music together after supper

She thought of that day nine years ago when she was fifteen and left home for good. She was a child then, confused and scared and unsure of herself. Now, all grown up, she knew she should get up and go back to her motel. She should pack her clothes and grab the first ride she could get out of town. But she was tired or running, tired of trying to survive and stay clear of police. She was tired of waking up hung over in hotel rooms with a strange man snoring next to her.

But if she stayed with her brother, she might be arrested for her stepfather's murder. And what about Jesse. If they arrested her, could he be arrested for not turning her in?

Chapter 10

Sergeant Frank Smith watched Lieutenant Roland Bitterman pour the last cup of thick black coffee into a stained mug. Roland took one swig and then dumped it down the drain. He took a carton of milk from the fridge and downed the whole pint.

The squad room next door hummed with early morning activity. Frank could hear the dispatchers in another room sending cars throughout the city in low dispassionate voices.

"Put on some more coffee, will you Sue?" Roland said to his secretary who had just walked into the room.

"Do it yourself." The secretary picked up a stack of papers and headed for the door. "I'm not your maid."

"Damned if you aren't cuter than a bug's ear when you're mad," he laughed.

"Sit on it, copper!" The door slammed behind her small bouncing frame. It just missed catching her red skirt.

"I don't know why I don't up and fire her." Roland told

Frank. Despite the twenty year difference in their ages they had become good friends since Frank joined the department. In those five years he had reached the rank of sergeant and for the past two years, a detective. He loved his job.

"Because, you old fart, you're still hoping to get a little of the action and you know it and she knows it and you're hoping your wife doesn't know it."

"Damn it to hell, you are blunt, aren't you?"

Roland grabbed his stomach and grimaced.

"Ulcers acting up?"

"How can you tell, doc?"

"You drink way too much coffee." Frank took off his jacket sat down at his desk.

"Since you're such a smart ass, I think I'll give you this call. It came in from the Palomino late last night, suspected kidnapping. Some guys in cowboy hats, probably drunk, took their stripper off the stage and hustled her away. The manager wants her found, says he's worried. That's a real laugh. He's worried, all right, about his loss of income. Still, we'd better check it out."

"What do you know already?" Frank stood up and grabbed his jacket.

"The cowboys left on a bus and the manager of the Palomino thinks they pulled into the Country Door. Sign on the bus said, 'One Night Stand.' Got a good description; she's early twenties, light brown hair, long and curly, 38-24-36, fair complexion, about 5'2", 120 pounds. Good looking dame, for a stripper." Roland reached into his desk and pulled out a paper bag. "The manager dropped off her purse this morning."

"Okay, I'll look into it." Frank took the bag and went out the door. He was hit in the face with a wave of hot desert air. *Of course Roland would have asked for her measurements,* he thought.

Belle yawned and stretched, then opened her eyes to bright sunlight. For a few minutes she wondered where she was, but didn't panic. She was accustomed to waking up in hotel rooms.

It had begun to worry her, drinking so much that she couldn't remember the night before. When she tried to quit she found that she couldn't go on stage. But three shots of tequila got her ready, stopped her hands from shaking. And she knew that in order to get a percentage you had to have drinks with the customers. It had to be the real stuff, she learned. Once she tried to substitute plain Coke but the customer got wise and demanded his money back. Then he belted her across the face leaving a black eye that kept her from working for two days. She didn't try that again.

She looked around the room and it came back to her how her brother had found her, how she had slept alone in the quiet hotel room.

It reminded her how quiet it was when she lived in the cabin in the mountains, before her Daddy died. Her days were full of swimming, music and church lunches. Her life, she knew, would have been a lot different if her Daddy hadn't died and her Ma hadn't married Bart. But now, all that seemed so long ago; almost as if it had never been.

A staccato knock on the door catapulted her from the bed. She sat shivering and naked on the toilet until the knocking stopped. The night before she stripped off the shirt Jesse had given her and showered, then crawled between the sheets. She liked to feel the cool sheets on her naked body. It felt soothing, like she was floating in a pool of water.

Belle rummaged through the dresser until she found a large blue silk shirt and slipped it on. She washed her face, scrubbing until all the makeup and smeared mascara was gone. She combed her hair with her hands, rubbed her teeth with soap on a washrag. She remembered that she had no makeup and felt naked without it.

She studied herself in the mirror for a minute. Belle knew she was pretty but saw only the flaws; the slightly too full face, the pale lips thinner than she liked, brown curly hair that tended to stick out every which way.

She paced the floor, turned on the radio, and turned it off, picked up the phone, dialed room service, hung up before they answered, and paced some more. She closed the drapes, lit a cigarette, opened the drapes, looked through all the drawers, then picked up the phone again and rang room service.

"Coffee, please, and bacon and eggs and potatoes." She ground out her cigarette. "And some sweet rolls and a bottle of champagne."

Belle ran to answer the soft knock on the door as soon as the voice on the other side said, "Room Service". She looked through the little hole in the door and saw the white-jacketed boy with a rolling tray of food. *Good,* she thought. *I'm so hungry. And I really could use a drink.*

She didn't see the man in a dark blue suit standing way to the left of the cart. She dropped the bolt from its track and opened the door.

Frank thought she looked rather appealing in the oversized blue silk shirt that matched her eyes. She was pretty, even without makeup. He noticed her smile freeze on her face when he took out his badge.

"May I come in?"

The smile returned and she motioned him inside.

"Of course, if you move aside for the food. I'm famished."

Frank stood inside the door as the white-jacketed Mexican boy pushed the cart into the room and with great ceremony, opened the champagne. He looked confused, and then finally placed the check in Belle's outstretched hand.

"My purse, it's at the club..." she stammered.

Frank produced the brown bag with her purse inside. "The manager at the Palomino dropped this off at the station," he smiled and handed it to her. She paid for her meal, tipping the waiter ten dollars. He nodded and bowed. "Gracias, Senorita!"

"I worked too long as a waitress not to appreciate tips," she told Frank when the waiter had quietly closed the door behind him. She turned her back to him, her hands shaking uncontrollably as she poured coffee into a white mug.

"I'm the same way, and I've never been a waiter." He said, talking to her back. "Miss Starr, I'm Detective Frank Smith and I'm here because of a kidnapping report filed by the manager at the Palomino Club. You don't seem to be in trouble, so if you'll tell me what happened I can file my report and we'll be done with it."

Belle turned her head and looked at him over her shoulder. "Please, call me Dallas." She poured herself a glass of champagne and downed it; readied another. Damn, was she about to be arrested so soon?

"All right." He said.

She moved away from the cart and sat down in a chair. Her hands had stopped shaking after the champagne. She sipped at the second glass and managed a smile. The detective was already sitting in the chair opposite her.

"It figures that the little bastard called you. He was pissed because I left in the middle of the act, I'll bet. But everyone thought it was part of the act and it went over quite well. They were still laughing and clapping when we left."

"What actually happened?"

"Jesse is my brother and the guys in the band were drunk and they thought it would be funny if they stole me from the stage." She brushed a loose curl from her face. "It caused me no small amount of inconvenience, plus the loss of my job, I'm sure. But how can I stay mad at such sweet guys?"

Her eyes studied him over her glass. She set it down and popped some bacon in her mouth. She offered him breakfast and champagne. He shook his head.

"Unfortunately, I'm on duty."

"How about some coffee?" Fear had drowned her appetite.

"Okay." He took the cup she poured for him.

"I'm curious, Detective Smith. How did you find me?"

"The Palomino manager saw the bus pull into this hotel. A few questions of the staff pointed me in the right direction." He sipped his coffee.

"Oh. Well, should I call you Frank?" She looked in his eyes with a practiced confidence.

"Frank will work for me. I don't stand on too much formality. This is Las Vegas." He felt hot, flushed.

"Okay, Frank. So you see I'm all right, don't you?"

"Yes, I do, but I have to ask. Do you have some identification, Dallas? And where are you living now?"

"I have my driver's license from Alaska. I recently moved here and I'm staying at the Green Dollar Motel downtown until I find a place."

"So you're planning on staying in Las Vegas then?" He leaned forward and spooned some sugar into his coffee.

"I have to admit, I'm a bit of a rolling stone, but yes, for now, that's the plan."

Frank sipped the hot brew, put his cup back on the table, and looked at her. "I suppose you've heard this before, but…" he lowered his eyes.

"What's a nice girl like me doing in the stripping game?"

"Something like that. It's really none of my business." He shifted in his seat and looked at her.

"Fate and circumstance, I guess. The money is good, and it really isn't going to be forever." She raised her eyes to his and caught him staring. "I might ask the same of you. You seem too nice to be a cop."

"Fate again," he grinned. "My father and grandfather were policemen. I guess you could say it runs in the family."

Belle thought he had a very nice smile. It made the skin around his eyes crinkle a bit. His eyes were warm and light amber brown and so was his curly hair. His build was on the slight side, but well-proportioned, like the after-picture in the 98 pound weakling ads

He stood up. Belle handed him her driver's license and he made some notes in his book. He flipped it shut and gave the license back to her.

"Better get a Nevada license soon, now. Thanks for the coffee." He walked towards the door. Her hands were shaking again.

"No problem. Come by and say hello when you're not on duty." Maybe that would erase any doubts he had about her, she thought.

He turned and looked at her. She hoped her face wasn't flushed. Why did she say that? She didn't want any more attention from the cops. As nice as he was, she couldn't trust him.

"Maybe I will." His answer surprised her.

She closed the door behind him and dropped the chain in its slot, then sank to the carpeted floor. Her legs had turned to mush. Then the tears came, hot and heavy.

The knock at the door was soft and tentative. She jumped to her feet, holding her breath.

"Sis?"

"Jesse!" She unloosed the chain, flung the door open and fell into her brother's arms.

"Jesse, they've found me. I just know I'll be arrested. A policeman was here because that manager at the Palomino Club called him. I gave him my stage name, the one on my license, but I don't know if he bought it."

"Now, go easy and tell me all about it. They haven't arrested you yet, have they?" He pushed inside, closed the door, and urged her to sit on the bed. He sat down beside her. He wondered if he shouldn't help her leave town. If he harbored her, he might go to jail as an accessory. But then, he would probably never see her again. He didn't want to lose her after all these years.

"Just remember, this is a nine-year-old case, and we're far from Tennessee. Why would the police be suspicious of anything? The detective just came because he was called. Besides, even if he is suspicious, it would take a while to get any kind of information from out of state." He squeezed her shoulders. "Everything would be in dead files by now anyhow."

Her tears dried after they talked awhile and Belle resumed her breakfast, swigging cups of coffee between gulps of champagne. She cleaned the plate of eggs, potatoes and bacon. Then she finished with sweet rolls and lit a cigarette. Jesse had watched her without a word. He poured some coffee for himself.

"Where are Jack and the boys?" She wiped her mouth with the white linen napkin.

"Down at breakfast. We rented another room so you could sleep. When you're ready, we'll go get your things." He smiled. "I had a talk with Susan in accounting and I got a cut rate for your room."

"I'm ready, more than ready. Oh, guess I'd look kind of silly in this outfit, though in Vegas probably no one would notice." She looked down at the shirt she was wearing.

"Just give me the key and we'll go get them for you."

"Okay. It's the Green Dollar Motel on Ivy Street, room #65. It's paid up through tomorrow. Here's the key. And Jesse, don't take too long. I'm scared."

"Don't worry, honey. We'll be back in a flash. Besides, we have an early show today. Want to come down and see it?"

"I guess. I don't know; do you think it would be safe?"

"Sure. No problem. Nothing can happen to you while Jack and I are here." He kissed her forehead.

Jesse closed the door behind him and Belle slipped the chain in the slot again, fell back into the bed and a restless sleep. Should she run again, the safest thing to do, or stay with her brother? It was so good to see them again, to have family. But her well-honed alert system told her that Frank didn't buy her story.

Frank scooted around in the hot seat of the squad car trying to find a cooler spot. He stared at the hotel he had just left. He'd learned long ago to listen to his instincts, and now his intuition was nudging him more and more insistently.

Something was wrong but what?

He started the engine, rolled down a window waiting for the air conditioning to take hold. He flipped his book open and looked over his notes, then slipped the car into gear and rolled onto Las Vegas Boulevard.

An hour later he was typing his report with two fingers, when Roland nudged his arm.

"What's the story? Tell me all the sexy details, will you?"

"Well, boss, looks to me like the girl wanted to leave, no real hanky-panky, but something's fishy about the whole thing. Maybe I'll go back when her brother and his band are available and talk with them."

"Yeah, yeah." Roland did a half smile at Frank. "What's she like, a real looker? Maybe you'd better bring her in so I can interview her, as your superior officer."

Frank made his mouth into a straight line and shook his head slowly. He got up from his chair, turned to Sue, and handed the license information to her.

"Check this out, will you, Sue?"

"Sure. Alaska, huh? Dallas Starr? Is this for real?"

"That's what I want to know. Thanks."

"No problem, Frank. It won't take me long." She looked at the picture on the license and pulled at her ear. "She looks familiar for some reason. Well, I suppose they all look alike at some point."

Roland poured a fresh cup of coffee that he just made.

"How come she's so damn sweet to you and won't even give me the time of day?"

"My fantastic personality, I guess." Frank pulled his report from the typewriter and handed it to Roland.

Chapter 11

Nashville 1955

Oliver Force walked through the front door at exactly 5:30 PM just like he always did. Charlotte handed him the Scotch and branch water she had poured when she heard his car in the driveway.

This talk, she determined, would come up as soon as she saw him begin to mellow and before he got drunk which, as near as she could calculate, happened somewhere between the second and third double Scotch. After seven years of marriage she knew when it was best to broach a difficult subject with her lawyer husband.

If she hadn't run into Laura McAllister, at Le Petite Shoppe that afternoon, it's possible that Charlotte would have gone another seven years without questioning her life.

"Charlie," Laura called out across the room, "it's really you!"

After exchanging hugs they sauntered into Fagin's for

drinks and lunch. Charlotte felt slightly drunk as she sipped her second glass of Chardonnay. She watched Laura's face as she talked about her new career and her first bit part in a movie.

"You look beautiful, Laura. Are you happy? "

"Are you kidding, Charlie? I can't tell you how wonderful it feels to be independent, to be earning my own money, and doing something as satisfying as acting. I don't even miss being married. And the people I meet, it's just incredible. Such beautiful and exciting people. All those years of struggle has finally paid off. Remember how broke we were in college? If it wasn't for dates, we wouldn't have eaten at all." She tossed her blonde head back and roared. Charlie thought she was twenty pounds slimmer than the last time she saw her.

Charlie took another sip of wine.

"Remember that Henry something or other you couldn't stand? He took you out to dinner three times a week." Charlie sensed that Laura was trying to catch her eye but she gazed intently at her glass of wine.

"Do I! It got tougher and tougher to get in the door without going to bed with him." She finally looked at Laura and laughed. "I told him I was a virgin and had promised my mother I'd save myself for marriage. Then, he asked me to marry him!"

"Charlie," Laura put down her fork. "Are you doing anything at all with your acting? Are you still in Little Theater?"

"Well, actually, Laura, I don't have time for that now. It was fun in college, sure, but now I'm married to a man who's very successful and busy. He needs me to entertain and hold down the home front. It's very exciting, really, and he does make an awful lot of money." She glanced across the table at Laura, who forked a small shrimp into her mouth, and wondered why it didn't make her feel any better to say that.

"But you were so good; you won the Most Likely to Be Famous" award at graduation, remember?"

"It's my own choice, though. Maybe someday…" Charlie dabbed her mouth with the napkin.

"Girl, you're already 32, an old lady in this business." Her tinkling laugh seemed a bit nervous to Charlie who realized that if she was 32, so was Laura. But she laughed anyhow.

"Oh, I know; you have children!" Laura pointed a manicured nail at Charlie. "Is that it, are you tied down with children?"

"No children. Oliver says this isn't a good time and I…" Her voice trailed off as Laura grabbed her purse and stood up.

"Darling, I have to be on Fourth Avenue in ten minutes and we're twenty minutes away. Can I call you? Or you call me. Here's my new number." She scribbled on the back of the wine menu and handed it to Charlie. "I'll be back in Los Angeles next week; come see me there."

It was another half hour before Charlotte picked up the check for the both of them and pointed the Corvette towards home. When she reached Silver Hills Estates she had a strange urge to keep going. She didn't know where she wanted to go, but she knew it was anywhere but there.

Still she pulled into the long circular driveway lined with roses. She took a deep breath through the open car window. The roses were worth every one of the long hours she spent pruning, watering and weeding them. Sometimes she sat on the bench there, just admiring their hues of crimson, gold, and stark white. She would close her eyes, intoxicated by their perfume, and dream of exotic places.

"Oliver..." She rolled his name on her tongue before letting it go.

"Yes, my dear?"

"Oliver, have you ever felt that life was passing you by?'

"Good heavens, no. Whatever made you ask a question like that?"

"Because that's the way I feel today."

Oliver smoothed thick black hair with his hand. Charlotte noticed beginning wisps of grey at the temples.

"Charlotte, what brought this on? Did you see a movie this afternoon?" His eyes narrowed as he finally looked at her. "What did you do today?"

"Good God, Oliver, can't you put the lawyer away for a minute?" Her face grew red.

"It's just that this is so unlike you, my dear. I only want to know what's upset you."

"I didn't say I was upset. I just wanted you to know how I'm feeling today." Was there a note of panic in her voice, she wondered.

Oliver turned his back as he refreshed his drink. Turning around slowly, he smiled at her. Lord, he can be charming, Charlie thought. She felt a bit sluggish from the unaccustomed afternoon wine.

"Come now, where were you today?"

"If you must know I ran into Laura McAllister. If you remember we were roommates in college. Now she's just landed her first good movie part and Oliver, she looks so happy. She reminded me of how much I loved acting in college, and how good I was."

"And you're wondering about your own career, what would have happened if we hadn't married isn't that true?"

"Well, yes, maybe a bit, but..."

"Say no more, I understand." He drained his drink and

patted her arm.

"Sweetheart, if you want to pursue your Little Theater again, you know it's okay with me. It's just that I depend on you so much, I don't know what I'd do if you weren't around to keep us going" He sounded grim.

Oliver turned to the bar to fix another drink.

"What about you?" He turned his head and looked at her, his eyebrows raised, his empty glass lifted into the air.

"No, thanks. Anyhow, I do plan to contact the Little Theater, just to get my hand back in. I thought of getting an agent. Do you remember Jeff Crawford? He always managed to get decent jobs for me."

"That was five years ago." The look on his face was definitely darker. "If you're sure that's what you want, perhaps I can find a better agent for you. I have a client, Roger Johnston, who might help you out. He has a lot of contacts."

"I think I'll stick with Jeff if he's available. But thanks anyhow."

"Oh, by the way, would you mark the calendar for Thursday the 14th; dinner party for two clients and their wives, politicians. Keep our drinks light, theirs heavy. I think roast beef would be appropriate, nothing with pork, I believe they're Jewish." He smiled and put his arm around her shoulders. "And Charlotte, wear your blue chiffon, the long one. Call the caterer's tomorrow, since this is rather short notice. There, that's a good girl." He patted her shoulder before letting go.

Oliver turned on the television and flipped the dial to the news. Charlotte stared at the back of his well groomed head for a moment as he moved to the black leather sofa, sat down and put his feet up on the coffee table.

"Dinner's ready in about 30 minutes. I thought we could talk some more. I have a table set on the patio. It's a rather warm evening."

"Of course, my dear. Call me when it's ready."

"All right." She climbed the stairs to bathe and change clothes. I'll get to him yet, she vowed, filling the tub with warm water and her most expensive bath oil. Deliberating a bit in front of her huge walk-in closet, she finally selected a black dressing gown with a very low neckline. She let down her straight long black hair and brushed it for a long time. Then she applied her makeup lightly, very carefully, as if she were seeing a boyfriend for the first time. When she finished, she inspected her face.

She was pleased with what she saw in the mirror. A lithe, toned frame that reflected her hours on the tennis court; a slightly too broad face, skin like cream and eyes, her best feature she thought, eyes so dark blue they seemed violet. Her lips were just right, pouty but modest in size. Her chin might be a bit too long, but it seemed to work well on her face. She knew that when she walked into a room, the women as well as the men turned to study her. Yes, she admitted, she liked the attention.

She put down her brush, took another look in the full length mirror on the closet door, and headed for the kitchen. The timing was perfect: Janet the cook had just taken the steaks from the broiler. Charlie checked the table on the patio. The wine was open and chilled in the cooler; the table set with good china on a white linen tablecloth, and two tall taupe candles in silver candlesticks flickered shadows on the table. The sun had dropped behind the peach trees. A slight breeze ruffled her gown. Perfect.

She walked over to the couch where Oliver had stretched out. The television hosted two grunting oversized wrestlers, one with long blonde hair, the other quite bald and fat.

"Oliver, we're ready to eat." She shook his shoulder,

first gently, then more aggressively. Finally he opened his eyes halfway and groaned.

"Okay, okay. Give me a minute, all right?" Then he promptly fell back to sleep.

She shook him again, harder. He shook off her hand without opening his eyes.

Ten minutes latter Charlie blew out the candles and closed the patio door. She said goodnight to Janet and slowly climbed the stairs to her bedroom.

Sometime in the night she was aroused from a deep sleep by Oliver's wet mouth on her right breast. She turned her face to the wall to avoid his breath which smelled of stale booze. Without a word he climbed on top and penetrated her. Sixteen strokes, she counted, as the warm wet liquid dripped down the inside of her thigh, exactly sixteen strokes as usual. Then he slipped off her, turned on his right side and fell asleep. His loud snores kept her from going back to sleep.

Charlotte stared into the dark room until dawn when she got up and showered. She pulled on some old jeans and a T-shirt, the one with Rudolf Valentino on the back. It was the one that Oliver hated and forbade her to wear. She slipped into her old leather sandals. Then she packed a small suitcase and went down the stairway, out the front door and into the black Corvette. The red and pink and white and yellow roses were a blur as she drove down the long driveway and turned the corner.

Interstate 40 out of Nashville was dry and the weather clear with almost no traffic. Forty miles out, Charlie pulled the Corvette onto the shoulder, put her head down on the steering wheel and cried long wailing sobs. Soon she dried her eyes, got out of the car and stretched. She lowered the top, then slid back onto the white leather seat and started the engine.

It was a bright June morning and the sun was warm on her shoulders, the breeze was cool in her hair. She felt wonderful.

At dusk that evening, exhausted and sweaty, she checked into an off the road motel in Texarkana. She pulled the dusty black Corvette under an elm tree at the door of her room, carried the small suitcase into her room, showered, and put on some clean jeans and a red t-shirt.

At the diner next door, she ordered a hamburger and beer from the skinny lady with salt and pepper hair and way too much makeup. Digging all the change from the bottom of her purse she went to the pay phone in the corner of the room and dropped the change. Oliver answered right away.

Suddenly Charlie was terrified. She hung up the phone without speaking and returned to her table. Now there were three men in the booth next to hers, looking her over, drinking beer and eating hamburgers. The big one poked his partner in the ribs with his elbow as she sat down. What was she thinking, running off like this? Would she end up raped and murdered in some motel room?

She drank her beer in big gulps, wondering what she would do next. She realized she hadn't eaten all day and was very hungry. She ordered another hamburger before she finished the first, and washed it down with a second beer. Then she got up, paid her bill, and went back to the phone. The three men were gone now.

"Oliver?"

"Charlotte! Good God, where are you? I've been worried to death. I've invited the Morrison's over for cocktails tonight and you're not home yet. What in the hell is going on?"

"That's what I called to tell you, Oliver. I'm not coming home." It came to her as she spoke; "I'm on my way to California."

"Are you insane?" She knew his face would be red just by the anger in his voice. "Now I'm a patient man, but my dear, I insist that you come home immediately. Where are you, anyhow?"

Charlie dropped the receiver into its cradle.

Chapter 12

Las Vegas 1955

"Ladies and Gentlemen, the Country Door proudly presents...One Night Stand, starring Jesse Williams and his band." Scattered applause filled the room.

Belle took the table to the side of the bandstand where it was darkest. She wasn't absolutely sure she should be here, but Jesse seemed to think there was nothing to worry about. She decided to relax and just enjoy the show. She hadn't heard her brother play music for a very long time.

She watched Dave unpack his bass guitar. It seemed strange that he didn't have his stand-up bass, but she realized that the band was no longer acoustic; they had gone electric. Dave's hands shook as he lifted the guitar from its case. He was still a good-looking man but his eyes were bloodshot and his skin had a grey pallor. The two women down front didn't seem to notice, though. They were flirting openly with him.

It was all Belle could do to keep from climbing on the bandstand with them. She wanted to sing with them again, like she did in the cabin before she ran away. She even liked being on the stage stripping. It made her feel powerful. When the audience clapped and smiled at her, it was the best high there was. There was definitely something erotic about being on a stage, no matter what she was doing there.

She ordered a shot of tequila. The waitress asked and Belle showed her ID. The waitress looked at her with eyebrows raised when she read her name.

"It's my stage name." She shrugged. "I'm a stripper."

"Oh," the waitress said, and handed her license back to her.

Jack looked at Belle from the stage and frowned. He turned his back and pulled his guitar out of its case. *What's eating him?* She wondered. *Wasn't she supposed to have a drink? Or maybe he didn't like what she was wearing.* Her wardrobe pretty much reflected her occupation.

Jesse climbed up last. He shot her a smile and a round okay with his thumb and forefinger. Belle waited for the band to start, sitting on the edge of her chair. She surveyed the room, still a bit nervous, and then noticed the slender woman with long black hair who hesitated at the doorway. Belle watched as the woman slid into a seat in the back of the room.

The lounge was cool, full of talking, laughing, clapping people. Charlotte wanted to be anonymous, to forget why she was here. She knew she would have to find a lawyer sometime soon, but for now she didn't want to think about what she would do next. She just wanted to have a drink and gather her thoughts. This seemed like the perfect place. She sank into a soft chair at a small table in the back of the room and ordered a Bloody Mary. Her days and nights had blended together, and here inside the casino time seemed not to matter. She knew it was sometime late afternoon. She was dog-tired from driving across the hot desert and not sleeping too well in the motels along the way.

Her last conversation with Oliver while she stayed in a Tucson motel had escalated into a screaming match.

"I'm just not sure where I'm heading, Oliver. I started for California but now I'm not so sure of what I want to do."

"Damn it Charlotte, you're really aggravating me now. Just turn around and come on home."

"I don't want to come back home yet. I'm sure of that." Her voice was strong, but she felt unsure of herself.

"What does that mean, yet? I'm supposed to sit here quietly while you try to make up your mind? What about my plans, my work?" He was shouting.

"Your plans? Your work?" She shouted back. "That's what our marriage has always been about. Now I want to think about my life as well."

"That's the stupidest thing I've ever heard. I've given you everything you wanted. You live like a queen."

"Everything but what I really want; the freedom to do something with my life."

"I'm warning you, Charlotte. Follow through with this nonsense and I'll see that you're cut off without a penny and you know I can do it."

"Go to hell, Oliver." She slammed the phone down hard.

Shit, what had she done now? Her private bank account where she had squirreled away a few thousand dollars wouldn't last long. Oliver didn't gain fame as a defense attorney without reason; he was good. And his threats weren't empty ones, she knew.

But it did make her realize that her marriage was dead and she wanted out, wanted a divorce. She remembered that her mother had quietly divorced her father in the then fashionable mode of a six week Nevada residence. She pointed the Corvette towards Las Vegas, and when she got there, stopped at the first hotel casino that had easy parking; the Country Door.

Charlotte watched as the band walked onto the stage. Jesse and Jack strapped their guitars around their necks; Dave plucked on his bass guitar after slipping the strap over his shoulder, stopping to twist a key now and then. It was still new to him, the electric bass. Before it was invented in the early 50's he played a stand up bass. When Jesse and Jack went with electric guitars, he had to go electric too. Tennessee sat behind the drums, grinning, hitting a few test beats with his sticks, twirling them now and then..

Charlotte swallowed a bit of the Bloody Mary the waitress put before her. It tasted so good she took another big sip, savoring the mellow feeling it brought.

The room was filling up to capacity. Four men at a nearby table, talking loudly and drinking fast, ordered another round. There were several couples and groups of people, but no other single women. No woman alone, beyond herself, except for a pretty young woman sitting near the bandstand. She was dressed in Levis and a tight tank top with lots of cleavage showing. Charlie thought that she was probably a hooker. She took another sip of her drink, then got up and looked for the rest room.

She saw her face in the mirror, tired and drawn. She resolved to finish her drink, get a room and go to sleep. Tomorrow, she would buy a new outfit, and some makeup. But she'd have to be careful with her money now. She splashed cold water on her face and combed her hair. If Oliver could see me now, she thought, in yesterday's shorts and halter that she had bought in some small town that she couldn't even remember the name of. Not exactly the picture of the wife of a successful defense attorney. She imagined serving cocktails to the Hendersons in this outfit and immediately felt better after a laugh. She sat down on the couch in the lounge and took off her sandals, rubbed her feet and put the sandals back on.

The lounge door flung open and Belle breezed through, smiled broadly at Charlie. The pretty young woman in front of the bandstand, Charlie recalled.

"Hi," Belle threw the greeting over her shoulder. "I gotta pee so bad I can taste it."

"Hello yourself."

"I saw you sitting alone. Come on over and sit with me." Belle shouted from the cubicle.

"Okay, for a few minutes. But I'm bushed so I'm going to get a room soon and get some sleep."

"Oh, I know what you mean. I slept 14 hours last night, ate breakfast and went back to sleep again. Absolutely pooped."

Belle emerged from the cubicle buttoning up her jeans and grinning.

"But everything looks better now after some rest, you know?"

Charlie liked her right off. Up front this girl, been around, but down to earth. But what if she is a hooker. It might be a big mistake to go sit with her. She wouldn't have asked her, though, would she, if she was waiting to pick someone up.

"What's your name?"

"Charlotte. Most people call me Charlie. What's yours?"

"Belle." Charlie looked up at her. Why did it take her so long to answer?

Belle asked, "Are you married?"

"Yes."

"Where's your husband?"

"Home."

"Where's home?" Belle ran water over soapy hands.

"Nashville. Say, you ask a lot of questions."

"What are you doing here, without your husband?"

"I'm getting a divorce." Charlie wondered why she was being so open with this girl she had just met. But it was easy to be open with Belle. She was outgoing and friendly.

"Mean bastard, huh?"

"Not really, but..."

"Come on, I want you to meet my brother." Belle was already at the door.

Seated close to the bandstand, Charlie looked up at the stage as Belle pointed out the band members and their names. A few more people drifted in from the slot machines, cleaning the black from their hands with tiny wipes and standing at the back of the room. All the seats were taken.

Belle ordered them both another drink.

Charlotte rarely drank alcohol before five in the afternoon. It didn't seem civilized. To her it smacked of alcoholism. Even after five, she didn't drink unless Oliver was home and wanted someone to drink with him. Somehow it didn't seem proper. But, she reasoned, it was probably after five by now.

Charlie's mother had taught her at an early age to always be a lady. Hazel Sutton would sooner go to market naked than go without a fashionable hat, gloves, silk stockings and heels, and of course the jacket with the real fox collar. The head of the fox rested on her right shoulder and the tail on her left.

"Charlotte, use your salad fork first. I have told you that one hundred times. And sit up straight." Hazel Sutton's well-manicured hand rested on Charlotte's shoulder when she spoke to her.

"Answer Mrs. Rogers, dear."

"Say 'thank you' to Mr. Jackson, Charlotte." Hazel Sutton delivered this with a smile at Mr. Jackson.

"Charlotte, you will not call him." This, in the advent of her first boyfriend. "A girl should never call a boy." Charlie still couldn't call her husband without good reason.

"You must never smoke on the street, Charlotte; never forget that. It makes a woman look like a lady of the night." Charlie always wanted to smoke on a street corner, just once, even though she didn't smoke.

"Always listen politely and attentively, my dear. And never be rude and interrupt when someone is speaking." *Then I would never be able to speak to Oliver.* Charlie thought

"A lady never swears or uses questionable language." *Would she be fucking surprised today.*

Charlotte was mostly an obedient child and told herself that her mother's life lessons were for her own good. She prided herself in being a sensible woman, doing what needed to be done with grace and dignity. She had worked hard to further her husband's career, as her mother said she should. Her mother's voice stayed loud and clear, though she had been dead now for almost a year.

Charlie ran her household well, doing much of the housework and gardening. She listened, smiling and nodding, while Oliver told her, in lengthy detail, about his court cases of the day. She asked a question now and then to prove she was listening. She murmured words of encouragement when he talked about his ambition, his desire to be a judge.

She thought she had done all a good wife should. She was the perfect hostess, an ever present sounding board. She supervised the housekeeper and cook (she even learned how to cook gourmet herself, since Oliver loved good food). She spent hours in the beauty shop every week; facials, haircuts, leg waxing, and manicures on an endless schedule. She showed Oliver, and herself, that she would do anything to fulfill her role as a successful attorney's wife.

"Then why the hell am I not happy?" She often wondered. Once, when her mother said again how lucky she thought Charlotte was, she asked her mother the question.

"Don't swear, Charlotte, it isn't at all becoming. You aren't happy because you haven't had a child. A woman is not fulfilled until she has a child. One is enough, possibly two. They are a lot of work."

"Oliver says it's the wrong time now..."

"Charlotte, you aren't getting any younger, almost 30 now, as I remember. There are ways to get around what a man thinks he doesn't want. Why, a son…Oliver would be in his glory. All you have to do is 'forget' your diaphragm."

"Isn't that a bit dishonest, Mother?" Charlie had looked at her in horror.

"That's foolish thinking, Charlotte." Her mother sniffed. "It's a woman's way to help the man she loves acquire something he doesn't yet know that he wants."

So she forgot the diaphragm and became pregnant. Three months later there was a painful miscarriage, no doubt in response to her weeping, vomiting, lack of eating, and general desperation and depression. Or maybe it was Oliver's cold disdain that froze her uterus. She never forgot the diaphragm again. And her mother never forgave her for emptying her womb so unceremoniously in direct disobedience to her wishes. Her mother died soon after from a rapidly growing cancer, still angry that she had no grandchildren.

It occurred to Charlie one rainy afternoon not long ago, while she was sipping tea at the kitchen table and watching large drops splatter on the window, that there might be more to life than what she was living now. Some women did seem to keep their identity and marriage intact all at one time. Why couldn't she do what she wanted, too? Then the rain stopped, the sun came out and she forgot all about it, for awhile.

She couldn't pinpoint the very day she decided that she would have to leave Oliver, but the final decision was made the night before she left. How long ago was that? She couldn't remember; five, maybe six days ago.

The music brought her back. *These guys are really good,* she thought, *that is, if you like country music.*

"Which one is your brother, Belle?"

"The one singing and playing rhythm guitar is my brother Jesse. The one playing lead guitar is Jack, his cousin. They grew up together. Well, really Jesse's my half-brother, but I never thought of him like that. My father's first wife died when Jesse was born. Jack is the oldest by two years, and he's the manager of the group. He says Jesse is the star."

Jesse shot a glance at their table just then. He caught Charlie's eyes and their eyes held for a few seconds. A curious chill went down her spine. Then he raised the neck of his guitar and looked around at the group. *Born to Lose* he said, and nodded his head for the downbeat. His voice had a guttural, sexy sound. As he sang the crowd's murmuring slowly faded away until the room was quiet. Dave rocked on his heels and thumped the bass guitar, a serious look on his face. Tennessee, open faced, grinning, eyes circling the whole room, set the pace for the group. If the drummer was off, then everyone would sound like hell. He hit a rim shot and glanced at Jack, who stood solid, watching his fingers race up and down the neck of his guitar. Jack never once looked at the audience.

Belle drained her shot of tequila, wiped her mouth with a cocktail napkin, and .signaled the waitress.

"Do you want another drink, Charlie?"

"No, thanks, I'm fine. Belle, are your mother and father still married?"

"No, my Daddy died. I should say he killed himself. Probably to get away from my Ma's nagging. She was always bitching about something." She looked down at her hands, her fingers tapping the table top.

"You mean he actually killed himself"

"Yep, shot himself through the head with his gun. You know, Charlotte, Charlie, he was a good man and I loved him a lot. I still miss him, even though I was pretty young when he died. Folks back home say that he was never the same after his first wife died. He just didn't seem to care about anything except his kids. We always knew he loved us, though."

"I'm sure you miss him very much. Did your mother ever get married again? Is she still alive?"

"Yes…to both questions." Belle's face grew solemn when she answered

"Oh, there's the break song. I'll introduce you to my brother now." She picked up the shot of tequila the waitress had just delivered and downed it in one swallow, again wiped her mouth on the tiny napkin.

She's sure changed the subject in a hurry, Charlie thought.

"Are your mother and stepfather still married?"

"Nope. He died, too. Got himself killed." Belle's head was fuzzy. It was the tequila.

"Who killed him?"

"Don't know. Anyhow, no loss." *Damn.* Her head cleared a bit. *Better shut up, you're talking way too much. She's nice, but you don't know this woman.*

Charlie started to answer but Jesse and Jack each pulled up a chair and sat down next to them. Dave drifted to the bar, and Tennessee joined the four rowdy guys at the next table. Jesse hitched his chair a little closer to Charlie.

"I really like your music, Jesse." Charlie smiled at him.

"Please, ma'm, you can call me Jess. And I thank you for the compliment. Where are you from?" His eyes lingered on her face.

Jack shot him a quick look.

"I'm from Nashville."

"Hey, so are we. Did Belle tell you? Well, not really from Nashville but about forty miles out; a place called Bear Holler. It's a couple miles from Bear Creek. How long are you here for?"

"I'm staying the six weeks or so that it takes to get a divorce. Then I'll probably head for Los Angeles to meet an old college roommate. How long are you playing here?"

"We can stay as long as we want, according to the manager. I don't think we've decided yet, but this contract goes through August."

"Then we'll meet again, no doubt."

"No doubt," Jesse smiled.

Charlie was thankful for the dim lights in the casino. She knew her eyes were red and her face without makeup was a bit pallid.

The tinkle of coins falling into metal trays in the background was foreign to her ears. She had never been to a casino before. She liked the sound; the free fall of money.

"I guess I'll have to try a bit of gambling. Do you gamble, Jack?"

"Nope. Not at all. That's just throwing money away in my book."

"How about you, Belle?"

"I'm sure going to try. Maybe some craps, or machines." She motioned for another drink. "I've really never tried before."

"Jess, do you gamble?" Her gaze lingered on his face.

He bit his upper lip and brushed his hair back with one hand.

"I do. But I like blackjack, not the slot machines."

"I don't understand that game. I guess I'll have to stick with the machines" She pushed her chair back a little, thinking it was time to go. "How hard can it be to pull a lever?"

"I'll be glad to teach you how to play blackjack if you want."

"That would be great. She looked at him and smiled. "I might take you up on it."

"And I might hold you to it." *Bold, wasn't he?*

"Good." She stood up and reached out for Belle's hand. "It was so nice meeting you, Belle. Let's have breakfast tomorrow morning, all right?"

"Sure, if it isn't too early. I'm used to sleeping in."

"So call me when you're up. If we miss breakfast, we'll catch lunch." She looked around the table. "Goodnight, Jack, and Jess. I'm happy to meet you. And good luck with your music. You guys are great."

They both stood with her, chairs rolling quietly on the carpet. "Goodnight, now." Jess smiled, bent close to Charlie and said something the others couldn't hear. Jack looked at his cousin and grinned.

The band climbed back onto the stage and Charlie headed for the desk to get a room. She came back to the lounge to give Belle her room number.

She saw that Jess was watching her as she came into the room. As she turned to leave, he sang, "Sweet Dreams, Baby." She could feel his eyes following her out the door.

Upstairs, Charlie took a shower, pulled back the covers and climbed into the soft bed. She thought of Belle and her family; her dead stepfather, murdered, and her father, killing himself. And her mother…where was she in all this?

And she thought of Belle's brother and One Night Stand. Especially she thought of Jess and the way he looked at her. It had been a long time since any man looked at her with such desire. She thought of his parting words, *so I'll see you in the morning, Charlie.*

She would have to make it clear to him that she wasn't interested. She was still a married woman.

Chapter 13

Las Vegas 1955

Jess pushed into the room. Jack, Dave and Tennessee were already in the coffee shop. It was two in the morning and their shift was over. Jess decided to join the group and bring up the subject one more time of introducing some rockabilly and pop into their act. He felt like going to sleep instead.

"Hey, Jess! Sit it on down here and have a cuppa," Tennie laughed.

"Very funny. You all don't mind, do you, if I want to be called by a name that says I'm a man, not a little boy. I want my name changed to Jess on all the announcements, too."

"Shit, you know we just like messing with you." Tennie reached over and ruffled his hair.

"Yeah, cousin, I do think you're smitten with that little old almost-divorcee," Jack said.

"I gotta admit, she's mighty fine. She could put her shoes under my bed any time." Jesse smoothed his rumpled hair back down with both hands, and then checked it out in the reflection of the window.

"Sure, like she'd fuck around with the likes of you." Jack looked over his shoulder for the waitress. "That lady's got class written all over her."

"Now do you want to make a little bet in that direction?" Jess picked up a menu.

"I'll take a piece of that action," Dave said. "But I'm betting on Jesse. I mean Jess."The laughs went around the table again.

"Okay, you smart asses, I'm gonna make you eat your words. Now will you let me get some breakfast and go to bed?" He rattled the menu in his hands. "I'm worn out."

Jess looked over the menu, trying to think of the best way to approach Jack. It was better to talk to him with all the guys present. Maybe they would take his side, or at least convince Jack to make some changes in their music.

A middle-aged waitress with dyed black hair and wearing a yellow uniform that was too tight came to take their order.

"I'll have bacon and pancakes, please ma'm. And these hogs will have any old slop you got."

She laughed, and took their orders.

"Hey Tennie, don't tell me you're sleeping alone tonight. What went wrong?" Dave punched his shoulder and grinned.

Tennie raised his eyebrows and looked at Dave. "A man's got to get some rest sometime. So are you jealous that the women won't leave me alone?"

"Not really. Just curious; we don't usually see this much of you after the show."

Dave said, "Not to change the subject, but Jess, you've

got to do that new one, "It Wasn't God Who Made Honky Tonk Women" every night at least once, maybe twice. It really brought the house down. Did you see the whole audience was standing at the end, clapping and yelling? And there wasn't a dry eye in the house," Dave said.

"Yeah, it's a good one, all right. I was thinking of making it the feature song when we cut a record."

"We'd have a winner; I think maybe sell a million if we keep it pure country with a honky-tonk flavor." Jack said.

Tennie nodded agreement. "Okay you country-type pickers, here's a question for you. What was the first country record that sold over one million copies?"

"Hmm. I'm seeing a bunch of blank faces all around," Dave said. "Okay, I give up, too."

"It was 1924, Vernon Dalhart; 'The Prisoners Song,' backed by 'The Wreck of Old 97'." He slapped the table with the flat of his hand and laughed. "He was a fucking Texas Operetta star."

"Tennie, how do you remember all that shit?" Dave pushed his plate back and called for another drink.

"Smart and savvy," Tennie tapped his forehead with a finger. "Hey, Jack, here's one for you, Mr. Lead Guitar Man. Who made the guitar a lead instrument?"

"That's easy enough; Mother Maybelle Carter. But she got it from Negros. They even called it niggerpickin'. And," he added, "I was listening to the Carter family when you were still shitting your diapers."

Jess raised his cup to the waitress, asking for more coffee.

"Speaking of changes in music, Jack; let's go ahead and try a little rockabilly, just to see if it goes over. It could put a little kick in the show; just a number or two to get the audience response."

Jess knew it could rile his cousin but really wanted to

try the Elvis touch. He loved his cousin but since he came back from the war Jack wasn't the same. He was irritable; quick to fly off the handle. Then he was quiet and moody sometimes, and that scared Jess, remembering what happened to his father. He didn't want to stir up a conflict with the guy he grew up with, the one who was like an older brother. Jack had always been the "boss" of the two of them. He made all the decisions and Jess never questioned his judgment. He thought of the time they were thirteen, or fourteen. They had been fishing all day and Jesse wanted to go home. Jack said no, they weren't done yet. They ended up yelling face to face, then punching each other. Jack beat Jesse until he cried "uncle". Then he sat on the river bank and waited until Jack was ready to leave.

Jack stabbed a forkful of pancake and waved it at Jess. "Why would we want to fix something that ain't broke? We're doing fine playing all country."

"Sure, we're doing fine now, Jack, but I can see the handwriting on the wall. Elvis Presley comes from country, and he's the biggest hit nowadays. And he mixes in jazz, gospel, and blues. He gets swamped wherever he goes. He's not much of a guitar player, just swivels his hips like a topless dancer, only faster. But people just go nuts over it, especially the young folks and the women. They're the ones that are going to decide what's good or not." Jesse's voice had a hard edge by now.

Dave stared at his plate, cut out a piece of egg, then looked at Jack.

"You know, Jack, he's got a point. Sure, we're doing great now, but we need to keep our eye on the future, too. Jess isn't the only one who thinks that country-rock is the wave of the future. I hear most of the record companies are looking for someone to compete with Elvis. Jess here could fill the bill. Some groups are throwing in pop as well. It seems like the old country swing is almost a thing of the past."

Jack took a sip of his coffee and didn't answer.

Jesse stared at Jack. "Look. There's no harm in trying a tune or two. If it doesn't go over, then we can drop it." He tried to keep the irritation out of his voice.

Jack looked from face to face, rounding the table. "Look here," there was patience in his voice, "think about someone like Webb Pierce. Pure country, making records hand over fist and lots of money along with it. "There Stands the Glass," "Back Street Affair", "Slowly"; how can you beat tunes like that? That new one, "In the Jailhouse Now" just blows everyone away. Sure, somewhat honky-tonk, but that reels them in every time. If you want some changes, let's add a pedal steel, like Pierce."

Dave and Tennie looked at Jess as if to say, well, what about that?

"You're right, Jack. We could use a steel. But how are we going to pay him? We're stretched about as far as we can go."

Jack waved a hand. "Those guys playing studio are making tons of money just playing country. I read where Chet Atkins said, 'Yeah, I'd like to buy me one of them Cadillacs, but everyone would think I was a sideman.'" Everyone laughed, easing the tension.

"You got a point for sure, Jack." Jess looked up at his cousin. "We need to keep up on all those things. All I'm saying is, let's add a number or two of rockabilly along with it. I'm not proposing rock and roll or anything too drastic. Just a little change of pace now and then."

The waitress brought the whiskey with a water back Dave had ordered. He drank the shot straight down and followed with a small sip of water.

"Jack," Dave said, "how about Eddy Arnold; his record

sales are flagging because he's sticking with his old style country." He picked up his bill and reached for his wallet. "Just give it some thought, okay?"

"I already did, and I'm against changing our style. Country's been around for a long time, and it'll be here when they forget all about country-rock and Elvis is nothing but a fucking memory. There's some country pickers in Nashville doing $50,000 a year playing studio country music; Chet Atkins, Floyd Cramer, Boots Randolph, Bob Moore and Buddy Harmon to name a few. They get together and jam, cut both sides of a platter having a good time they can't even call work; then go home to their wives at night. No more one night stands. How much did Elvis make last year?"

Jess sighed. "I don't know, but what I'm saying is that it's all starting to change. Did you hear about Elvis playing Kilgore, Texas? They say he wore red pants, a green coat and pink shirt and socks. Mind you; I'm not saying we should do that, but you can see the young folks want more entertainment and variety." Jess held Jack's gaze. "I hear that Elvis stood before the mike for five minutes before he hit a lick, kind of sneered, hit his guitar and broke two strings right off. I never broke two strings all at once in my lifetime. Hell, he just stood there with the strings dangling and started moving his hips and swiveling around. You couldn't hear any music for the girls all screaming and fainting. Gives me chills just thinking about it. I heard that the studios are happy as all get out that they found a white man to sing like a Negro."

The silence was ominous. Then Jack's voice rose and his face flushed. "I still say no; end of story."

"Hell, I'm with you, Jack." Tennie wiped his mouth and pushed his empty plate away. "I'm a country picker and I don't care to learn no rockabilly shit."

"You know what, we're all tired now. Let's talk about it some more tomorrow, okay?"Jess stood up and threw some money on the table.

"There's nothing left to talk about, Jesse. I'm the manager here, and I say we aren't changing our style."

Jack got up, and left Jess and Tennessee and Dave staring at his back as he stalked out the door.

"My cousin's being hard-headed. Let me talk with him tomorrow because I'm determined to throw some country-rock into our routine." Jess finished his coffee and they all headed to the door.

In his room, he stretched out on the bed, his mind still racing. How could he get Jack to listen to reason? He already offered to just try a song or two a night to see how it went over before committing full time. He told him that if it didn't work, they could abandon it right away. But Jack seemed immoveable.

What was he going to do about the money that's disappeared with their agent? There was no reaching him and they were short on cash right now. Jack arranged to get the next pay coming directly to them, minus the agent's cut, but that was two weeks off.

And he couldn't get Charlie out of his mind. Belle was spending every day with her. Three times she had come into the lounge with Belle but each time she had one drink and left.

It was a month since they first met before he managed to "accidentally" get to the coffee shop at the same time as Charlie and Belle. He pushed into the booth beside Belle.

"Morning, ladies."

"Hi, Jess." They spoke together, looked at each other and laughed.

He had a hard time keeping his eyes off Charlie. At first

glance she was rather plain looking without makeup, but he kept returning to her face; her delicate dark eyebrows, black hair that fell straight and shiny as silk onto her shoulders. Long black lashes swept her cheeks when she blinked. Her shoulders were white and bare in a sleeveless midriff top of lavender that accented the deep purple in her eyes. But what he wanted most at that point of time was to see her without clothes.

He was captivated by the way she picked up her coffee cup with both hands, her small thin fingers pointing in his direction. She slowly put it to her mouth. With the tip of her tongue she licked a small drop of cream from the side and then she sipped, eyes lowered and lips curled around the edge. He wanted those hands around his dick. Her eyes lifted and caught his; he smiled and looked long into her face until she looked away. He was sure that her body was fine, her nipples dark and breasts firm, buttocks tight and legs shapely. Then she rose from her chair with a fluid graceful motion and he saw that she wore shorts. Her pale flesh didn't diminish the beauty of her legs. She smiled at him and said, "See you later, Jess," and his heart was pounding like Dave's bass guitar.

He was hard just thinking of her and that usually didn't happen until the girl, and it could be almost any girl, was naked in his room. He relieved himself right where he lay before falling into a restless sleep.

Chapter 14

Belle stretched herself full length on the lounge chair and with a long practiced habit slowly scanned the pool area. Her eyes stopped when she spotted Detective Frank Smith coming towards her.

"Hello, Frank." She sat up on the side of her chair. *Damn, what does he want?* She willed herself to keep her voice steady.

"Hi there, Dallas." He sat on the lounge chair next to hers. "I had an interview in the hotel and when I finished, I thought I might as well stop and say hello. The desk clerk said you were at the pool." He seemed nervous. "Can I buy you a cup of coffee?"

"It's a little hot for that, but I could go for an iced tea."

"Good." He beckoned to a waiter making his rounds at the pool. He came back soon with coffee and iced tea.

"Have you decided yet if you'll stay in Las Vegas?" He sipped his coffee. "Darn, you were smart to have something cold." He placed the cup on the table beside him.

"I'm still not sure, Frank. I like it okay, but I do get restless after a while."

"I'd kind of like it if you stayed. Maybe we could take in a movie sometime."

"That would be nice. Right now I'm kind of busy, though, trying to get settled and look for another job." She set her tea down next to his cup. "Maybe later, though."

"Oh, sure, I understand. I don't mean to pressure you. It was just a thought." He looked around the pool. "That water sure looks inviting. Do you swim?"

"Actually, I do. We used to swim a lot where I grew up."

"That was Indianapolis, wasn't it?" He looked into her eyes.

"Yeah." She felt herself grow weak.

Belle said, "I'm looking for a job outside of stripping." She wanted to change the subject.

He smiled. "What kind of work are you looking for?"

She hesitated. "I'm not quite sure what else I can do, besides waitressing. Maybe I could do office work; answering the phone or filing. I even thought of trying for a job as a showgirl, though I hear it's hard to get into."

"That's what I hear, too. And I know they look for very tall girls." He stood. "But you're pretty enough, that's for sure." His face grew red. "Well, my break is over and I have to go back to work. If I hear of any promising jobs, I'll let you know. Here's my number; call me when you're free. I'll see you again sometime, Dallas."

"Sure. I'd like that, Frank. Oh, Frank, Dallas is my stage name. Just so you know. But that's what I go by all the time. I've almost forgotten my given name." She lied, but she was good at it. He took her hand briefly, and she smiled at him. "So call me Dallas. I like it best." Frank nodded, smiled, and then headed for the hotel door.

Belle looked up to see Charlie coming their way. "Hi, Belle." She looked at Frank going through the pool door into the hotel.

Charlie grinned at Belle, not saying anything. After a few minutes, Belle looked at her and said, "Well, what's on your mind, lady?"

"Just; who is that handsome man?"

Belle wanted to tell Charlie who he was and how she knew him. She wanted to tell her everything about her life and how she was wanted for murder. But she couldn't. She had already said too much the first night they met. Since then, Belle carefully avoided any talk about her past. If Charlie asked, she passed it off as unimportant or changed the subject. She liked her a lot, but wasn't sure if she could trust her.

Belle had never known anyone like Charlie. She was beginning to see her as the big sister that she always wanted. Charlie was elegant, smart and sophisticated. Charlie was comfortable in any company. She was polite and considerate of others. Belle wanted to be like her

Belle thought of the women she knew when she was growing up; her Ma, her Grandma, and the women of Bear Holler. Some nice, some not so nice, but mostly simple folk who's lives were geographically and socially limited. The waitresses and strippers that had been her companions for the past nine years weren't on the same level as Charlotte Force. Charlotte was educated and beautiful, too. She exuded that elusive quality called class.

But most of all, Belle appreciated that Charlie liked and admired Belle. No woman had ever looked at Belle with admiration before. Charlie said she was in awe of Belle's sense of adventure.

Charlie had asked who Frank was. Finally, Belle said,

"He's a detective that I met when I was shopping one day. We had a cup of coffee and some conversation. But I'm not really interested in him so I've discouraged any further contact."

"Well, he's very handsome. If he's nice, too, maybe you should reconsider." She lowered her sunglasses and looked at Belle.

"Take my word for it; he wouldn't be any good for me." Belle got up. "I'm going for a swim. Want to come?"

"No, I'm just going to relax for a while. You go ahead." She laid back on the lounge next to Belle's and closed her eyes.

Belle hoped that Frank took the hint and would go his way and leave her alone. She couldn't risk getting any closer to him. Besides, he made her nervous for some reason.

She dived from the side of the pool and felt the warm water envelop her body. She liked the feel of water on her skin. It was soothing. It made her feel pure and clean.

Chapter 15

Jess woke to the rattle of dishes in the hallway as the maids made their rounds of cleaning and picking up trays of dirty dishes left outside the doors. He yawned and stretched. Jack's bed was empty. The bed was still made so he hadn't come in at all. He must have gotten lucky. Either that or he was angry with Jess and decided to stay with the guys in their room.

It was noon, straight up. He remembered that this was their day off, their only day off on this gig. Tonight there would be a wimpy local band called Desert Country on the bandstand. The manager would be happy to see One Night Stand back tomorrow night.

So what to do with the day of freedom? No need to call practice. The guys played together so much that each of them knew what the others were going to do before they did it. And Jack wouldn't learn anything new.

He hoped that Jack remembered to check payroll for their money. They had run up a big bill at the hotel for food and drinks. There was still no sign of their agent. His office was closed and the phone disconnected. He was gone, and so was their money.

Belle said she was spending the day at the pool, building a tan.

He thought about bringing her up on the stage. She always had a good voice and a girl on the bandstand was a draw. He'd have to mention it to the guys. He thought it would be okay. She's been in Vegas almost two months and no one was asking about her. It was almost certain that no one was looking for her anymore, especially when they were way across the country from Bear Holler. But on the other hand, if they did arrest her it would be his fault. And, couldn't he be arrested, too, for not turning her in. He really didn't want her to leave now that they had found each other. *Hell, we can't live our lives in fear, no matter what.*

He showered, put on some shorts and a T-shirt and not bothering to shave went to the hotel coffee shop. He sat down at the counter and ordered breakfast. The hot coffee brought beads of sweat to his face. The caffeine lifted his awareness and woke him fully. He felt the air conditioning flip on, cooling his face. The temperature, he saw by the gauge just outside the front door, was over one-hundred degrees. He finished ham and eggs and wandered to the lobby, thought about buying a book and joining Belle by the pool. He wasn't much of a reader, but maybe he could find a detective magazine in the gift shop.

Then she was walking toward him, smiling. She was wearing shorts and a frilly scarlet top. His breath hung in his mouth and it was a few seconds before he could speak.

"Good morning, Charlotte; er, I mean afternoon. I kind of lose sense of time when I sleep half the day."

"Hi, Jess. And my friends call me Charlie. What are

you doing today?" Did he imagine that her face was flushed?

"Oh, just hanging out. It's our day off, you know. How about you?"

"I've been up to my eyeballs in lawyers and their papers, but I think it's pretty much finished. The papers are filed at last, and now I just wait for the six weeks to go by. And time is really dragging. I just want this over with as soon as possible."

She opened the map in her hands." Say, Jess, do you know how to get to Red Rock Hot Springs? I hear it's a good place to go see and not too far from here. I thought I'd take a drive out."

"Sure, I know where it is." He could smell her perfume; subtle and musky. "There are several springs in the Red Rock area. Actually, it's my day off so I could take you. Uh, that is, if you have wheels, which I don't, except for that smelly bus that carries a bunch of raunchy guys around."

The hesitation was unmistakable but in the end, she said, "That would be great"

"I'll just go upstairs and get my shades. Meet you back here." He wanted to shave.

"Okay. See you in an hour?"

It was after four and still too hot to put the top down on the Corvette. The sun hung bright above the horizon. She offered to let him drive and he declined. Not that he didn't want to; he had never driven anything like a Corvette before.

Along the highway the sandy landscape was dotted with cactus. It was flat and dry all the way to the distant mountains. The air was still except for heat waves rippling above the sand.

Conversation was easier than he thought it could be, given their diverse lives. He wondered what they could have in common, but words flowed like water over rocks, gathering momentum and volume.

Jess wanted to ask Charlie about her husband, but wasn't sure he should. They had only known each other less than two months, yet he felt as if they were old friends. They often had coffee together, mostly with Belle, too. Or they chatted at the pool. Before now, she had always avoided being alone with him.

Suddenly out of words, they drove silently through the late afternoon. Then Charlie said, "Oliver wants me to come back home." *Where did that come from? Was she warning him off?* "But I'm going to California and meet up with an old college friend, as soon as the divorce is final." She brushed her hair back from her face; Jess noticed that she did that when she seemed on edge. Maybe he was more aware of it because he had the same nervous habit; slicking his hair back with both hands and running his fingers down the line of his ducktail.

"California? What will you do there?" he felt his stomach lurch.

"My friend works for Universal Studios. She just got her first speaking part in a movie and she thinks she can get me work, too."

"Are you an actress?" Jess shifted in his seat. His back was sticking to the leather in spite of the air conditioning.

"I'm a pretty good actress. I played lead in two college plays, spent five years in Little Theatre, did some off Broadway the first few years I was married and living in New York." Her cheeks flushed red and she laughed. He thought it was the sweetest laugh he ever heard, soft and deep and sexy.

"I've been putting on plays since I was ten. My first

show was a spoof on radio commercials and my friend and I charged five cents for admission. We pinned fake fruit on our heads and sang, 'I'm Chiquita Banana and I'm here to say…you should never put bananas…in the refrigerator.'" She laughed again. "My Mother thought it was pretty undignified but we made 65 cents even though some of the kids were gone to summer camp. I've been hooked ever since."

"Wow. I had no idea I was in the company of such talent."

He glanced at her and rested his left arm on the back of her seat. It was so casual that he thought she didn't notice

She shot him a sideways glance. "Well, it's tough to make money as an actress and," she reached over and turned up the air conditioning, "I am over the hill for most roles."

"I'll be rooting for you, though I would hope that you'll change your mind and stick around here instead." She stared out the windshield.

"You know what, Jess? I do like Las Vegas. I've kind of settled in here. I thought about getting a little apartment and hanging out for awhile. But Laura is pushing me to come soon because there are some parts opening up. She wants me to try out."

Jess was silent, looking out the window. "It would be great if you stayed. But I understand. When you have a talent for acting, I suppose you want to be acting."

"Speaking of talent, Jess; I think you have a great voice. I was mesmerized."

"Good. I wouldn't mind hypnotizing you." He brought his arm from behind her seat and raked his hair.

She looked at him with eyebrows raised. "Hmm. Someone tried to hypnotize me once and it didn't work. Seems I'm not a good candidate."

"Maybe he wasn't good enough." Jess smiled and looked sideways at her.

Her eyes scanned the road ahead. "So what do you plan to do with this-mesmerizing-voice, anyhow?"

"Go straight to the top, what else?" he didn't laugh. "Look, Charlie, at the risk of sounding like an egomaniac, I have to say that I know I'm good enough to go as far as I want to in this business. And I've got a great band. But if they don't keep up with me, then I'll go on without them."

"Belle said that you and your cousin were at odds about what kind of music to play."

"Yeah, that's right. What we need to do with the group now is to introduce some country-rock into our routine, but Jack is dead set against it. And I'm just as determined to do it. Jack needs to wake up to changing times. It's causing a rift between us and I don't like that but I've got to think of my future. I'm not going to play honky-tonks and lounges forever."

Charlie nodded her head slowly and said she knew he would figure it out. "We almost came to blows three years ago when I pushed for us to go to electric guitars. I told him, Jack, we can't even be heard in honky-tonks if we stay acoustic. It's noisy here in Vegas, too, what with the clanging machines and the drunks hollering. All the groups are going electric, even the Grand Old Opry. They have drums now, too. We have to do it." Jess rubbed his neck; he didn't know what to do with his hands when he wasn't smoking.

"Jack said he didn't want to play any honky-tonks anyhow. Well, he finally agreed because the guys were for it and we all pressured him into it, but he's still mad about it. He wants our agent to get jobs where we can play acoustic."

Charlie touched his bare arm with her hand. "I think you're right, Jess. I'm speaking as a music fan now." Her touch sent little electric shocks up his arm and settled in his head.

Theirs was the only car on the road leading to one of the hot springs. Jess told Charlie to pull off far into the side of the road and behind a stand of cactus so as not to be seen from the road. No need to tempt highwaymen.

"Are you sure this is right?" she asked and he nodded. He might have shown some doubt because now she would know that he's been here before, and he had, more than once. He got out of the car and opened her door, offering his hand to Charlie. She hesitated but finally took his hand and stepped out of the car.

Climbing over boulders and dodging cactus, their feet sinking into the sandy path, they finally came to a small bubbling pool that smelled slightly of sulfur. Around it was mounds of sand and the whole area was hidden by a circle of boulders.

She knelt down and dipped her fingers into the pool, and then turned her head to smile at him. "This is great." Her nose wrinkled at the smell of sulfur.

"Go ahead, get in," Jess said.

"I didn't bring a suit." She sounded like she regretted not thinking of it.

"You don't need a suit. I'll turn my back if you want."

"Are you going in?"

"If you say it's okay."

She sat back onto the sand cross-legged. She raised her hand from the water and brushed a wisp of hair from her face. She left a wet spot on her right temple and he wanted to wipe it away, but didn't. He wondered if she was considering his suggestion or if he had insulted her. He sat down beside her and took her hand in his.

"Look, Charlie, you don't have to be afraid of me. I

think you're the most beautiful woman I've ever seen and I wouldn't do anything to hurt you."

She looked at him, seemed surprised. "Do you really think I'm beautiful?"

"Yes. Why would you doubt it? Don't you ever look in a mirror?"

She laughed. "Sometimes opinions come from someone else. Before you know it, you believe it, too. Thank you for giving me a different opinion."

Still unsure but glad that he had taken time to shave; he put his arm around her shoulders and kissed her forehead. Not too bold, he thought, and hopefully reassuring. It was true, he didn't want to hurt her or force her in any way, even though he fairly ached at the sight of her nipples outlined on her halter top. He could wait, but it wasn't easy. If she had been any other girl he wouldn't have hesitated.

"Jess, Belle told me you aren't married, but do you have a steady girl?" He wondered, *is she trying to keep things cool; or is she interested?*

"Nope. Just played the field, until now." He scooped water from the spring and splashed her legs.

"Hey," she looked at him, mocking indignation, "that's a really old line."

"Well, sometimes it still works." He wiped his face with both hands. "So, not to change the subject, but why don't you tell me about your husband and why you're getting a divorce."

Charlie stared at him, her lips parted. "Do you really want to know?"

"Sure, that's why I asked." He leaned both elbows onto his bended knees, heels dug in the sand. She turned to face him.

"Oliver is a very successful defense attorney, maybe the best in the country. He's good at what he does and he makes a lot of money. However, he has recently reminded me that it's not my money. He gave me whatever I wanted and as long as I supported him in his business, I could pretty much spend my time as I wanted. He didn't beat me or go out with other women. He drinks a bit too much but he's not a mean drunk." They both watched a crow fly overhead. "I really don't have any reason to divorce him."

Jess stared at the bubbling pool.

His voice was soft and low. "Does he make you feel like a woman?"

Charlie didn't answer. Her eyes just followed his into the pool.

Jess got up, took off his shirt and spread it on the sand for her to sit. But she stood too, took his face in her hands and pulled him to her, her mouth hard on his. She smelled like a summer day in the Smokies; a whiff of bare breeze with the hint of honeysuckle. He held her as gently as he might capture a wild bird.

He kissed her neck, her cheeks, and the tip of her nose. He held her face in his hands and his tongue explored her mouth. He untied her top, fingers shaking. He was right about her breasts; they were firm and the nipples dark. They fit into his hands like they were meant to be there. She whispered to him that *it felt strange, being with another man.* He said, *Of course, why wouldn't it?* He laid her gently down on his shirt and though the sun was behind the distant mountains, the sand was still warm. He buried his face in her neck. His tongue made a path between her breasts. He sucked one breast, then the other. He found the zipper and peeled off her shorts. He saw her slowly pull her hands from her face and look at him.

He stood and dropped his shorts, naked before her. He was glad he had spent so much time swimming in the hotel pool. His body was muscled and tan. He lay down beside her, kissed her again and moved his mouth over her belly, to the inside of one thigh. She raised her hips and sighed; *Jess.* Then he was on top of her. Her hands were tight on his buttocks. She pulled him deeper inside her. He slapped her gently where her ass met her thigh, like he might urge a filly. The slap brought her sharply into him. The sand was gritty on his knees. Her skin felt soft and pliant under him.

Then it was so quiet he could hear the sulfur pool spitting hot streams of water into the desert air.

They lay side by side. He lit a cigarette and handed it to her. She took a short drag and handed it back. She hadn't smoked since college but it seemed like the thing to do. The smoke choked her but she didn't mind. The sand was starting to cool beneath their bare bodies. They watched stars dot the sky and surround the half-moon.

Charlie thought that making love to Jess was as different from sex with Oliver as a hot spring from an iceberg. She turned to him and they were both on their sides facing each other. He rubbed her cheek with his chin. The hint of stubble on his face excited her. She ran her fingers down his back. He murmured, *Charlie, Charlie.* She felt his breath on her lips and kissed him. It was hot and sweet, like the first time.

They dozed with his arms around her until he woke and moved his arm. She sat up beside him. He lifted her into the hot spring water and climbed in beside her. Then he reached for the iced pack he had carried from the hotel. He pulled out two bottles of beer and snapped them open; first hers, then his. The beer felt cool and soothing on her throat. She kissed his cheek.

"Thanks, Jess. That goes down just right."

"Hey, sweet thing, you deserve the best. Next time, champagne."

She laughed. "Whatever you say."

The air was still warm when they climbed out of the pool and put clothes onto damp bodies. She wondered that she didn't feel ashamed. She was not yet out of her marriage and she was with another man. What was a decent waiting period anyhow? Was it the same as in a death, divorce being like a death? Should one wait a year before a new romance? What would her mother say?

She knew very well what her mother would have said and decided to put that out of her mind. But what would Jess think of her; that she was an easy woman, that she slept around? That she did care about. Would he want to see her again? And what right did she have to do this to Oliver, anyhow?

Oliver had been her first. He was all she had ever known. Their lovemaking wasn't bad; just routine. She had realized that orgasms were escaping her when she overheard a conversation one day at the Mason Street Salon. The women were describing sex as out-of-body experiences that were foreign to Charlie.

She was surprised that there could be more to lovemaking. Skin on skin with Jess inside her she could only ride the waves, moan and call his name. She couldn't have stopped if God himself had stood beside them shaking His fist.

Jess kissed her forehead, as he did in the beginning. Even if she never saw him again, she determined to remember this night. She was beautiful; didn't he say so?

They retraced their path to the car and Jess slid into the driver's seat. He put the top down and drew her to him. With the night air washing over them and her head on his shoulder, they drove slowly back into the lights of Las Vegas.

Chapter 16

Days blended into weeks and the phone calls from Laura were fewer now. Charlie began to wonder what she would do when her divorce was final. Would she leave Jess and go to California, or stay in Vegas.

She was falling in love with Jess, she knew that much. The musician's life was so foreign to her, living on the road and sometimes not knowing where the next job was coming from. But she could see that he loved it. Sometimes, she loved whatever he loved. Other times, she missed her house, her garden, her easy life. Sometimes she even missed Oliver.

One late afternoon, on the way back from the pool with Jess, Charlie saw Oliver sitting in a chair near the elevators. His legs were crossed, hands folded in his lap, and eyes straight ahead. Then he stood quickly and walked towards them. His hair was slightly rumpled and his face dark and grim; the lawyer-look that she knew so well.

She thought her knees might buckle under her but for Jess holding her up.

"I've come to take you home, Charlotte." Oliver glared at Jess.

"I'm not leaving, Oliver." Charlie turned to Jess and said, "I'll see you later, okay?"

"Will you be all right?" he asked. Charlie saw Jess take measure of Oliver's stocky frame, his Armani suit. Oliver was just tall enough to look down his nose when he spoke to Charlie.

"Yes. I'll be fine. I'll see you later." She squeezed Jess' hand and looked into his eyes before pulling away. Jess jabbed the elevator button without taking his eyes off Oliver. Oliver took Charlie's arm, not roughly but with a firm hand. He steered her to the 24 hour coffee shop. She heard the faint ding of the elevator bell as they walked through the lobby.

They found a table in the corner. Charlie ordered coffee. Oliver brushed the waitress off with a wave of his hand when she asked for his order. He sat across from Charlie in the booth, staring at her. She felt his eyes taking in her wet stringy hair and short swim suit cover.

He folded his hands and stared at the table top. "Charlotte, in spite of it all I'm willing to forgive this lapse of yours and take you home." He sighed. "But I would expect there would be no repeat of this scandalous behavior."

"I'm not going home, Oliver, and all I need from you is to leave me alone. I've filed for divorce." Her voice was flat.

"You're not thinking straight right now. I'm sure it's the influence of that punk you've obviously taken up with." He brushed imaginary crumbs from the table. "I can assure you, Charlotte, I would have no problem suing him for alienation of affections. Who is this guy anyhow, and how do you know him?"

She looked at him and dropped her chin into her hand. There were bags under his eyes and she thought he looked tired.

"He's the brother of a young woman I met here. Nothing for you to be concerned about; actually, none of your business."

"Anything to do with my wife is my business, Charlotte. I'm not only concerned, but very upset as well. Do you know what I've been through since you left?"

"No, I don't, Oliver." She was sure that he would tell her.

The waitress, a pale-faced young girl in a slightly stained yellow uniform, brought a mug of coffee and set it before Charlie. She asked if there was anything else. Oliver again waved her away.

"I'll tell you what I've been through. As embarrassing as it was, I had to cancel plans with the Hendersons at the last minute with very little explanation." Oh, yes, she remembered, the cocktail party. "Then I was forced to send Bobby Jackson, who was totally unprepared, to attend my court case the next day. Since then I have spent endless hours tracking your trip, even hired a detective to find you. I had no idea if you were alive or dead or what on earth might be going through that head of yours."

She felt a pang of guilt. "I am sorry, Oliver. It was inconsiderate of me. But I'm not changing my mind."

"I'm going to stay here until you do. Let me see you gallivant off with this...what's-his-name...again and you can take the consequences. Right now, I'll be off to my room and, Charlotte," he stood and looked down at her, "I'll be filing a response to your divorce petition in the morning."

"Don't, Oliver, please don't."

But she was talking to his back.

Oliver shoved his key into the hotel door, skinning his knuckles.

"Shit!" Frustrated, he twisted the lock hard and jiggled the knob until it opened. Inside, he turned on the shower; and then poured half a glass of Scotch from the bottle he brought from home. He drank it straight down without the usual ice and branch water. It left a comforting burn in his throat. He stripped off his clothes and sat on the bed, dropping his head in his hands. He thought of the day when he came home and Charlotte was gone.

He had pulled the BMW into the garage, clicked the door shut, and sat there for a few minutes. Damn, he just wasn't looking forward to going inside that night.

He was on time so Charlotte would have his drink waiting. He could have a bit of anesthetic before the "discussion" started. Maybe she wasn't angry after all. Perhaps he was just imagining that she would be.

He meant to stay awake the night before and not drink so much. But the conversation turned to Charlie meeting up with Laura McAllister. Laura had inflamed her with the wild idea to return to acting. It goaded him into pouring another and yet another until the drone of the television lulled him off to sleep.

It had been a stressful day, he told her. But sometimes he thought that Charlotte didn't appreciate the pressures a defense attorney experienced on a daily basis. Oh, yes, she listened attentively, smiling and nodding, when he told her. But did she really understand what he was going through? She didn't experience first hand the well-heeled murderers, the smug white collar criminals, the flirty middle-aged adulteresses that he had to put up with. He thought she didn't understand why he had to keep up appearances. At times, he felt her resentment leaking through her calm demeanor.

She could have tried again to wake him up for dinner. Instead, he awoke in the middle of the night and lumbered up to bed chilled and hungry. Sure, he woke her up but what's wrong with a husband wanting to make love to his wife?

"Charlotte?" The house was unusually quiet; no radio or TV playing. And what was for dinner? He could smell nothing. No rattle of pots and pans from the kitchen. That's right; it was cook's day off. Okay, Charlotte was still angry. He would take her to Bertoni's for dinner. She was always saying that she wanted to go out more. And it would be hard for her to argue with him in a public place.

He checked the answering machine for messages. There were none, except a reminder for a dentist's appointment the next day for Charlotte. Maybe she had to go to the market for some last minute item. But she always managed to be home when he arrived from work. He'd emphasized early in their marriage how important that was to him. The only time she missed in seven years was when she had car trouble and was stuck at the repair shop. Even then, she called him the minute he arrived home. Another thought shot into his consciousness. Could she have been in an accident on the highway? Was she lying in a hospital emergency room somewhere?

Oliver walked through the house. Nothing was disturbed. He remembered that he hadn't seen her that morning when he left for work. He assumed that she was on her usual morning walk. He opened the front door and peered down the driveway. Even the gardener was absent. He must have left early. And Charlotte hadn't even watered her precious roses. The soil looked parched. He looked out back. The Corvette was gone.

Back inside, he poured himself a drink and opened his briefcase spreading papers onto the dining room table. The phone rang.

He picked it up. "Hello?"

Silence. "Charlotte?"

A click and he stared at the receiver for a few seconds before setting it down He paced the floor, and then returned to the papers for the Jillian trial. He still had a lot to do before tomorrow. What if something has happened, though? He'd have to send that twerp Bobby Jackson to court in his place. He was sure to fuck something up.

He poured another drink, then rummaged through the refrigerator and made a cheese sandwich. The bread was dry and he couldn't find any mayonnaise.

The phone rang again, and he grabbed it right away. "Hello!" Irritation made his voice like sandpaper.

"Oliver?"

He poured more Scotch into his glass, sat down again on the side of the bed. His head ached with emotions unfamiliar to him; anger (*how could she*); fear (*would she really leave him*} grief (*what was she doing with that punk*}.

He rose and walked into the bathroom, climbed in the shower. The hot water stung his back. *So she wanted a divorce. Well, she was not going to get away with it.*

Oliver's threat, Charlie remembered the next morning, was to contest her divorce. She wondered if he really would carry through with it. She dialed the desk to learn his room number and rang his room. No answer.

She turned on the shower and the phone rang. It was Jess.

"Hello, darlin'. Is everything okay?"

"He's going to contest the divorce. But yes, I'm fine.

More than fine." She smiled even though she knew he couldn't see.

"Can I come up to your room?" She wanted to say, yes *come as fast as you can.*

"Better not, Jess. Oliver's in a foul mood and I don't want you to get involved."

"I'm already involved."

"You know what I mean. Give me some time to take care of this mess, all right?"

"Sure, whatever you want. But I'll be suffering you know."

She laughed. "That's funny, you made me feel better."

"I'll be thinking of you and if you need anything, anything at all, you know my number. You do know my number, don't you?"

"Yes, I do. But now I've got to get in the shower and go see my attorney, I guess."

"Want me to wash your back?"

She giggled. "Some other time, I'm afraid."

"Come to the club tonight, Charlie?"

"I don't know, Jess. It might not be a good idea."

"I'll be looking for you."

Charlie said goodbye and smiling, dropped the phone in its cradle.

Two hours later she opened the door to the plush air conditioned offices of Dunn and Dunn, Attorneys at Law. She sat in the soft leather chair across from the desk of Mark Dunn, her purse tucked beside her.

"There's been a slight complication, Mark. Oliver is in town and he says he's filing an answer to my divorce." She felt for the tape in her purse reassuring herself that it was still there. "I have something to tell you in the strictest confidence."

That night Charlie and Belle sat together at the same table near the bandstand where they had first met.

"Oliver's in town." Charlie said. "He cornered me yesterday afternoon just as Jess and I came back from the pool."

"Damn. What did he say?" Belle lit a cigarette. She felt a wave of panic. What if Charlie went home with him just as they were becoming good friends? And it sounded like Jess and Charlie were more than friends. Belle liked that idea. She liked it very much.

"He said he was going to contest the divorce. But I've seen my attorney today and everything is all right."

"Are you sure? You said Oliver was a good attorney."

"Absolutely; Mark Dunn assured me there's nothing to worry about." She caught Jess's glance and smiled at him.

Belle watched the guys climb the bandstand stairs and pick up their instruments. Her eyes darted about the room. She paused at a back table. Wasn't that Frank? He was sitting alone. But what was he doing here? Did he come to see her or was he on some other mission? He returned her gaze and raised his hand in a wave. She pushed down her fear and waved back with a smile. The band started their second set. Next break, she thought, I'll go say hello if he doesn't come over here.

Jess opened with "Maybelline" and the dance floor filled up. Belle noticed a man in a suit sitting at the table next to Frank. He was staring at their table. She looked at Charlie.

Charlie had her eyes glued to Jess, dark eyes sparkling in the dim light.

"Do you know that guy staring at us?" Belle nudged Charlie's' arm.

Her face turned pale. "Yeah. That's Oliver." She looked back at Jess. He was glaring at Oliver.

"Maybelline" ended and Jess looked down at Belle. "Folks, my sister is a hell of a singer and she's here tonight. What do you say, should we get her up to do a number?"

The crowd clapped.

She waved him off, shaking her head. She didn't want to call attention to herself, especially with Frank sitting at a back table.

"Hey, Belle, come on up."

Someone shouted, "Come on, Belle."

Again she shook her head. She looked different now, than the day she disappeared. She was older, her hair was longer, and the teen baby fat in her face was gone. She was slimmer, too. But why call attention to herself and take the chance of being recognized?

Jess came down from the bandstand and took her hand, pulling her to the stage.

Could she remember all the words to any song? She hadn't played or sang for almost nine years. Okay, she'd take a chance. She smoothed her hair and slowly climbed the stairs with Jess till tugging her hand.

"How about 'San Antonio Rose?'" It was one of the first songs she had learned and she thought she'd never forget that one.

Jess grinned, said "Sure." He nodded at Jack to start.

It was midway through the song, just as she was feeling high, like she was back home, when her eyes fell again on Frank. He was watching her with interest, but not smiling. *Damn,* she thought. *Jess had called her "Belle."*

The audience clapped and hooted, yelled for more. She did "Your Cheating Heart", and then returned to her table. Charlotte's face was flushed and she was still clapping.

"Belle, you were wonderful. You have a beautiful voice."

"Thanks, Charlie." Belle looked at Frank's table. It was empty.

But Oliver still stared in their direction.

"Belle, I think I'll leave. I don't want to encourage any confrontations here. I'll see you tomorrow, okay?" She picked up her purse and stood.

"Wait; I'll go with you. I'm ready to go to bed." Belle wanted to tell Charlie about Frank, and about everything. But she couldn't; not yet.

The next morning Belle came down to the café for breakfast and found Jess and Charlie there. They sat close, their heads bent together. His arm was around her. Belle watched for a minute before saying hello. Then she slid into the seat across from them.

Charlie put her hand on Jess's thigh. "Belle, you might as well know that I like your brother a lot."

"Charlie, nothing could make me happier. Well, maybe if I could get a cup of coffee, that would be a close second."

"Are you okay? You seem quiet this morning."

"I'm fine. Just tired I guess. I think I'll hang out in my room and read this afternoon." She took a sip from the mug the waitress had brought. "What are you guys doing today?"

"I'm going to make the rounds of some other clubs with the guys." Charlie cut into her French toast.

"It's my day off and I'm not letting her out of my sight," Jess said. He gave a tug at Charlie's shoulder, pulling her towards him. "Do you want to come along, Belle?"

"Thanks, but not today." She drained her cup. "Okay, now you guys are boring me. I'm going to go upstairs, turn on the TV and order room service. See you later, okay?"

Chapter 17

It was midnight and the early shift was done. Jess walked into the room when Dave answered his door.

"Hey, guy, I know you've got a drink in here somewhere."

Dave poured two fingers of Jack Daniels into each water glass and handed one to Jess.

"Thanks Buddy. I could use this. I just had an argument with Charlie. "I told her we'd been fired. She suggested that she could help me find some other kind of work. I guess I was on edge but that rankled me and I yelled at her and stomped out of the room."

"Do you know anything about the group that's replacing us?"

"Not really, except that they do some rock and pop. At least, that's what the manager said when he told Jack we were through."

Jess raised his glass in a salute. Dave did the same. "Yeah, this isn't the best time to be fired, is it?"

"Sure isn't, but it pisses me off. This is what I've been telling Jack all along. We better change or we'll be out of luck." He smoothed his hair with one hand, took a sip of the Daniels. "But Charlie thinking that I might quit music really got to me, Dave. That's all I ever wanted to do, play music, and I won't ever quit."

"Well, maybe she's got the right idea. She's a good woman, Jess. And she's a beauty, too."

"But what would I do if I quit music?"

"Yeah, I know." Dave set his glass on the bedside table. "Still, sometimes I think there's another life and maybe we're missing out on something important."

"Not me. I can't ever imagine not playing music" Jess sipped his drink. "Problem is, I can't imagine losing Charlie, either."

"Do you think she might go back to her husband when money runs out?"

"Naw. She's made up her mind." He smiled. "I helped her along with that one."

"Just a little word from your buddy here. You've only known her for a few months."

"But you know," Jess said, "Some people you just have a feeling about…she's honest, and kind; and smart, too. And," he wiped his mouth, "she is movie-star beautiful. I can't lose her."

"You do have different backgrounds. How will you get around that?"

"They say love conquers all, my friend. And how can she resist this?" He spread his legs to a wide stance and opened his arms, palms up.

"So what will you do if she says give up the music or else?"

"Won't come to that, Dave. We can talk about anything. I never thought I'd meet a woman like her."

"I'm sure you'll figure it out. Hell, she must know that we'll find other work."

"She says she's afraid it will be in another city, just when she's settled in here."

"That's a real possibility."

"Well, I'm going to hit the sack. See you in the morning. Thanks for the drink. Oh, Tennessee said not to expect him back to the room tonight. He hooked up with some babe in the lounge."

"Okay, see you. Sleep well." Dave shut the door.

Charlie knocked on Jesse's door. She'd apologize, she thought. After all, who was she to tell him what to do with his life. If she couldn't deal with it, then she'd just say goodbye. But she didn't want to do that either.

No answer. No light under the door. He was a sound sleeper so he might not hear her knock. She hoped he was asleep and not out with someone else. Better to wait till morning anyhow. Things might look better in the daylight.

She saw a light under Dave's door as she walked by. She stopped and knocked softly. He opened the door right away.

"Hi, Dave. Is Jess here?"

"He's just gone to bed, Charlie."

"Do you have a bit more of whatever you're drinking?"

"Sure, come on in. Have a seat."

He picked up Jess's glass and washed it in the bathroom sink. Then he poured her a drink and slid his chair up close to hers.

"So, how are you doing? Jess said you had an argument."

"Yeah, true. I don't get it. This is such a rough business and all the hassle to get paid a measly paycheck. Why not do something else? That's what we argued about, you know. I love the guy but I'm scared where we'll end up. Now you're all going back to Bear Holler and he admits you'll end up playing one night stands who knows where?"

"That's about right. But we've done it before." He looked at her. "What will you do, Charlie?"

"I'll go back to Nashville as soon as my divorce is final. I've given up the idea of California. It's a nice dream, but not realistic." She stood and stretched.

"You know, I can give up a dream that looks like it won't work out, but he has trouble doing the same. I have to hope that he'll change his mind about playing." She sat down again. "But I also know that I can't tell him what to do."

Dave stood up and paced slowly across the hotel room. Charlie watched him between sips of her whiskey. It bit her tongue and it felt good.

"Look, Charlie, this is none of my business, but I know musicians, so maybe I can shed a little light on this for you. I like you, and I like Jess. Only you two can decide what's best for you. You're worried about one night stands and traveling. Those things don't really matter to someone like Jess. A picker will do anything to be on stage."

He sat down again in the chair next to Charlie's. She noticed a faint bit of perspiration on his forehead and thought, he would be a good looking guy if he quit the booze that loosens his tongue and makes his flesh puffy, puts bags under his eyes. He was the calm one of the bunch, the wise one who kept them together. She liked him.

He was an enigma, though. Charlie never saw him with a woman. He drank steadily day and night but he never missed a show. He was kind, sympathetic even, but distant and private at the same time. She had never heard him talk as much as he was this night.

"What do you mean by that, Dave? Will a musician

really do 'anything?'" she asked.

"Well, a picker's goal of course is to be working steady playing music, and if there's good money involved, even better. And to be famous would put the icing on the cake. Here's what it's like for a musician; all he wants to do is play his music. Just starting out, he's going to jam sessions and sitting in with whatever band will have him, for free, of course, one night at a time. He'll sell his grandmother's body for a chance to get on the bandstand.

"Say he's been buying beer for the leader for two sets now, and he's listened to every other two-bit picker in town thinking that he's way better than that. He figures it's his turn next and has decided to do "Live Fast, Love Hard, Die Young" because everyone says he sounds like Faron Young. He's considering what to do for a second piece, something like "All Right" so he can leave them wanting more. It's damned sure he won't get more than two numbers so it had better be a good."

Dave finished his drink, got up and poured another. He raised his empty glass, asking Charlie if she wants another. She shook her head. She lowered her eyes, swirled the whiskey around in her glass. She wanted to hold back the threatening tears.

Dave went on. "Then the leader comes to the mike and announces, 'break time; we'll be right back'. Now this poor bastard has to sit through another fifteen minutes and buy the asshole another beer. He's already spent $5 plus tips and hasn't been up yet. The wife is going to raise hell when he gets home since that's his last change until Friday. But you know what, Charlie?

"He doesn't give a shit; after break time, it's his turn and after he comes down from the bandstand, he'll be high for hours. It's better than a line of coke. He's god. He has the power to turn people on, and there's nothing like it."

"Sounds a little like good sex," she says.

"Better. Can I get you that drink now?"

"No, thanks." She searched his face. "It sounds like this guy doesn't even need a woman."

"It's not that. He really does need someone. But if that someone doesn't go his way, well, he figures there's always another one that will. He won't have to look any farther than the front of his bandstand."

Charlie thought of her conversation with Belle yesterday. Belle tried to explain what it felt like being on the stage. She talked about the high, the feeling of elation and power. She found that she actually understood how Belle could love the attention and at the same time, not like stripping. Playing music must be something like that; the high that stayed with you for hours.

Dave stared out the window at the street full of neon lights.

"Hemingway once said that you can't be in love and write at the same time because they are both run by the same motor. I would say that goes for a musician who is after all, an artist just like a writer."

Dave was pacing again; just four strides each way in the small hotel room. He stopped long enough to splash more whiskey in his glass. Charlie knew that the bottle would be empty soon and tomorrow a new one would stand in its place.

"Now, Charlie," Dave kept walking the floor. There was a bit of slur in his voice, but his step was steady. "About our imaginary picker. If he gets seen by someone who has a band and remembers him the next time his lead guitar is out with a hangover, he'll call him up for a one night stand. Maybe that will work into a Monday and Tuesday job, and eventually he'll play five or six nights a week, even seven nights. He'll take any of the above. If he has a day job, and he might have one if he's able to pay his bills, then he won't have much time for his lady. Or sleep, either. So maybe he pops some bennies to keep going."

Charlie sighed. "Dave, you really paint a dark picture."

"I know, I know. But the music always comes first; before God, before mother, children or woman. Not too many women want to put up with that for long. If he needs a new amp, they'll sleep on the same lumpy mattress a while longer. If he has a chance to go on the road, more one night stands, he won't see the family for awhile and they'll just have to get along without him. If he gets lonely, he can pick up someone to keep him company from the cute things that wiggle their ass in front of the bandstand every night."

"But surely all musicians aren't like that, Dave." Her voice faltered.

"Of course not; only 95%. The rest are clean-living straight arrows."

"You sound bitter."

"Not really. It's just that I've known a lot of pickers." He set his glass on the nightstand and rubbed his eyes. He went on. "So, even if you have some success, make a hit record, the average life span of a record is so short that you only have so much time to go on the road and cash in before it dies. And once you're famous, it would be like throwing money away if you don't go on the road. The pay is fantastic. So our musician packs up his group, says goodbye to the wife and kids, and hits the road again."

"Are you like that, Dave?" Charlie sipped her drink. It tasted bitter now.

"Sure. I'm a picker, aren't I?"

He sat down in his chair next to her.

"So you don't think Jess would ever quit music?"

"Nope. He'll see this firing as a little glitch on the way up. But he won't quit; I'd bet on it. Instead he'll be spending 250 days a year on the road promoting his record; the one we'll cut when we go back home." He patted her knee. "But I could be wrong. It's probably the booze talking. Don't even listen to me, okay?"

"Will you go on the road, too?"

"Of course. What else would I do? How about you? Would you go?"

"If it meant losing him instead, maybe I would. I really don't know at this point." She stood up and handed her empty glass to Dave. He put it on the nightstand, took both her hands and kissed her cheek. Then he walked her to the door, said goodnight, and closed it behind her. *He's a good friend*, she thought. *I wonder if he's right.*

She walked down the hall to her room; put the key in the door.

Jess was stretched out on her bed and he looked so sweet; hair tousled, boyish grin in place and arms open wide.

"Hey, darlin', I've been waiting for you. Come on, let's forget all this shit. I'm sorry."

"Damn, Jess. It's not that easy to forget. We've got a real problem here."

"What's the problem?" He got up and sat on the edge of the bed.

"If you can't see it then I'm not sure I can explain it to you." Charlie pulled a chair close to him.

"Charlie, you just can't ask me to give up my music. You wouldn't really give up what we have because of it, would you?" He rubbed the back of his neck and bit his lip.

"Oh, Jess. I don't want to. It's really none of my business to ask you to do anything, and I'm sorry that I mentioned it. All I can tell you is that it's hard for me to trust that it's the right thing for me." She folded her arms across her chest. "What will you do now that you're leaving Las Vegas?"

"Just get work somewhere else. We always have. And it won't always be like this, Charlie. I'm on my way up, no matter how it looks now. I'm asking you to hang in there for awhile." He lay back down and propped two pillows behind his head. "We'll have money some day, and a better life."

"I'm just not sure that it will make any difference in the long run, Jess."

"I'm sorry as hell if I upset you. Just give me some time, okay?" He took her hand and pulled her down beside him. "You know I love you."

Charlie lay down and closed her eyes but they still burned hot and wet.

Chapter 18

Belle

It was seven the next morning when Frank and the policewoman Sally knocked on my door. I was groggy, having drunk a lot the night before. I didn't think about how I was opening the door without looking. They were nice enough I guess, but that didn't make it any easier. I was beating myself up for not running. Deep down I had the feeling that I would finally be arrested. But I almost didn't care any more because I didn't want to leave Jesse again.

Sally patted me down. She let me get dressed but stayed right with me all the time. She wanted to handcuff me before we left but Frank said he'd be right close by and it wasn't necessary.

They put me in the back seat of a squad car and Sally slid in beside me. I was sobbing, hiding my face from the people who walked by, staring.

"How did you know about me?" I couldn't help but ask.

I caught Frank's eyes in the rear view mirror.

He didn't answer at first. I thought he actually looked disappointed, as if I had brought home a failing grade from school.

"Our secretary recognized you. She remembered a flyer in the mail many years ago, and dug it out of the files." His answer was short, staccato. "When I heard your brother call your name at the club the other night that cinched it."

So it was ended. My life was over. They would find out everything, and I would stay in jail forever. They would say why did I run if I wasn't guilty. I couldn't stop crying.

Charlie came to see me the same day I was arrested. She asked me about my life; what had happened to put me on the run. It spilled out, all about Bart. I told her about the rapes and how it looked to the police like I killed him.

I could see that it upset her a lot. But she said, "Belle, I'm not really a strong Christian, but I remember a quote from Jesus that my Granny always said to me. 'There is nothing that enters a man from outside which can defile him: but the things which come out of him, those are the things that defile a man.' This is something I really believe."

She sat down beside me on my bunk and hugged me.

I told Charlie about how much I missed my Daddy after he killed himself. I told her how I blamed my Ma because she nagged him all the time. And how my Daddy paid attention to me and my Ma hardly knew I was alive. I told her how sad I was when Ma sent my brother away after Daddy died. I said I knew she wasn't really his mother, but I missed him, and Jack, too.

"Belle, you've been through so much. I admire the way you've taken care of yourself." Charlie took my hand in hers.

"Look at me now. I haven't done that good of a job, have I?"

"Everything that's happened to you is not your fault. You were a victim, a helpless child. Then, you were on your own and somehow learned to survive. I think that's amazing." Charlie was looking at me, smiling. I lowered my eyes.

"You don't know, Charlie, what I've done." I pulled my hand away on the pretense of pushing my hair from my face. "You wouldn't think so highly of me if you knew."

"Tell me. Let me be the judge of what I think."

I did. I told her about the old gray-haired lech that picked me up going out of Los Angeles and how he tried to rape me while his wife was shopping at Sears.

"I stole money from a guy I was sleeping with at Muscle Beach, and then I left him when I thought I was going to be caught. Sure, I sent it back later, but that was his rent money."

"You did what you had to do." She brushed my hair from my face with her hand.

"Once I slept with a guy I just met, because it was cold out and I needed a place to stay."

"Anyone would have done the same."

"I drank way to much, all the time. Sometimes, when I woke up in the morning, I couldn't remember the night before. I wouldn't even know the name of the guy in the bed next to me."

Charlie patted my knee.

I stood and paced the small cell. "I stole tips from the tables in restaurants. I slept with my friend's boyfriend."

There were tears in Charlie's eyes now. "Belle, we all do things that we later regret. The thing is, we forgive ourselves and go on."

I could feel the tears on my cheeks, even though I tried

to stop them.

"I took up stripping just for the money. I hated being naked in front of all those leering men, but I loved being on the stage. I hated that I loved it. It seems sick that I loved it." I sat down on my bunk and dropped my head in my hands.

"Belle, none of this has touched your spirit. No one can take your soul from you. No one. Nothing you have done has ruined you. You're a beautiful, talented and kind-hearted woman."

"You don't even know what I did to Bart." I stared at my hands.

"And you don't have to tell me. It makes no difference at all to me." Charlie got up from Belle's side and looked down at her. "He deserved what he got." Her eyes were blazing.The tears just flowed and I sobbed until Sally came by to see what was wrong. Charlie gave her an okay sign and she smiled, and then walked on.

I've been sitting in this jail for two weeks now, waiting to be extradited back to Nashville. They appointed me a lawyer, Miss Crawford, and I'm pretty sure she doesn't believe my story. To tell the truth, I'm tired of running and always looking over my shoulder. But if they convict me, I could spend my life in jail, and that's scary. Yeah, it would have been better to run.

I can talk to women in other cells but we don't have much in common, besides being locked up together. They're mostly hookers and don't stay long before someone comes and bails them out. Sally said it's their pimps. She also said that I'm the only serious criminal here. Sally brings me books to read which helps a lot.

When I first came, a nurse by the name of Mary Hocker examined me. She said everyone gets an examination to make sure they don't need any medical attention while they're in jail. Mary said I was in top condition, except for the shakes from coming down off the booze. She said I should quit smoking but now isn't the best time. Sally told me that Mary was the first nurse in the country to be a jail matron. It seemed to me she liked her job and she was sure nice to me.

Jack and Jesse come see me every day.

"They're letting us go, not renewing our contract." Jesse told me.

"Yeah, some country-rock group is coming in." Jack frowned. "Just watch, they'll empty the place out and the manager will be begging us to come back."

"I'm sure sorry to hear that," I said."Did you find your agent yet? And your money?"

"Nope. We did arrange for the hotel to pay us directly, though."

I told them to take the $1300 I had hid in the hotel room, in a pocket of one of my shorts, and to use it any way they needed to. Jesse swears he'll pay it back and I believe him.

Sally brought me a fried chicken dinner today and it put me in mind of Sunday dinners the summers I stayed at Grandma and Grandpa's farm. Sometimes Jesse could come at the same time, and Jack was welcome, too, though they were our Daddy's parents and not related to Jack. They treated Jack the same as they did me and Jesse.

Grandma would start early in the morning wringing the neck off the chickens. She'd take them by the head, and then spin them around until the body flopped to the ground and ran around for a little bit without its head. I thought it was awful the first time I saw it. I made up my mind I wasn't going to eat that chicken. But later, I'd smell chicken frying and start to reconsider.

The neighbors came by unannounced and you never knew how many would show up uninvited. Grandma always said, "Set yourself down and eat something."

Seems like the women did all the work, though, except for Grandpa bringing in the wood for the cook stove and maybe going down to the cellar to fetch some canned peaches, or to the truck garden for lettuce and tomatoes. And while the women were cooking and gossiping, the men all went behind the corn crib and smoked cigarettes. Grandma wouldn't tolerate that, even on the porch. Sometimes we kids would hide inside the corn crib, crawling over the loose corn already shucked and peeking through the slats. We could hear most of what they were saying. That's where I learned some of my worst language. We could see them passing around a bottle of white lightening, as they called it. Grandpa pulled the bottle out from under the crib.

Then Grandma would holler for everyone to come eat. There'd be fried chicken, slices of ham, mashed potatoes thick with real cream and home churned butter from cows we milked ourselves, corn on the cob and peas from the garden, and home made biscuits and gravy. There were lots of fresh picked vegetables, too, especially green beans with some hog jowl for flavor. My mouth is watering, just thinking about it.

After dinner, everyone spread out on the lawn on blankets under the shade of the trees. Or they sat on the porch swing and complained about how full they were. The men loosened their belts and sat around belching. The women and kids did the dishes and cleaned up. We didn't like it much but we knew that later there would be cold watermelon or home made ice cream. The men turned the handle of the ice cream bucket, packing it with ice and salt all around. They would check it every now and then to see if it was set yet.

Sometimes I'd stay all summer with Grandma and Grandpa, or maybe just a week or two. Once in a while Jack and Jesse would stay, too, or my cousin Jim. I liked Jim but I never let on. Everyone knows you can't marry your cousin or all your kids would be idiots. There were three kids from the Johnsons who were first cousins and all three of them were slow.

One thing just as bad as watching Grandma wringing the heads off chickens was when Grandpa and my two uncles would stick the hogs, they called it. What they were actually doing was cutting their balls off so they could grow fat for market. It made me feel like throwing up just listening to the squeals and seeing the blood squirting everywhere.

Don't get me wrong, I loved being on the farm. But sometimes it seemed too harsh, that life. Another thing I hated was how Grandpa got rid of too many kittens. They were so cute and helpless. But the cats were only there to keep the mice under control and they were wild, not house cats. When they reproduced too fast, some of them had to go. I saw Grandpa putting six new little kittens in a gunny sack.

"Grandpa, where you taking those kittens?"

"Sis, I'm giving them away. We got way too many cats."

It was Jim who told me Grandpa threw that gunny sack in the river. I was mad at Grandpa for days, but he just put his arm around my shoulders and said,

"Sis, that's how life is on a farm. You might as well get used to it."

Grandpa always called me Sis, why I don't know. I guess that's where my Daddy got the idea because he called me Sis, too. But Daddy told me he loved the name Belle and that he picked it out himself.

Every morning, as soon as the roosters began to crow, Grandpa came into my room and shook my shoulder. He said the roosters were his alarm clock. Sometimes I was scared and for just a minute I forgot where I was. I thought it was Bart coming to my bedroom. But then I realized it was Grandpa even though my eyes were still closed, because he had one stiff leg that shuffled when he walked. Daddy told me once that Grandpa had an accident at the saw mill where he worked as a young man, and he was hurt so bad they wanted to cut off his leg. He said no, thanks, I'll just keep it as long as I can. They said he'd die, and he said, we'll see. Well, he proved them wrong. And he worked his ninety-eight acres just as good as any other farmer.

Anyhow, when he came in to wake me up, the room still dark just before dawn, he always said the same thing,

"Sis, get up now. You're burning daylight." I didn't want to move from under the warm featherbed cover if it was cold, but if it was summer I'd jump up to see what the day would bring. I knew it would always be something fun.

Grandma would be out priming the pump and getting water for coffee. Then she cooked bacon and sausage and eggs and oatmeal while the coffee perked.

The whole day stretched in front of me like a county fair with too many choices. It was hard to decide what to do first. I could take the .22 once I was twelve years old and had the lesson in gun safety from Grandpa. I could shoot at squirrels and rabbits and birds in the woods. Trouble is, I never hit them, because I'd go all soft-hearted just as I was about to pull the trigger. The gun would veer a little to the left and I'd miss by a country mile.

Or I could ride bareback on Old Grey while Grandpa

plowed weeds from the watermelon patch. There was always the river to take a swim as long as we didn't ever go alone. Jesse, Jim and I and maybe some of the kids that lived in the log cabin by the river would swing out on a rope over the water and drop into the cool bath. Then we'd swim back to shore and fight over who was next, watching out for water moccasins.

One summer I got a bad case of poison ivy. Several times a day, Grandma dabbed diluted bleach on my body, until it all dried up. It itched so bad I couldn't sleep.

The summers at the farm were the best. I was away from Ma and Bart. But my time would run out and eventually I had to go back. Every time I went back home, I made up my mind that I wouldn't let Bart touch me but then I would be too scared to fight him and give up. He said God would strike me dead for not respecting a man of God. I thought a lot about why God gave Bart what he wanted but wouldn't listen to me. It must have been because he was a Preacher. If God really talked to Bart, though, He could tell him to leave me alone if He wanted to.

Every time I think like this, I start crying and can't seem to stop. There's only a piece of metal where a mirror ought to be, but I can see my face and my eyes are all bloodshot.

Damn, I hate this place. How come I have to be here? It just doesn't seem right that Bart is still causing me pain and grief. I hope he's burning in hell and I'm glad he's dead. I'll never forgive him for what he did to me. And I hate Ma for making my Daddy kill himself. I always wondered; did she know what Bart was doing to me?

Chapter 19

Oliver picked up the phone in his hotel room. "Hello?" His voice was gruff.

"Oliver, my attorney will be calling you this afternoon about the divorce." Charlotte's voice was soft, almost friendly. "In the meantime, I want to ask you to represent a friend of mine, Belle Williams. She's a young woman who is accused of murdering her stepfather nine years ago."

Oliver didn't answer. Charlotte continued." I'm not sure if she's innocent but he was raping her for years. So if she did kill him, she had good reason."

Silence. He was stunned. *What nerve*, he thought.

"Are you serious? You're divorcing me and you have the gall to ask a favor?" His voice was sharp.

She hesitated just a few seconds. "Would you mind if I came to your room and we talked about it?"

"Okay, Charlotte. Come on up." Oliver wanted to see her again. He still missed her. Sometimes he sat in the lounge for hours, waiting to see if she would show up. But when he spotted her at the table near the bandstand his stomach sickened at the look on her face as she watched Jesse.

He should be getting back to Nashville, back to work. But he didn't want to leave without Charlotte, so he stayed on.

Charlotte settled in the chair opposite Oliver. Her face was drawn. She moved to the edge of her seat.

"Does this young woman have money?" Oliver asked.

"Not much. Just a few hundred dollars."

"Then how would she plan on paying me?" He got up and poured a drink. He offered one to Charlotte.

She shook her head. "I want you to do it pro bono."

"And why the hell would I do that?" He turned to look at her, his face registering surprise..

"Because, Oliver, at one time I meant something to you. For old times sake, please?"

"And what would be in it for me?" He didn't mean to sound harsh.

She was silent, staring out the window. He looked at her face. He was afraid she was going to cry. He hated it when women cried, especially Charlotte.

"Oliver, this woman is like a sister to me. The sister I never had. She's been through hell, on the run for nine years. I really want to help her." She turned in the chair to face him. "We can reach an agreement that is beneficial to you in the divorce settlement; whatever you want. That's what's in it for you. Please, just help her."

"Where is she now?" Maybe if he seemed interested Charlotte wouldn't cry.

"She's in Las Vegas City Jail. But any time now, she'll be sent back to Nashville. It would be easy for you to see her since she'll be in the same city. That is, when you go back."

Oliver paced the floor. Everything was swirling around in his brain. This was not like him, he thought. Usually everything was so orderly in his head. His life was so perfectly mapped out, until Charlotte left him.

Then it came to him. He could turn this complication around to his advantage.

"Charlotte, I want you to come back home. That's my price. If you can't do that, then look for another lawyer."

She stared at him. "Oliver, I'm in love with someone else. Surely, you can't expect me to just come back as if nothing has happened."

"In love? In love?" He was shouting now. "Isn't that what you told me at one time, that you loved me?" He jutted his chin forward, eyes intense and face flushed.

"Things change. I didn't want them to, I didn't will it. Oliver, I'm really sorry, but let's go on with our lives. You'll find someone else."

"But I want you. I miss you, Charlotte." He reached for her hand. She pulled away.

"All right then." He looked down at her. "Those are my terms, Charlotte. Come home or find someone else to do your dirty work."

He watched as she stood and walked out the door. "Let me think about it, Oliver."

In her room, Charlie broke into tears. She spent months getting to know Jess, learning to trust him. She thought she wouldn't ever find a love like his. Now, if she wanted to help Belle, it would mean giving up Jess. It seemed like there was no good answer. Return to Oliver and give up Jess, or leave Belle, whom she also loved, to her fate. She knew Oliver could save Belle if anyone could. Oliver was the best.

The next day Charlotte went to see Belle.

"I'm arranging for my husband Oliver to represent you, Belle. He's on his way back to Nashville now and he said he would see you when you get there."

"I'll be leaving tomorrow they tell me." Belle said. "They said someone from Nashville will be picking me up. Charlie, I'm so scared." She was shaking as she talked.

"Don't worry, Belle. Oliver is a crackerjack defense attorney. He'll give you the best defense possible. I have the feeling that this is all going to come out all right." Charlie hugged Belle, smoothed her hair from her face.

"Does he know about you and Jess?" Belle asked. "Why should he represent me anyhow; I can't pay him."

"He's doing it pro bono. Guaranteed. Don't worry, I have my ways." Charlie gave a wan smile, and patted Belle's shoulder. "Yes, he does know about Jess."

"Charlie, are you coming back to Nashville since the guys are going back home?"

"Absolutely. And I'll see you there."

Now it was time to tell Jess. This was the hardest part. She waited until the bus was packed up and the guys were ready to leave.

"I'm sure going to miss you darlin'. Don't be too long coming back home, okay?" Jess took her in his arms and kissed her forehead, like he'd done dozens of times before. She stayed a long time like that, measuring the warmth and strength of his arms.

"Jess, I have to tell you something." She pulled away from him. "I'm going back to Nashville, but it will be with Oliver."

He startled and held her at arm's length. His eyebrows arched and he looked at her, mouth open. "What? Are you putting me on, Charlie?"

"No." Tears streaked her cheeks and she wiped them away. "That was his price for defending Belle."

"The bastard; I'll kill him. Then you won't have to worry about him ever again." He pulled her close. "Tell him to fuck off. We'll find someone else to defend her."

"I've seen him work, Jess. He's never lost a case. I don't know any other defense attorney in the country that can say that. He's the only one who can get her off, I'm sure of it. If she's innocent, he'll prove it, even if she did run and the evidence looks bad. If she did it, he'll prove self defense. I can't take a chance with Belle's life." Charlie clung to Jess.

"I can't stand the thought of you being with that jerk. Come on, Charlie, don't do that. We'll find some other way. Maybe we can sell the cabin and raise enough money to pay him."

"He won't take the case for any amount of money. He made that clear to me. There's no other way, Jess. But don't give up hope. I can always leave again after Belle is free." As soon as she said it, she knew it wasn't true. It could be years, and by then Jess would probably find someone else. "But Jess, please don't ever tell Belle. She doesn't know. If she did, she wouldn't let Oliver defend her."

Charlie pulled away, backed up far enough to see the guys at the window of the bus. They were yelling for Jess to hurry up, they wanted to go home, too. She waved at them. Then she turned and before he could speak again, she walked back to the hotel.

Part Three

It may be that two souls meet and it is not destined that they are to be together in this world. They touch each other and part. They have other work to do. Yet the meeting can never be forgotten; it is ingrained on the soul itself.

Reshad Field

Chapter 20

Las Vegas 1955

Frank opened the report in front of him, then closed the folder, opened it again and thought, damn, just put it away and forget her. She's gone, and should be forgotten.

But he read through the report again. Something just didn't seem right, but he couldn't quite put his finger on it. He closed the folder.

When he had picked her up in her hotel room more than six weeks ago, she didn't look surprised, just sad. She wore the face of a scared 12 year old. When they first met in the same hotel room, she had seemed mature and self assured, confident beyond her years. He knew now that she was a skillful liar, practiced and secure in her ability to convince others she was telling the truth.

In the squad car on the way to the station, he glanced at her in the rear view mirror. Her hair was straggling, eyes still sleepy, head lowered. Tears and last night's mascara streaked her cheeks.

She raised her eyes to his as if she sensed him looking at her.

"Frank, help me. Call Jesse, please. She wiped her face with her hands. "I've been on my own since I was 15. I'm tired of running." She cried and he looked away.

"Frank, I didn't do it."

He didn't answer. How many times had he heard that from someone he arrested? I didn't do it. The prisons were full of innocent people.

Don't get involved, he told himself. *The courts will sort it out. This is none of your business. She'll have a lawyer to help her.*

But he could let her call her brother, no problem. He turned her over to the booking officer with a request that she could call Jesse right away.

This would be good on his record, catching a killer. It might even help him make Lieutenant. He imagined the good-natured razzing he would give Roland when they lifted a beer in congratulation at the local bar.

He told himself he was just passing time when he opened the folder again and started to write on a yellow legal pad. He remembered the conversation with the deputy on the other end of the line when he called Nashville to say he had arrested Belle.

Suspect was seen on the path where victim was found by two reliable witnesses Saturday night, around the time of death. The Sheriff hinted there might be a third witness who heard Belle say she finally killed the son-of-a-bitch.

A charm bracelet with a broken clasp that her classmate says belongs to suspect was found on the ground near the body. Belle's mother couldn't find Belle's bracelet.

Local Sheriff recalls suspect telling him she would kill Bart if he ever touched her again. Was it true that this minister was molesting her or was it the lies of a rebellious teen?

Mother states suspect was at home early in the evening of the crime but cannot swear that she was there later, because she, Nadine, went to bed early with a severe headache.

Belle ran away before she was ever accused of anything. This was the most damning part of all.

Frank drew a heavy line across the page and wrote in capital letters:

SUSPECT SAYS SHE DIDN'T DO IT, BUT SHE'S A LIAR

The two witnesses were old, probably have bad eyesight. Maybe they weren't even alive now. Who knows if the third witness had a grudge against Belle?

She could have lost the bracelet anytime, or it could belong to someone else.

She was young and scared. She could have made empty threats to the Sheriff, who didn't seem too anxious to help her.

Mother could be the killer. You'd think she'd swear that her daughter was home at the time.

It didn't look good, he admitted to himself, but still, it's all circumstantial. A good attorney would establish reasonable doubt. So why hadn't it been thrown out in the preliminary? Going to trial could ruin Belle's life, no matter how it came out.

He pulled out his notebook and dialed the number that Charlotte had given him, that of her husband Oliver. Well, she had said, she was no longer his wife officially but she had promised to go back to him. She told Frank that Oliver would be defending Belle.

Frank wasn't sure of the reception he would get. But, he told himself, he just needed to confirm that Belle was getting the best help available. Why it concerned him, he couldn't say.

He was put right through to Oliver Force by his secretary.

"Mr. Force, this is Detective Frank Smith of the Las Vegas Police Department. Thanks for taking my call."

"No problem. How can I help you, Detective?"

"Please, call me Frank. I'm curious about a young woman I arrested about six weeks ago. She was extradited to Nashville, and I understand you're her attorney. Her name is Belle Williams. I'm curious how she doing, and what you can tell me about your plans for her?"

"Well, Frank, she's doing all right, considering. I'm not sure yet which way we'll go. First, of course, we'll try to get the charges dropped for lack of evidence. Right now we're waiting for a court date. I'm afraid that could take years; I can't tell you how much longer. I've asked them to speed up the date but no response so far."

"Have you talked with her recently?"

"I saw her only yesterday. She's spending all her time reading. She's taking instructions on getting her GED and studying law books as well. A very motivated young lady, I'm impressed with her.

"The downside, Frank, is that this community has a long memory and the victim was a respected Minister. And the Sheriff has added his testimony as to her threat. Now there's a third person who places her at the scene. The evidence is all circumstantial, but she did run which doesn't help her case. If we only had something to confirm her alibi..."

He let the sentence hang in the air. Frank could hear another phone ringing in the background and Roland walked into his office about that time.

"Thanks. I won't keep you any longer. If you don't

mind I'll check back with you from time to time."

"Of course, that's no problem. Call me whenever you want. But you realize, of course, that I cannot discuss all the details of the case with you."

"I do. I thank you for your time. Goodbye for now."

The lieutenant looked at the folder lying on Frank's desk and shook his head.

"Can't let it go, can you?"

"It does prey on my mind. Maybe I need a vacation. How about I take a couple of weeks off and go fishing?"

"Guess you could. There's not much going on here and we have a full staff this time of year." He sat down on the corner of Frank's desk." You wouldn't be fishing the lakes around Nashville, would you?"

Frank smiled but didn't answer.

"I'll start tomorrow if that's okay."

"Go. But Frank, be careful. Get too involved and it could ruin a man's career."

"I'm not going to fuck her, just try to get all the facts. Sweet kid, really, and I'm not sure she did it. I can't explain it, but I just have the feeling that she's been the victim here, not the perpetrator." Frank stood and grabbed his jacket. "There doesn't seem to be anyone to help her out, to dig up some more information. Her brother doesn't seem to know what to do from here. According to him, the lawyer was sort of forced into taking her case for free, so he probably won't give it any priority."

The highway was almost deserted at 4 AM on a Saturday morning. Frank couldn't sleep any longer so he thought he might as well hit the road. He pushed a Louis Prima tape into the dash, and turned it up loud. He really liked the big band sound. He pulled onto the highway and pointed the Dodge towards Nashville.

His excitement, he thought, was just like he always felt when he was onto a case. It was also the excitement he felt when he was on the road to anywhere. And, he told himself, it had nothing to do with Belle.

He remembered trips every summer as a child with his Mother and Father. They were long and boring car trips mainly, but now they were bringing back memories. Once they all had arrived at the lake, or grandparents' house, or Aunt Jane and Uncle George's house, it was a lot of fun. He could bicycle to a swimming hole, explore the woods, fish with his cousins, and play board games with his parents at night.

He thought he was lucky, really, to have such a normal childhood, and parents who stayed together and took care of him. Sure, they were a bit cold and distant in some ways, but that was the time when parents figured their job was over when they provided a roof and food and clothes and discipline. It was usual for boys to go to military school, as he did, and girls to go to boarding school, like his sister did. It didn't seem strange that kids didn't always live at home, or have close relationships with their parents.

Frank would never have thought of asking their advice on anything. He would never have told them his secrets or talked about the things that worried him. Still, he knew they loved him, and he missed them. They were both gone now; Mom first from cancer, Dad next from grief. And Sarah, his only sister, died in a car crash two years ago.

That's it. He was feeling a bit lonely, more sad than not. He had no family in Las Vegas and very few friends. He worked long hours and certainly didn't have much in the way of a social life. He'd tried dating off and on, but hadn't met anyone he wanted to keep on dating, let alone marry and start a family. He still had plenty of time. He told himself, no need to hurry.

The sun was rising hot on his windshield. He lowered the visor, pulled the tape out and shoved another Prima tape into the player. Merging onto I-40 and the plains of the Arizona desert stretching as far as he could see, the loneliness faded and a new sense of purpose emerged. He finally admitted to himself that he was looking forward to seeing Belle again.

Chapter 21

Bear Creek 1955

An oak tree just outside room 41 in Metzer's Motel shaded Frank from the already hot morning sun. He pulled a chair outside and just sat, sipping very black morning coffee furnished in the motel waiting room. A bird that he couldn't see sang from one of the upper branches. It was early but already muggy. Sweat formed on his forehead and started a slow trickle to his upper lip. He could taste the salt. It was late September but still hot and muggy. Here in Bear Creek, far from the dry heat and neon lights of Las Vegas, time seemed to amble through the summer at a leisurely pace.

It was easy for Frank to organize his thoughts and plans. He had always been a planner, a list maker. His father and mother were both planners and left notes on his desk, hanging from the refrigerator, and on the bathroom mirror.

"Hang up your clothes."

"School books!"

"Lunch in frig"

So he wrote a note in his mind;

Drop in on Sheriff.

Go see Belle.

Visit Belle's mother.

Have tea with the Witherspoon twins.

It was a loose list for sure, but it would get more detailed as he went along.

He was skeptical that Belle killed her stepfather. That was the message from his gut and like any good cop, he paid attention to intuition. He believed that intuition was nothing but an unconscious and conscious accumulation of facts and impressions that people liked to call intuition. Still, he knew himself well and he knew that he tended to be a perfectionist in his police work, if not in his life. He had a need to be sure, one way or the other, if Belle was innocent or not.

He had sent her a short note saying he would be in the area soon and planned to visit her, if it was all right. She replied saying she looked forward to seeing him.

On the drive to Nashville in the quiet hours alone with his thoughts and gazing at the endless plains through Texas, he admitted to himself that he was as much interested in Belle as he was in whether she was innocent or guilty of murder. Until now he had pretty much denied it.

He was aware that he didn't really know her at all. Maybe she was some kind of manipulative liar. He already knew she could lie. Maybe she was going to prison for a very long time. Maybe she wasn't interested in him at all. There was a ten year age difference.

Still, his gut (again) rejected all these arguments. Hadn't she flirted with him a bit, and she had already lived many more years than those of her birthday. Anyhow, how would he ever know what might happen if he didn't follow through with this? Still, he was a bit surprised at himself. He wasn't prone to making impulsive leaps.

He picked up his chair, carried it back into the stuffy room and turned on the fan. It rattled in the window and sent warm air into his face. He closed the door and dialed information.

Sheriff McMann picked up the phone himself and agreed to meet Frank for lunch at Johnson's Café in Bear Holler. It was about a two mile drive. Frank walked in the door and spotted the Sheriff sitting in the second booth. He would be hard to miss; Stetson hat stained with sweat, plaid shirt that held a shiny badge, Levi's with a belt that supported the belly that fell over it. The buckle was huge and had a metal carving of a deer in the center.

The Sheriff rose to shake Frank's hand, then pulled a wrinkled handkerchief from his back pocket and wiped his face.

"Meg, bring this fellow a cold beer, will you? Detective, have a seat."

"Sure, but please call me Frank."

"Okay. And my name is Horace. Horace McMahan."

Meg brought two glasses of brew to the table and took their lunch order.

"Sheriff, I sure don't want to step on any toes, especially yours, and I know that I don't have any jurisdiction here. But if you're willing, I'd appreciate your telling me all you know about this murder that Belle is accused of. All I know is, it was her stepfather and he was a respected man in the community. She also told me she ran away because she had no alibi as to where she had been the night he was killed. Her mother went to bed early with a headache, so couldn't vouch that she hadn't left the house."

Frank took a bite of his tuna sandwich and dipped a French fry in ketchup.

He continued, "She said everyone knew that she and Bart didn't get along, and she seemed to know that she would be accused of his murder. Also, she said she once told you he was raping her. And that's about all I know."

Horace drained his glass in one swig and signaled for another. Sweat ran down his neck in little trickles and he wiped it away with a napkin. His body was short and round, he had dull brown eyes and when he took off his Stetson and put it on the seat beside him a gray fringe of hair poked out behind his ears.

"Well, Frank, you're right so far. You know, when Belle was about 12 she told me that he had raped her several times. But she didn't want me to talk to her mother about it, and without any real proof there wasn't much I could do."

Frank watched Horace down another glass of beer in one big swig.

"Girls that age don't know how these things work. Belle and the Reverend didn't get along at all, so maybe she thought I'd throw him in jail and he'd be out of her hair. At the time I doubted if what she told me was true. I knew the Reverend pretty well, and he was popular in the area. He was known for always giving a helping hand to someone in trouble."

"So nothing was ever pursued about her accusations?"

"Nope."

"I'm not saying it was wrong, but just wondering why you never talked with Nadine about Belle's accusation."

"I did, once, just after she ran away." Horace took a bite of his hamburger.

"What happened?"

"Of course, she denied that it was even possible. She

said Belle was giving her grief long before the Reverend came into the picture." Horace wiped his mouth with a napkin. "In fact, she thought marrying him would help straighten Belle out."

Frank studied Horace as he swallowed more beer. "All I heard was that there was a bracelet found near the body, and that some ladies saw Belle on the path close to where the Reverend was found. That, and the fact his head was bashed in with a rock by someone."

"You got all that right. I don't think the bracelet will prove much. It was the kind that all the girls were wearing at the time. They collected charms and added to it all the time. And, the charms on this bracelet were identified by Belle's friends. But still…" His voice faded.

Frank stood up. "Well, thanks, Horace. Guess I'll be heading back to town."

"There's one more thing I can tell you, Frank." He thanked Meg for another beer and asked for the check.

"What's that?" Frank sat down again.

"I questioned some of Belle's school friends at the time. I had almost forgotten about it. It was so long ago. There was one in particular, a sweet girl by the name of Bonnie. She had just moved to Nashville and got married. She had something interesting to say."

Frank leaned forward across the booth. "What was that?"

"She said Belle called her after she left town. She said Belle told her she had finally killed the son-of-a-bitch."

Frank sat back on the bench, mouth open. "Do you think that's true?"

"Doesn't matter. It's hearsay anyhow."

"Still, that puts a different light on things."

Horace pulled out his billfold and handed some bills to Sara, who walked to the cash register across the room.

"There's more."

"Bonnie said she left the dance that night late, and the path home took her by the murder site. Belle was coming down the path just in front of her." He stood up and grabbed his hat." It was just after the time of death, according to the coroner."

"But Belle said she was nowhere near there, that she was home all night." Frank felt his stomach flip. Was he dead wrong about Belle?

"Her mother won't confirm it, says she went to bed and didn't know if Belle stayed home or not."

"Can you tell me where Belle's mother lives? Also the older ladies who saw Belle that night. And how about Bonnie? Does she still live in town?"

"Sure. Everyone knows the Witherspoon twins and where they live. Out this highway south till you see an old gas station on the right, then turn left and go to the end of the road. Theirs is the only house there."

"Thanks. And Nadine, I think her name is?"

"She's in Bear Creek, really close to your motel, just off the main drag where the Caterpillar sits on the corner. The only way you can turn is right. You'll pass it on your way back. She's three houses down on the right. But I don't think she'll answer her phone or the door."

"Why wouldn't she answer?"

"She's been that way since Bart was killed and Belle left town. She hasn't even been to the jail to see Belle since she got back in Nashville. She doesn't go out of the house at all. Once in a while, her neighbors see her in the back yard, but if they talk to her she goes right back inside." They reached the door together. "The last time I talked to her was the day after Bart was killed, when they found the body and I went out to tell her. She was pretty upset I'll tell you."

"Do you think she had anything to do with it?"

"I don't think so. Belle says she was in bed all evening. But on the other hand, no one can say for sure that Belle was there. They could have done it together for all I know."

"So is that all the evidence they have against Belle?"

"So far as I know. The big thing is that she ran away, and that she was seen at the spot where he was killed. Now there's Bonnie, which is pretty strong evidence. There was the charm bracelet near the body. But how could they prove that it didn't belong to someone else? And even if it is hers, maybe she killed him in self defense." He opened the screen door. "I've been subpoenaed as a witness, so they might not tell me everything. I get the idea that they don't have much more than you know already, though."

"If that's all they have, I'm surprised it got past the preliminary."

"I'm a little surprised myself."

"What about Bonnie? Is she sticking to her story?"

"I have no idea. I was told not to talk to her. She's married, has two kids, and lives in Nashville. I don't have her current address. She married a foreigner, a Nashville man." He laughed and put his hat back on his head.

"Do you know anyone that could tell me her last name?"

"I'll have to think about that. Maybe her mother still lives in town. I'll check it out for you." Horace rubbed his neck with his hand.

"I appreciate it, Horace. And thanks for lunch. I'll stay in touch."

"Yeah. I'll be interested in how this all turns out."

They walked into the blistering afternoon air together.

Chapter 22

Belle

Three weeks after I was arrested they put me on an airplane and extradited me back to Nashville. It was okay with me. One Night Stand got fired and all the guys are back at the cabin in Bear Holler anyhow. As for me, at this point I just want to get everything over with, no matter how it comes out. Charlie is still in Las Vegas

Mr. Force came to see me two days after I arrived in Nashville. He pulled a chair up beside my bunk and spread some papers out on the bunk in front of him. Then he leaned back in the chair and folded his hands in his lap.

"Belle, if I'm going to help you, I need for you to tell me the absolute truth about everything. What you tell me is confidential. But I cannot do a good job of defending you if you aren't honest with me."

I studied his face. How do I know that I can trust him? I think he's smart but I don't like him all that much. His hair is too slick and his voice is too soft. He smiles a lot with his mouth but not with his eyes. But if he can get me out of here, and Charlie seemed so sure that he could, then I can put up with him.

"I'm scared, Mr. Force. Really scared. I don't want to go to jail for life. Do you think they would execute me if they say I'm guilty?"

"You need to tell me the truth about everything before I can answer that question." His eyes got softer and he looked square into mine. "Tell me everything, Belle, and I do mean everything."

So I did. I still didn't trust him 100 percent but I made the decision that he was my only chance to get out of here.

I told Mr. Force everything about Bart. I told him how he raped me for those years when I was young and how I didn't get along with my Ma. I told him about my brother and how we were separated when he was nine and I was six. I told him how Jess had accidentally found me in Las Vegas. I told him how Charlie had been so good to me and how grateful I was to her.

He got up and walked back and forth in the cell when I mentioned Charlie's name. He frowned and said, "What I want to know is what happened up to and including the day your stepfather was killed." He stopped pacing and looked down at me.

I hesitated for a long time. I told him about the day before the killing, and the day the Sheriff came to tell Ma her husband was dead. Then, I told him what I had done. I told him everything.

I dropped my head in my hands and rubbed my forehead. I was getting a blistering headache.

He actually patted my shoulder. "I understand why you did it, Belle. It was foolish of you, of course. But understandable." He gathered up his notebook and papers. "Rest assured that everything you say to me is strictly confidential. No one, not even a judge, can make me repeat it. It's covered under attorney-client privilege."

Then he said that he would represent me. I thanked him over and over. I don't know why, but I felt much better knowing he was on my side.

They had my preliminary hearing to see if there was enough evidence for me to go to trial. It was touch and go for awhile. Mr. Force was impressive, though. His voice became strong and sure. He made a motion right away for dismissal, which the judge denied.

Jesse and the guys were there. Charlie had just got back in town and she was there, too. Mr. Force was flustered at first when he saw her, but he regained his composure right away.

In court, the district attorney showed a charm bracelet that he said belonged to me. It was on the ground close to where they found Bart. I told Mr. Force that I had one like that but I think I lost it or gave it away. He said not to worry; lots of girls had that kind of bracelet

The Witherspoon twins were there and they both pointed fingers at me and said they saw me the night Bart was killed. They remembered that it was a full moon and the path was moonlight bright. Margaret said she didn't really think that I was the kind of girl to kill anyone. And they didn't see me do anything at all. Florence kept dabbing at her eyes.

I told Mr. Force that most folks thought Margaret was a little slow. She never married and her sister Florence always looked after her, even when Florence's husband was still alive. Mr. Force didn't suppose it would make any difference in her testimony. She was still believable.

Sheriff McMann testified as to how I ran when he came

to the house looking for me the day Bart was found. He told how I said that I would kill Bart if he ever touched me again. He also said as to how the Reverend Hollister was so respected by everyone. He told about all the things Bart did for the community and how his congregation loved him, and how the crowds flocked to his tent meetings.

Then he talked about what Bonnie said to him. This was a surprise to me. It seems that the Sheriff had just found the notes about his conversation with her, and brought them in as evidence at the last minute. Then the prosecutor let Mr. Force know just before the hearing, like he was obliged to do.

The Sheriff said when he interviewed Bonnie she told him she had a phone call from me and I said to her that I had finally got rid of my stepfather. She even told him that she saw me on the path that night. Mr. Force objected and the judge said, "Sustained" after Mr. Force said that was hearsay. He said if they wanted to present the evidence then they should subpoena Bonnie for direct testimony. I think it convinced the judge to go to trial, though.

Bonnie never liked me since her boyfriend asked me for a date when we were freshmen in high school. He was a real jerk, but I went out with him anyhow. He never asked me out again because I wouldn't have sex with him. Bonnie found out that I dated him and never talked to me again. She gave me dirty looks every time we met in the hallway at school. Why would I call her anyhow? I couldn't stand her. She was outright lying. But the prosecutor said he would get a statement from her and subpoena her for the trial.

I'm afraid. Mr. Force said the trial might not happen for years because there's always a waiting list for court dates. I could be found guilty and could spend the rest of my life in jail or even be sentenced to death. Mr. Force said, don't worry, but I couldn't help it.

The judge won't let me bail out since I ran away before. Even if they would set bail, I don't know anyone with enough money to bail me out.

They took me back to my cell. When the door clanged behind me, I sat on my bunk with my head in my hands for a long time.

I had a letter from the detective in Las Vegas who arrested me. He said he was coming out this way and wanted to see me. I was really surprised to hear from him. He pretty much ignored me when he picked me up. He said in his letter that he wanted to know my side of the story. But coming all the way out here? Maybe he had some friends or relatives in the area. It's hard to believe that he would come all this way just to see me. I wrote that I'd be happy to see him. I told him that Oliver Force was defending me. He wrote back and said I was lucky to have him, so even Frank knows who he is.

It's pretty boring here most of the time. They keep me in a cell all by myself since I'm the only one here accused of murder. Sometimes I can hear the other women talking and telling stories, and that makes me feel lonesome. I wish I could sit down with them and hear about their lives. I have the feeling that they're just like me. Maybe they've had bad luck, just like me.

I read a lot. I've always loved reading but never had enough books. Now there are plenty of books and I'm taking full advantage of the little library here. There are books on philosophy, law, and psychology. There are novels that I never wanted to read in high school, like Moby Dick and Great Expectations. I figure if I'm here for awhile, I might as well take advantage of the time I have.

Charlie came to see me as soon as she was back in

Nashville. She did tell me that she and Jess are through and that made my gut ache. I asked her what happened since I had dreams of her being my sister-in-law. She just said that musicians are married to their music and didn't have room in their lives for a real relationship *I'm a musician*, I thought, I wondered if I was like that.

I asked Charlie if she was going back with her husband, and she just stared at the floor and then changed the subject. She never said, but I think the answer was yes.

Ma hasn't come to see me, though. I know she doesn't leave her house. You'd think she'd come see her only daughter. Maybe it's just as well. We never did get along too well and even if I think I want to see her sometimes, maybe it's better this way. I've been thinking that I treated her badly after Daddy shot himself. I really blamed her for being so bitchy all the time and I could see that it got to him.

But lately, I've been remembering how Daddy was depressed a lot of the time, how he talked about Jesse's mother Emma Sue and what she was like and how he missed her. Maybe Ma felt that in him and it made her the way she was.

I was mad at her for bringing Bart into our house. Funny thing is she said she married him because she thought being a preacher and all maybe he'd be a good influence on me. I was always giving her a bad time, arguing with her and defying her, staying out past curfew, even drinking and smoking with my friends.

That's a real laugh, though, about Bart being a good influence on me. I kept thinking there must have been some way she should have known about him. I wondered if she did know, but just didn't want to face it. I've been reading in psychology books about how sometimes a person doesn't realize in their conscious that they have blocked something out. Sometimes men who came back from the war couldn't remember things. Jack said he couldn't remember everything that happened to him. But my Ma was not in any war.

The other thing on my mind is, Ma is getting kind of crazy. And she was getting pretty tired of Bart, the way he was disappearing all the time and not spending any time with her. Maybe she suspected what he was up to with me. And I wondered, if he was doing that to me, was he bothering other girls, too? Maybe that's why Ma doesn't come out of her house

A few minutes ago, I woke up with a start. The door to the cell next to mine clanged shut and a woman's voice was yelling. She sounded crazy. I'm sure sick of this place.

"Come on you mother-fuckers, I'm ready for you. Come on and get it."

I could hear William the guard bang the metal bars with his flashlight, telling her to quiet down.

"What's the matter, am I too much woman for you? What are you liver-lilies scared of anyhow? Let me out of here and I'll show you what for."

"Come on, Louise, settle down. You're getting on my nerves now."

Louise is talking to herself, so low that I can't understand what she's saying. Her voice rises a little, and then drops to a whisper.

Once when I was seven I came on to Ma doing that same thing, talking to herself so low I couldn't understand what she was saying. It was two weeks after Daddy died and it was my birthday. I didn't have a birthday party because we were still in mourning. It was all I could do to lie on my bed and cry. Even now I can still see the way he was laying on the floor of the shed with the hole in his head and his eyes wide open. It didn't even look like him and I said so, in between the screaming. Maybe Ma was thinking about that, too, when she was mumbling to herself. She wasn't crying, though, so I thought maybe she was just going crazy on me.

When I think about the day Daddy shot himself, of all things, I remember those chickens scratching around on the ground, and that rooster all proud and cocky, strutting through the crowd of hens and cock-a-doodle-dooing. He was waving his head back and forth and looking them all over. What a stupid thing to think about, when your father is dead on the floor. When Ma started wailing again, the chickens all scattered, running scared every which way.

Oh, God, Louise is screaming again.

"Help, help, help! The bastards are killing me…someone help."

"Okay, Louise, that's enough." William shouted. That wasn't like him.

But she did stop yelling after that. I thought maybe she fell asleep.

That's the trouble with being here; too much time to think. I'll get a new supply of books this afternoon, something to take my mind off things.

I hear William's footsteps coming on his usual rounds. He's one of the nicer guards and he nods to me as he walks by. His footsteps stop in front of Louise's cell.

"Louise…oh damn!"

Then I see it; a little trickle of red coming from a corner of Louise's cell. My heart was racing and I tried to say something but my voice wouldn't work. I heard William's muffled voice on the phone and pretty soon the hall was filled with uniforms.

Later, I heard the guards talking. It seems Louise got a small pocketknife in by carrying it in her rectum. She was so violent and loud that they put her in the cell right away while they were waiting for a female guard to come in and shake her down right. I never did see what she looked like. But it made me cry, just the thought of her dying like that, even if she was crazy.

Chapter 23

Getting in to see Belle was easy for Frank because of his credentials and Sheriff McMahan's introduction. By the time he got Oliver Force's okay as well, they gave him unquestioned access to go into her cell. But he didn't know what he would say or do. Did he believe her or not? Now that he knew about Bonnie and the Sheriff's testimony, doubts had reared up in his mind again. He doubted her innocence one minute, then the next he could see her face and feel sure his gut reaction was right.

And what was his motive anyhow? He admitted to himself long ago that his interest was more than that of freeing an innocent woman. He was attracted to her, but a stripper? Not exactly the type of girl he would take home to Mother, or even Father for that matter. He knew what they would say if they were alive. But still; there was something about her that was different, that was sincere. Not only was she beautiful, but elegant in a down home sort of way. He had the urge to take her in his arms every time he saw her, even the day he arrested her. She looked so vulnerable; scared, but with an air of righteousness.

She rose from her bunk as the cell door clanged open, walked toward him. She was thinner, paler, and her eyes were dulled. What he saw was not the vivacious woman that he met in Las Vegas.

"Frank! Thanks so much for coming to see me. Tell me, what are you doing in Nashville?" She reached out her hand and he took it in his.

"I came to see you, Belle. I wanted to see if there was anything I could do to help you out of this mess."

"You mean that was the only reason for your trip?"

He laughed. "I told the Lieutenant that I was going on vacation to get some fishing in. I don't think he believed me. But this morning I did go to the creek by Sheriff McMahan's place and we took a couple of nice trout for breakfast, so it wasn't a total lie. I plan to go visit the Witherspoon twins and see what they have to say. Later I'll go to your mother's house. I'm told she doesn't answer her door or phone but I'll give it a try. I'm not even sure if she can be of any help, but I'd like to explore all avenues. But tell me, how are you holding up?"

"Most of the time I'm hanging in there. I'm actually reading a lot. It's something I've always loved to do but I never had enough time, or books. But now…it seems I have nothing but time and plenty of books. Still, it's lonely; and you know, just last night a crazy woman in the next cell killed herself. Look, you can still see the blood stains over there." She pointed to a dark red streak in the walkway near the corner of her cell

"That must have been scary." He patted her shoulder. "Belle, I'll do everything I can to help you, I promise. I'm afraid you have to be patient, though."

She sat down on the bunk and indicated that Frank take the only chair in the cell. He watched her try to smooth the wrinkles from the dark blue prison dress. Her hair was dirty and stringy and she tucked it behind her ears. Even so, and without makeup, she was still attractive to him. She was appealing in a way he couldn't explain to himself.

"Why would you do this for me?" She met his eyes.

He squirmed in the chair and looked through the cell bars. How could he explain without sounding foolish, or lecherous?

"I'm thinking that you might be innocent, Belle, and I feel partly responsible for the mess you're in since I'm the one who arrested you."

"Is that the only reason?"

"Well…that's the main reason, for sure," he stammered, still looking out the bars as if he expected help to arrive at any moment.

"Then I'm grateful. I'm surprised that you would do this for me" She managed a sad smile. "Frank, I have to admit that I think you're a very nice guy and under different circumstances I could…" her voice trailed off to a whisper.

"I know," he turned to look at her, and then rose to sit by her side on the bunk.

"Is your brother still in Las Vegas?"

"The guys are all back at the cabin in Bear Holler. They got fired when the casino hired a rockabilly band. I guess they'll play Nashville until they can get another road trip. The worst of it is their agent stole all their money and they can't find him. So they're broke, too, and without an agent on top of everything else. It seems like troubles all come at the same time."

She chewed on a nail, the hangover of a bad habit from her teens

"But things aren't all bad, you know, Frank? I have the best attorney in the country, and I have my brother, and a little money that I've saved to help him out for awhile. I have Charlie, too. And now, you're here to help me. It could be a lot worse."

Frank looked at her face and draped an arm around her shoulders. *She's amazing,* he thought. *Not only is she beautiful, but she has a good heart. And she's brave.* He'd never know anyone quite like her. He fervently hoped that she was innocent. But even if she wasn't, maybe she did it in self defense.

She looked up and smiled at him. She reminded him of a frightened deer that he saw once when he was hunting with a friend. He put his arms around her, held her tight for a short moment and then kissed her cheek. *What are you thinking*? He told himself. He let her go abruptly, standing up at the same time. His face blushed red and he signaled for the guard.

"Belle, what about Bonnie's testimony? Is there anything to it?" He stood by the bars, waiting for the guard.

"She always hated me since I dated her boyfriend once in high school." Belle stood, too. "I don't know why else she would say those things. They're all lies."

Belle stood in front of him and looked in his eyes. "I'm not totally innocent, Frank. I'm trying to be honest here. That's more than I should tell you."

That didn't make any sense to him, but the guard was waiting for him. He let it go.

"Okay. I think I'd better go now but I'll see you soon, Belle." The guard unlocked the cell door.

Back at the motel, Frank spread the copy of the coroner's report and Sheriff McMahan's police report on the table. Death was by a skull fracture, a piece of bone piercing the brain, caused by a blow from a heavy object. There were small fragments of rock in the wound and they matched the large rock that was found near Bart's body. Dr. Jake Jergins, the coroner from Nashville, noted several abrasions on the body, mainly his right arm and leg where he hit when he fell to the ground. He noted that there were no other injuries. The coroner's conclusion was that Bart was hit in the head with a large rock by a person or persons unknown.

Sheriff McMahan had carefully bagged the rock and sent it for fingerprinting. There were no discernable fingerprints. The rock was covered with blood, perhaps washing away any prints that might have been there. In his report Sheriff McMahan noted many scuffled footprints around the body, matching the boots of the hunter who found him the next morning. The bracelet, found nearby, was bagged separately and kept for evidence, along with the rock. The Reverend had been fully clothed and his clothes had a few splatters of blood on them.

Frank stared out the window. Strange. Wouldn't lots of blood have dripped onto his clothes before he fell? The head has a large blood supply and even the smallest wound can bleed profusely.

There was a short perfunctory note that Horace had interviewed several classmates of Belle's and the only information recorded was that Bonnie had seen Belle on the path that night, and that Belle had called her after she ran away. Bonnie said that Belle admitted to her that she killed the Reverend.

There was also a note that the Witherspoon twins had seen Belle on the path when they left the dance.

All this was circumstantial. There was no direct evidence against Belle. Still, all these things pointed to her. Frank considered abandoning the whole project, leaving the trial up to Oliver and the court. Then he remembered how Belle looked sitting on the bunk in the Nashville jail. His gut reaction remained; she couldn't have done this. He had to find the answers before he left town.

Chapter 24

Frank's car raised a cloud of dust on the long road to the Witherspoon house. There were no shade trees and the sun was relentless. It was the hottest part of the day, mid-afternoon, and his clothes stuck to his body like glue. He thought about putting off the visit until tomorrow early when he could start out cool at least. But now he was getting down to the end of his two week leave and since he had to have three days to get back home he had asked for more vacation time. Roland wasn't happy about extending his time off for another two weeks, but Frank made it clear that he wasn't going to leave until this was done so Roland gave his okay.

It was the beginning of October and the heat was stifling. When did it start to cool off here, he wondered.

The small frame house, neat but cluttered with tools and swings and plants on the front porch, sat on a small hill. There was a tool shed next to the house, the door swung open. He peered inside, and since no one was there he knocked on the front door. No answer. So he knocked again, louder this time. The door opened to a slight elderly woman who smiled and asked him who he was.

"Ma'am, I'm Frank Smith, a detective from Las Vegas. Sheriff McMann said you might talk with me. I would just like to ask a few questions about Belle Williams if you don't mind."

"The District Attorney said that we shouldn't talk about this case because we are going to be witnesses. I'm sorry." She started to close the door.

'I know, and I promise not to ask you about the case. I just want to know what you think about Belle, and what her stepfather was like." He smiled, wanting to put her at ease.

"Well, I guess it would be okay." She didn't sound like she believed it but she opened the door for him.

There was a welcome breeze through the open doors and windows as they sat in two parlor chairs in front of one of the windows. Frank took the lemonade she offered in both hands and placed the cold glass on his forehead. He smiled at Margaret and asked about her sister Florence.

"Florrie is bringing in a bucket of water from the well. She'll be here in a minute."

"I want to ask you how long you've known the Williams' and the Hollister's."

"I've known them all their lives, except of course, the Reverend. I attended his church and so did my sister."

"What do you think of Belle?"

Margaret pushed a damp strand of gray hair from her forehead. "I think she's a bit on the wild side, and it was wrong of her to run away like she did. And even before she ran away, she gave her mother a lot of grief. Nadine is a very religious woman and now she's gone a little strange what with all that happened to her. She doesn't even go to church anymore."

"Do you think that Belle could have killed the Reverend?"

Margaret shifted in her chair, looked down at her hands, suddenly rubbing them together as if she was washing them.

"I don't know. I would have to say that I don't know. But it must be very hard to kill someone."

"You're right; it's a lot harder than most people think it is." He made an effort to catch her eyes in his. She was still looking at her hands which lay folded in her lap.

Florrie came to the door and stopped abruptly when she saw Frank. After the introductions, she sat in the chair next to her sister's and chatted with the two of them for a few minutes. The breeze had stopped and it was becoming hotter by the minute.

"Ladies, did you both know the Reverend?"

"Oh, yes." They answered in unison.

"Did you know about trouble between him and Belle?"

"Well, she never liked him. She was a wild one, too." Florrie said. "And the Reverend was strict with her. But he did a lot of good in this community."

"If you think of anything that might shed more light on this, would you let the Sheriff know and he'll tell me?" They both nodded their heads.

Frank got up to leave.

"Oh, do you have to go already? Won't you have some more lemonade?"

"Thanks, Ma'am, but I need to get back. I want to thank you for your time." He took a step towards the door. "Ma'm, are you sure it was Belle that you saw on the path the night the Reverend was killed?"

"Absolutely sure. I've known that girl all her life. And there was a full moon that night so it was very bright out."

She walked with Frank to the door. "You be sure to

come back anytime now, all right? It's nice to have company. We don't get much because we're so far out of town."

A door slammed in a back room and Frank looked down the hall but didn't see anyone.

"It's just Maddie," Margaret said.

"Who's Maddie?"

"Why, that's my niece." She said. "We raised her from a baby, Florrie and me. Her Mama died when she was born." She opened the screen door for Frank.

He stepped outside, turned back to Margaret. "How old is she?"

"She's twenty-five. She's a little slow, if you know what I mean, but she's a lovely girl; wouldn't hurt a fly. We're real close, her and me."

He nodded. This is the first he heard of a granddaughter and niece.

The car door handle was hot to his hand and inside was like an oven. He headed back down the long dirt road, lost in thought. He had to come back and talk with the sisters again. And Maddie. He needed to talk to her as well.

Frank found Nadine's house in the late afternoon. It was slightly cooler now, but still too hot for comfort. It was a different kind of heat than what he was used to; humid, making him sweat constantly. Not at all like the dry heat of Las Vegas. Most of the places in Las Vegas boasted air conditioning, while here it was only a few bars that had it.

There was no answer to his knock. He knocked again, and again. He had been warned that she might not answer the door. Maybe he would try later. He stepped off the porch and then looked up to see a figure in the back yard, bent over rose bushes. He followed the sidewalk to the back yard, stopping close to the woman.

He coughed and said, "Mrs. Hollister?"

Nadine, jumping, turned and stared at him. Frank realized that he was between her and the back door. Eyes wide, mouth open, she stood motionless. She wore a torn housedress with red and white stains down the front. It was too big for her thin frame. Fading red hair streaked with gray reached almost to her waist and fell into her face when she took a step backwards. In her right hand she held pruning shears.

"Please, don't be alarmed. I'm not here to harm you. I'm with the Las Vegas Police Department and I'm a friend of your daughter's. I want to talk with you about Belle."

"I don't know. I'm not sure…" she stammered, her eyes seemed to be searching for a way past him.

"Why don't we go inside, would that be all right?" Frank put his hands in the pocket of his Levis, thinking that it might put her at ease, but she didn't move.

"No, no, I have to finish my work. What do you want?"

"I want to know about your daughter. Do you think she could have killed your husband?"

"What? Belle is my daughter and she wouldn't kill anyone. Bart, he was a holy man. He was so young when he died." She waved the pruning shears at him. "God took him home too soon. And the Reverend took care of Belle like she was his own. He loved her. She wouldn't kill him."

She turned and snipped a thorny branch. This is not the right time for pruning, Frank thought. Not that he knew much about gardening, but pruning in this heat?

"How can you be sure she didn't kill him?" he said.

"Belle went away to school. She's been gone for…" She frowned. "I don't remember for how long now. She didn't kill him."

"Didn't she run away?" Frank was puzzled now.

"Of course not. She just went off to school. I don't

know what she's doing now."

"Did you know that she's in Nashville jail awaiting trial for murdering your husband?"

Nadine stopped snipping branches, stood frozen, and then headed for the door, skirting Frank and the sidewalk he was standing on.

"Mrs. Hollister, please, stop and talk to me for a minute."

She again stopped, staring straight ahead, and then turned to look at him. He stepped back, aware of the shears still in her right hand.

"I don't know who you are, but you're crazy. Stop bothering me. My daughter is at school and my husband is dead, God rest his soul."

"Mrs. Hollister, I talked to the Witherspoon twins a little while ago. Do you know Maddie? Did Belle know her?" Frank felt better with a few feet between them. His stomach rumbled and cramped.

"Belle knows Maddie, she was her friend. The Reverend counseled Maddie and with the help of Jesus he made her well. Praise be to God! Praise be to God!" She raised both arms and looked up at the sky. "Now I have to go. Goodbye."

Frank heard the door lock behind her, turned and walked back to his car. He thought he would go back to the Witherspoon's farmhouse early tomorrow. If he could get Sheriff McMann to go along, so much the better. He was leaving with more questions than answers. Did Nadine kill Bart and the shock make her crazy? Or did Belle really do it and her mother didn't know how to help her. And Bart was counseling Maddie? Could she have killed him if he tried to molest her?

The more he learned, the more questions he had.

Chapter 25

Belle

This is the worst time of day. Dinner is over. All the visitors are gone. I'm sick and tired of reading. Worst of all, it's way too early to sleep.

I walk as far as I can in the cell, back and forth. I'm stopped by the bars. There's no one around at all. This feels weird. It seems like I could just walk out and go home. I grab the bars and rattle them. Someone screams from far down the hallway.

Suddenly I'm hit, really hard; enveloped by an overwhelming sadness. Tears fall down my face like a waterfall. It comes to me that I'm alone. I think I'm going to die, right here behind these bars, in this very room. For the last nine years I've had this feeling, off and on. Before I ended up in jail, it hit me more often when I first woke up. That was the time when I was totally sober, or most likely hung over. If I happened to be in my own place, if I had my own place, I'd open the fridge and grab a beer. In a hotel room, I'd call for room service. If it was a sleazy motel, I'd throw on some clothes, splash water on my face and race to the nearest bar. With the first swallow of the golden brew, a mellow feeling spread over my body like a warm blanket. It crept up my neck and filled my head. Then, everything seemed all right.

I can't do that in jail. At first I missed the booze. My hands shook and I was jumpy. After a week or so, it eased up. Sometimes, like now, I wish I had a drink or two. Or a joint.

I lie down on my bunk. I force myself to think of other things, like I always did when Bart raped me. I think of Old Red with his floppy ears. Jesse told me Red died two years ago and it made me sadder to think about it. I think of my Daddy's smile and how he called me "sis". Most often I remember the meadow behind the barn where field daisies spring up out of nowhere and cover the ground in the spring. Now it seems like a sign of renewal, of faith that all will be new and clean.

I think of something Margie taught me. I close my eyes and concentrate on nothing. I see myself going out of my body. It actually works. My body stays on the bunk and I'm floating above it. My breathing slows and a feeling of peace washes over me. After awhile, I return and I'm not sure how long I was gone. Once again, I'm sure that I can handle this. I have lots of help and support. And I have Frank. And Charlie. And Jack and Jesse. Even Tennie and Dave come to see me.

What I really want is my Daddy. But he's dead. And Ma. But she hasn't come. Charlie tried to go see her but she wouldn't answer the door. Frank is the only one who got through to her. He says she's real shy of seeing anyone. He didn't say so, but the way he described her made me think she's losing her mind. Maybe I'll never see her again. Can you be an orphan when you're a grownup and your Ma is still alive?

Frank comes almost every day to see me. He's nice enough but I see questions in his eyes. Besides, he's a cop. And my experience with cops hasn't been good; especially with Sheriff McMahan. He could have stopped Bart when I went to him, and he didn't believe me. He's the only one I told, and he just sloughed it off like I was a liar, or crazy.

But maybe Frank is different. Otherwise, why would he keep coming to see me? Why is he going to all this trouble to try to help me? I can tell he's attracted to me, even though I'm not looking my best these days. And I like him, too. I look forward to his visits and try to keep myself presentable by combing my hair, washing my face and brushing my teeth. I pinch my cheeks to bring a little color.

Frank told me about his family, where he grew up, and how they took road trips every year when he was a kid. He told me about seeing my mother. We talked about what it was like growing up in Bear Holler. We talked about everything except what was on his mind, what he really wanted to ask me. Did I kill Black Bart? I'm glad that he never asked.

Chapter 26

Bear Holler 1955

The Sheriff sounded like he wasn't quite sure if it was on the up and up to talk with Maddie since he was to be a witness at the trial. But Frank reasoned that Maddie was not a witness so there was really nothing wrong with the Sheriff talking to her. And Frank wasn't a witness, so what was the harm? Frank could even do most of the talking and Sheriff McMann could just lend his presence.

The sisters seemed happy to see him again, and they fawned over the Sheriff as if he were a long lost relative.

"Come in, come in, and set a spell, the two of you." Margaret plumped up the pillows on the parlor settee, sat down next to Florrie and indicated that Frank and the Sheriff should sit in the two easy chairs. She jumped up in a moment and headed for the kitchen for lemonade and cookies, promising to be right back. Florrie, though, looked a bit uncomfortable.

"Well, Sheriff, to what do we owe the pleasure of this visit? Not that we aren't happy to have the company." Her smile seemed forced to Frank.

"Florrie, we're here to visit with you two ladies and I can tell from the sweet smell in the air that you've been baking those cookies just this morning," Horace said.

"You'll be sampling some of those cookies in just a few minutes. Margaret just went to fetch them. We don't get much company, you know. In fact, the only time we have a visit with anyone is when we go to church. We've had three more preachers since Reverend Hollister," there was a catch in her voice, "but none are as good as he was. Why, he was here twice a week to counsel our Maddie and he never showed up without something in hand from his garden. He was an old fashioned fire and brimstone preacher and could light up the congregation like no other since then."

She got up to help Margaret carry a tray of lemonade and cookies.

"Yes, indeed," Margaret agreed. "Reverend was one of a kind all right but not everyone liked him. Some thought he was a bit harsh. I like Reverend Dixon just fine, though. He's very down to earth. And he's such a nice man, too, with a lovely family."

Frank noticed a frown on Florrie's face. It sounded to him like they had a bit of difference of opinion; subtle but real.

"What was he counseling Maddie about?" Frank asked.

"My granddaughter was orphaned as a baby. And she's a bit slow, too. She never could make it in school. So she was having trouble understanding the Bible. The Reverend was patient with her and he spent a lot of time reading to her from the Bible and explaining what it all meant. She was obstinate at first and didn't want to listen, but eventually she warmed up to him." Florrie smoothed her hair from her face and placed two glasses of lemonade on the table between the men. "They would take walks in the woods and sing hymns. He was a good man."

"Thank you, Ma'am." Sheriff McMann took a big swallow from his glass and reached for a cookie offered on a plate by Margaret.

Frank, too, put the cool glass to his lips and savored the sweet-sour liquid. The cookies were still slightly warm, full of nuts and chocolate chips. "Yes, thanks so much for your hospitality."

"Is Maddie home now? I would like to meet her," Frank said.

"Yes," Sheriff McMahan said, "and we need to ask her some questions, if you don't mind."

'Oh, I saw her walking down the road towards the barn a while ago. Maybe later you can see her before you go." Margaret wiped her damp face with an embroidered handkerchief.

"But she's back now, sister. She came in the back door while I was in the kitchen. She'd be glad to meet you, and glad to see the Sheriff again I'm sure." Florence called down the hallway, "Maddie? Come on out."

Shuffling slowly down the hallway, eyes on the floor in front of her, Maddie finally reached the parlor and stood in front of the group. She held her hands rigidly at her side and riveted her eyes to the floor in front of her. She swayed slightly back and forth.

"Hello, Maddie," Sheriff McMahan said. He stood and reached out a hand to grasp hers. She pulled it away and folded her hands in front of her dress. She wore a flowered dress with long sleeves. It was too big for her gaunt frame. She towered over her grandmother and great aunt by several inches. Frank thought she was about Belle's size. Her hair, long and straggly, was the color of dishwater.

"Maddie, this is Frank Smith. He's a policeman from Las Vegas and we would like to ask you some questions about Belle. Would that be all right?" Horace said. When she lifted her eyes Frank saw they were a very pale green that gave her a ghostly look. She wasn't unpleasant to look at but she wouldn't hold an observer's glance for long. She wore the countenance of one who does not comprehend everything that goes on around her.

She nodded and dropped her chin to her chest.

"Do you want to go outside on the porch and sit where it's a bit cooler?"

She nodded again and shuffled towards the front door. The Sheriff and Frank got up and followed behind. The sisters looked at each other and Frank saw Margaret open her mouth, then close it again without speaking.

"Don't tire her out now, you hear? She gets tired real easy." Margaret called out after them. *It sounds like Margaret is worried about something Maddie might say,* Frank thought.

Settled on the porch, Maddie in a swing and Frank and Horace in chairs, Frank said, "Maddie, I understand the Reverend Hollister was telling you about the Bible, and Jesus. Is that right?"

"Yeah."

"Do you remember singing hymns together and walking in the woods?"

"Yes. He saved me so I won't go to Hell."

"How did he save you?" Frank folded his hands in his lap.

"He told me about Jesus." She scratched her head.

"Maddie, what do you think of Belle?"

She stopped swinging and raised her eyes to his. "She's

my best friend."

"Do you think she killed Reverend Hollister?"

"No."

"Why do you say that?"

She started the swing again with a push of her right foot. "Because I killed him."

Startled, Frank looked at Horace, who said, "How did you do that, Maddie?"

"I walked in the woods with him. We were friends."

"Did you hit him with something?"

"He was my friend and he loved me." She rubbed her eyes with both hands. "I think that was a long time ago. He's dead now."

"But why did you say that you killed him?"

"Because I walked in the woods with him and then he was dead."

Horace threw up his hands and looked at Frank, who shrugged and raised his eyebrows.

"But Maddie, someone hit the Reverend in the head with a rock. Was that you?" Frank said.

"I walked in the woods with him and then he was dead."

Frank stood and walked the length of the porch. His stomach was queasy, and he felt nauseated in the heat. He watched Maddie as she repeated again that the Reverend loved her. He walked back and stood in front of her.

"Why do you say that he loved you?"

"Because we had secrets and he said he loved me so we could have secrets."

"What kind of secrets?"

"I can't tell you or they wouldn't be secrets, would they?" She jumped out of the swing and hurried down the path towards the barn.

Frank wiped his face with a handkerchief. They stepped

back inside, chatted with the sisters for a few minutes and downed some more lemonade and cookies before taking leave of them. They climbed into the Sheriff's old pickup and drove down the dusty road back to the highway.

"Well, what do you think of all that?" Frank asked.

"Uh, can't say for sure. Maddie has always been different so I can't put too much stock in anything she says. Why would she say she killed him, but didn't hit him?"

"I don't know." Frank was tired and thirsty, in spite of the lemonade. "Let's have a beer, what do you say?"

"Sounds good to me."

Frank leaned back in the seat and closed his eyes.

"Can we go back and talk with Maddie again?"

"Don't know why not, though I don't think it will do much good."

"How about tomorrow?"

"Okay with me."

"Let's take her for a walk in the woods to where Bart was killed."

The pickup stopped in front of the Black Bear Inn and they entered the cool air-conditioned interior and sat down at the bar.

"I saw Belle and her mother, too." Frank said.

"How are they doing?"

"Belle is okay, but she looks bad. She's getting really frustrated. Her mother? Crazy as a loon, I think. She's convinced that Belle is in school."

"She always was a little crazy, but nothing like she is now."

They downed their beer and headed back to the motel after agreeing to meet early the next morning to talk with Maddie and the sisters again. Frank chewed some Rolaids, turned the cooler on high, and went to bed early. He didn't want to think about all this right now.

The next day they walked with Maddie into the woods and asked her to show them where she last saw the Reverend.

"We always sit down here," she pointed to the tree where Bart was found.

"Were you sitting here the night of the dance?"

"I don't remember." She looked at the ground and twisted her fingers together.

"When was the last time you sat here?"

"I don't know." Her eyes shifted from side to side as if she wanted to run.

Frank squatted down beneath the tree, wanting to put Maddie at ease. The leaves had turned and were shades of burnt umber, orange and pale gold. He picked one up. Beautiful, he thought. Then he thought of the horrible thing that had happened in this lovely spot. He was grateful that the weather had finally cooled some.

Horace McMahan was pacing and acting like he wanted to wrap this up and leave.

"Maddie," Frank said, stretching his hand and offering her a bright orange leaf, "if someone does something bad to you and tells you it's a secret, God says that you don't have to keep it a secret. God says you have to tell someone because bad things shouldn't be kept secret."

She raised her eyes and looked at him. "Are you sure?" She bent to take the leaf from his hand, turning it over and inspecting it.

"Yes, I'm absolutely sure. Besides, secrets aren't secrets any more when the person is dead." He picked up another leaf, one of varied shades of brown.

"Oh." Maddie looked at the blue sky above as if she expected some heavenly guidance. She watched cumulus clouds drift slowly by. Her feet shuffled side to side.

"Do you want to sit down here with me?" Frank patted

the ground beside him.

Her eyes widened and she stepped back. "No, no."

"That's okay. You don't have to." *Careful, you'll frighten her and you'll never get the truth.* He sat cross-legged, elbows on his knees, hoping to take away any threat.

The sun behind the trees dappled the ground in front of Frank. He stared at the dancing sun spots. Horace had stopped pacing and shoved his hands in his pockets, watching Maddie. The ground was getting cold and slightly damp under him, but he was afraid of making Maddie uncomfortable if he got up again.

"Maddie, you can tell us. Did the Reverend do any bad things to you?" Frank plunged ahead, not sure if he was right to be so forward with this girl.

"He only loved me like he said God wanted him to." Maddie stopped moving her feet and stared down at Frank.

"How did God want him to love you?"

Her voice was a whisper. "He put his thing in me because God told him to." Frank looked up at Horace who stood staring at Maddie. Frank wondered; *did I hear her right?*

"That's good that you're telling about it, Maddie." Frank felt sorry for this simple girl who trusted Bart because he was a Minister. "Please go on and tell us everything."

"Sometimes it hurt and he said that was okay because that is what God wanted and he knows because God talks to him." Her voice was still a whisper, barely heard. "He read it to me from the Bible. The Bible is the word of God. I learned that. The Bible said it was what God wanted, for him to put his thing in me and love me."

"Maddie," Frank tried to keep the anger out of his voice, "the Bible doesn't really say that. I'm afraid the

Reverend was lying to you. And it isn't your fault. He was an evil man, pretending to be holy."

She raised her eyes to his. "The Bible doesn't say that?"

"No. I'm sorry." Frank held her gaze.

Horace said, "Maddie, do you know what happened to the Reverend? God would want us to know how he died, wouldn't he?"

Maddie pointed to the ground under the tree where Frank was sitting. "He fell down right there. Are you sure the Bible doesn't say that?"

She began walking in a circle, ever widening, wringing her hands and crying.

"The Bible doesn't say that. Maddie, it's okay. You're doing the right thing to tell us what happened."

"He fell down," she repeated.

"He fell down and hit his head on a rock?" Frank stood up. He tried to keep the excitement out of his voice. *Be careful; don't put words in her mouth.*

"He fell down and hit his head on a rock..." Maddie was crying even louder. "My Aunt Margaret was mad at me because I lost my bracelet that Belle gave me. It broke."

"Why did he fall?" Horace pushed on.

She was sobbing now. Frank rose and put his arm around her shoulder. He handed her his handkerchief. She wiped her eyes, blew her nose and put the handkerchief in her pocket.

"Maddie, did he stumble? What happened?" Frank's voice was gentle.

"He said his stomach hurt and he bent over and he stumbled and fell and hit his head. I was scared. The rock was all bloody."

Frank and Horace looked at each other.

"I've had a stomach ache," Frank said.

"You know what? Me, too. I thought it was the beer

and pig's feet."

"There was rat poison in the shed." Frank remembered that he looked inside the Witherspoon shed as he passed the open door.

"Yeah, rats can be a problem in this part of the country. They'll eat up all the shucked corn in the crib if you don't keep them under control."

"I was scared," Maddie said. "I was scared."

"Let's take you home. I want to have a talk with your Grandma and Aunt Margaret." Frank offered her his arm but she walked ahead so fast that it was hard for him to keep up.

Margaret and Florence sat on the front porch swing. They wore sweaters for the evening air was crisp and cool. Maddie, Horace and Frank climbed the porch steps. The sisters looked up at them and smiled.

Frank hugged Maddie and said, "Thanks, Maddie. You're a very brave girl. I know that this isn't easy for you." Maddie ducked her head and rushed on past them to her room. They heard the bedroom door close.

"Hello, Horace. Hello, Frank. Florence got up from the swing. "I'll be getting you a little coffee to warm you up."

Horace said, "No thanks, ma'am. I have some business with you today. Could we go inside?"

The sisters looked at each other. "What's wrong, Horace?" Florence asked.

"We want to tell you a story that we've just heard from Maddie."

Settled inside, Margaret picked up her knitting from the table beside her. She mouthed the words, *knit one, purl two.*

Horace told the sisters what Maddie had said. Frank verified everything. They spoke quietly, gently. They didn't want Maddie to hear them talking about her.

Margaret dropped her knitting into her lap. "Well, Horace, Maddie doesn't lie. She might be backward but she doesn't lie," Margaret said.

"Did you know what was going on?" Horace took off his Stetson and wiped his forehead with his sleeve. He laid the hat on the table beside him.

Florence shook her head. "I can't believe it. This is truly a shock, Horace."

Margaret looked at him. "Well, I suspected he was taking advantage of her. I followed them into the woods one day. He was hugging her when I found them but he said it wasn't anything to worry about. He said she was sad and he was consoling her. She said there wasn't anything wrong, and that they were friends. But I knew better than that." Margaret looked at her sister, who was staring at her. "I wasn't born yesterday." She wrapped a strand of yarn around a needle and pulled it deftly through, wrapped another strand around it.

"So why didn't you call me? That's what I'm, here for, to take care of these kinds of things." Horace said.

"I thought you wouldn't believe it, Horace. Besides, how could I prove it? I didn't want to cause any upset for Maddie. There would be questioning, and she would be scared." Margaret said this with a tone that said it made perfect logic for her to try to solve the problem herself.

Frank thought she was right. Maddie would have been too scared to say anything while the Reverend was still alive. And if Horace responded the same way he had to Belle, then Maddie would have kept that secret forever.

Florence, mouth open, watched her sister as she pulled another strand through.

"I didn't know," Florence said. She turned her gaze to Horace, then to Frank. "I didn't know."

"That's okay, Florence, I took care of it myself." Margaret said. "You didn't have to know. I'm sorry that you have to know now." She picked up her knitting again. "I told the Reverend in no uncertain terms to leave Maddie alone. I don't know how he got her away from the dance that night. Mabel Hawkins was supposed to be watching her."

"Margaret, I wish you had told me. It's my granddaughter, after all." Florence gazed out the window. The wind had come up and was whipping the lone maple tree, now almost bare of leaves.

"I couldn't get you to see the truth about the Reverend. I know you liked him a lot. Maddie wouldn't say anything except that they had secrets, and that he loved her. But he didn't fool me."

Florence frowned at her sister. "I had a right to know."

"I didn't think you would believe me. I really had no evidence, and Maddie wouldn't talk, except to say they had secrets. I knew that no one else would believe a retarded girl instead of a Minister." Margaret let a tear roll down her cheek. "I love that girl so much. She had to be protected." She dropped the knitting again. "She didn't know how to protect herself."

"I love my granddaughter, too, but Margaret; covering this up" Florence stared at her, wide-eyed.

"I just wanted to scare him off." She picked up her knitting again. "I thought if he knew that I was wise to him, then he would leave her alone."

Horace picked up his hat and spun it in his hands, elbows on his knees. "Margaret, did you give the Reverend anything to make his stomach hurt? Anything like rat poison?"

"Horace, I would never do anything like that. I'm not a murderer."

"Well, Frank and I have had a stomach ache, too, so we

were wondering if there was a little something in those cookies…"

"I'm shocked, Horace, that you could think that of me. Truly shocked." Margaret's voice was angry.

"Do you think Maddie could have done it?"

"That sweet girl? Not on your life." Florrie chimed in.

"Well, we're going to ask for another autopsy and we should know more by then. In the meantime, please don't go anywhere out of town."

"Horace McMahan, where on earth would we go? We live here."

Horace stood. "Well, ladies, you know that Maddie will have to come in tomorrow and make a formal statement.? Will you bring her?"

"Of course, Horace." Florence said. "Please be gentle with her, all right? She is a sensitive girl."

"I'll have a matron there as well. Jane Simmons is one of the most sympathetic women I know."

Horace and Frank said goodnight, stood and walked out the door.

Horace drove straight to the tavern. "Now I really need a drink," he said.

Frank grinned. "Me, too. Let's celebrate."

It didn't take long for Judge Mathews to issue an order to exhume Bart's body at the request of Sheriff McMahan. Maddie's written testimony was submitted to the Judge by Oliver Force. When the coroner had finished his exam two weeks later and all the reports were back, they showed just what Frank and Sheriff McMann expected.

Since Maddie said that Bart complained of stomach pain, the coroner ran toxicology tests. To almost everyone's surprise, Bart's body contained rat poison; warfarin, which is a blood thinner. Rats consume the sweet liquid it's in, and then bleed to death internally.

But that didn't cause the Reverend's death. The amounts of rat poison would have caused stomach pain and weakness maybe, but it wasn't enough to kill him.

The cause of death was changed to accidental. The coroner said Bart died from falling and hitting his head on a rock. This was sustained by Maddie's testimony as well as the absence of blood on Bart's clothing. Re-enacting the scene, Frank and Horace testified how it happened. The rock was large and had a sharp edge, and Bart, being a very big man, fell with enough force to cause a skull fracture.

But where had the poison come from? Margaret? Frank had seen rat poison in their shed, but that doesn't necessarily mean it was there nine years ago. Still both Horace and Frank had stomach discomfort after eating cookies at the Witherspoons.

The coroner, Dr. George Clemmens, also concluded that the previous coroner's report was in error. He said that coroners in rural areas in 1946, when many doctors were off to war, were usually older family practitioners. They may or may not have had additional training in forensic science. They could go years without doing an autopsy. Errors were not uncommon.

Dr. Clemmens said that the previous coroner, Dr.Jake Jergins, had died in 1950. Dr. Clemmens was convinced that Dr. Jergins had assumed murder from Sheriff McMahan's report that he suspected foul play. He gave a cursory exam of the body, after clothes had been removed, looked at the X-rays, and wrote his conclusion. There was no reason to test for poisons at that time.

Oliver Force filed a motion for dismissal of Belle's murder charge. Judge Morris granted it with no objections from the District Attorney's office.

"Frank, you did a good job. Thanks for bringing me along on that road." Horace held out a hand and shook Frank's. He gave him a clap on the shoulder. "Come on over for a little fishing tomorrow and we'll knock back a few beers as well."

Frank liked this small town Sheriff. He did his job with an ease that Frank didn't see too often. His offhand manners could fool someone into thinking he wasn't too bright, but Frank had seen how well he handled people. His manner was laid back, offhand, but most effective.

"Thanks, Horace, but I guess I'll be picking Belle up from jail if all goes well and she's released tomorrow."

"I understand. But you know the invitation is always open."

"I appreciate that. I also thank you for all your help" He rubbed his aching neck. The motel bed wasn't all that comfortable.

"You know, Frank, I am curious about one thing and just never got around to asking. If it's not too forward of me, do you plan on hanging out here once Belle is free?" He took out his handkerchief and wiped his forehead. There were small beads of sweat on his brow, despite the cold weather, "I mean, are you in love with her?"

"Uh," Frank was taken by surprise. The question was out of character for the burly Sheriff. "I guess I am, Horace. I don't have any idea how she feels about me, though. But I'm going to take a chance and try to find out."

"Good luck, my man. And if you get tired of the gambling town, we might be able to find a spot for a talented cop on this force. Of course, the pay isn't all that good, but the benefits speak for themselves." He swept the autumn landscape with a red puffy hand. They both took in the rolling hills beyond a blue water lake, the low white clouds overhead, and the trees where leaves had turned crimson and burnished gold.

"You know what it's like in the summer and the fall here. Stick around and see how beautiful winter and spring can be in the Smokies."

"Thanks. And if things work out for me and Belle, who knows, I could settle here as well as anywhere." Frank put his hands on his hips and looked around.

"Horace, do you have any idea where that poison came from?"

Horace shook his head. "I sure don't. Our tests came back negative and my stomach doesn't hurt any more. It must have been the pig's feet and beer after all. So maybe it was Margaret. Maybe we'll never know."

Chapter 27

Belle

The day I got out of jail it was raining. November 29, 1955. I looked out the waiting room window at the bare-limbed trees. The wind bent their branches, tossing them back and forth. Torrents of rain splattered onto the windows. Leaves, faded brown and yellow, sat in lumpy heaps on the ground.

The heavy barred gates clanged behind me and I walked into the waiting room. I saw them; Frank, and Jack and Jesse and Charlie too. My eyes burned and I ran to hug them one by one, not even trying to stop the tears. Charlie gave me a handkerchief.

Jack opened the outside door and I walked out, free. Even if I was happy to be out, it felt strange to leave the place I had lived for almost four months

Sheriff McMahan and the Witherspoon twins were coming up the walk with Maddie trailing behind. Frank had told me how Bart had lied to Maddie and forced her to have sex with him. She looked up at me and smiled.

"Belle," she said. I reached out my hand.

"Maddie, thank you for helping me get out of jail. I think you're a very brave woman." I held her hand. Maddie pulled back and fussed with her purse. "Can we still be friends, like we always were?" I said.

"We are best friends, Belle. We are best friends. I told the Sheriff that." She looked at Horace. "I came to see you today."

"Thanks, Maddie. I'm happy to see you."

"I had to make a depo…depo…" Maddie frowned.

"I know, Maddie. I know what you mean, a deposition." I smiled at her. "I'll come see you after I get settled, okay?" I said. She waved and then walked with the others to their car.

I told Frank I felt sorry for Maddie. Having to go to a police station was probably very hard for her. Frank told me that it was just a formality. The sisters took her right back home after she signed her statement.

On the way to the bus everyone talked about who would drive me home. But wait, I hadn't thought. Where is home? Not with Ma. Frank was staying with the guys in the cabin and it was too small for even one more person. Besides, cooped up with five guys? In the end, we all piled into One Night Stand's bus, even Charlie, and squeezed into the booth. We sat in the parking lot, huddled inside, and talked it over.

"I could stay in the bus," I said.

Charlie wouldn't have it. "It's getting too cold for that. You're coming to stay with me in Nashville. My house is not huge but it's plenty big for the two of us."

I searched her face.

"You're not with Oliver?" I said.

Jess' head snapped up and he looked at Charlie.

"No. I never moved back in." I was stunned. After she broke up with Jess she told me that she was going back to Oliver.

Frank had his arm around my shoulders. "Belle, I think that's a great idea, staying with Charlotte in Nashville until you get your bearings."

"No objections from me, for sure." I looked at Charlie, still puzzled. "Thanks, I accept. And as soon as I'm working, I'm paying rent."

"We can talk about that later, okay? Right now, let's get out of this parking lot before they chase us out." Charlie stood up. "Besides, we have some serious partying to do," she said. We climbed off the bus and into Charlie's car.

Charlie said her house was modest, but it was nicer than any place I had ever lived. She showed me to a beautiful guest room. Charlie lay across the bed while I unpacked the few things I had with me.

I had to ask her why she didn't go back to Oliver.

"I just couldn't go back, Belle. I don't love him anymore. I don't want to spend my life under his thumb." She sat up on the edge of the bed.

"Then why did you break up with Jess?" I closed the last drawer and sat down beside her.

"I broke up with him at first because I was going to go back to Nashville with Oliver. The only way he would agree to defend you was if I came back to him. I agreed because I couldn't let you down." She looked down at her hands, avoiding my gaze. "I didn't want to tell you about that before, but it doesn't matter now if you know."

"I can't believe you did that for me, Charlie." I stared at her face. "I just can't believe it." I felt little shocks all through my body. No one had ever done anything like that for me.

Charlie didn't seem to notice. She went on, "Anyhow, the more I thought about going back to my old life, the more anxious I became. I finally decided that there was no way I could go back. So I pulled out my ace in the hole."

"Your ace in the hole?" She had my interest for sure. It put me in mind of Daddy's poker game pals who kidded each other about keeping an ace up their sleeves.

"Oliver left Las Vegas before me. He was way behind on his cases and had to get back home. I was supposed to withdraw my divorce petition, and then follow him back to Nashville."

Charlie got up and said," Hold off a minute and I'll get us a drink." She returned with a tray of cheese and crackers and two whisky and cokes.

"Anyhow, I called Oliver at home from Las Vegas. I told him I wasn't coming back to him. You can imagine his response, Belle. Of course he said in that case, he wouldn't be representing you. And, he would see that I was cut off without a cent. He was furious. He accused me of lying to him to force him to leave Las Vegas." Charlie stared straight ahead.

"When he was through ranting, I asked him, 'Do you remember the Martinson versus Alabaster Recording case?'" She took a sip of her drink. "Well, it was real quiet on the other end of the line."

I bit into a cracker. "What was the case all about?"

"I'm getting to that." Charlie got up and walked the floor. "I said to Oliver, 'I have a copy of the wonderful tape Jim Martinson gave to you. It's beautiful, really. He starts out by telling his name, gives the date, and then sings two songs he wrote. I especially liked, "Standing in the Sunshine of Your Love."'"

"Charlie," I said, exasperated. "What did the tape have to do with anything?"

Charlie ignored me. "Well, Oliver sounded like he was choking. 'You made a copy of the tape?'"

I told him, 'Yes. Actually my attorney has it now. Are you sure you don't want to help Belle? She needs you desperately'." Charlie sat down on the bed beside me

She went on. "Oliver coughed. Finally he said, 'Well, I could talk with her and see what it's all about. I won't make any promises, though.' That's when I knew I had him." Charlie's face shone like that of a long distance runner just crossing the finish line first.

Then she explained to me what the tape was all about. It proved that Jim Martinson wrote Alabaster's best selling song that Gregory Dunlap claimed to have written.

It seems Gregory was in Jim's band at one time. He heard Jim sing "Standing in the Sunshine of Your Love." Gregory wrote out the music like it was his own and took it to Alabaster Recording. That record, "Away in the Night" and "Standing in the Sunshine of Your Love" made a lot of money for Alabaster with the famous John Walker recording it. When Jim Martinson heard it on the radio, he brought the tape to Oliver Force to see if he could get paid for writing the songs.

Oliver didn't tell him he was representing Alabaster Recording. Instead he convinced Jim that he didn't have a case and he might as well drop it. Jim believed him. Being a backwoods country boy, he just went home to the Smokies thinking he got off easy because Mr. Force didn't charge him anything for his services.

Then Alabaster bought the tape from Oliver for $20,000. But before that, Charlie had found the tape in Oliver's player. She made a copy because she liked it. She didn't know the circumstances around it until she heard the song on the radio and asked Oliver how come someone else was recording it. He sloughed off her questions. That made her angry enough to go through his records until she uncovered the whole story. The memory of what he did disgusted her. She ended up using it to her advantage, knowing that he could lose his license to practice law if this ever got out.

"Belle, he was angrier than I've ever seen him. But there was nothing he could do about it. I had him over a barrel." She raised her eyebrows and looked at me. "But that's not all. I made Oliver send $20,000 to Jim Morrison and tell him it was for the song he wrote." She smiled. "That cleared up my own conscience a bit."

"That is some story. You know, I'll always be grateful for all you've done, Charlie. But what about Jess?"

"I have to be honest, Belle. I love your brother, but I'm not ready to give up my freedom. It would be the same old story. I'd be living my life according to him and his music. I can't trust that I would have any life of my own. I've been quite content to be independent, to be on my own."

I said, "That breaks my heart. But I understand what you're saying. As sweet as he is, I'm finding it hard to trust Frank. I don't think I can put myself under anyone's control ever again." I know that my eyes were misty. "Anyhow, we'll always be sisters, won't we?"

"Sisters forever." This time she hugged me.

After I settled in at Charlie's house, the two of us headed for the cabin. I could hear the music before we turned the last bend. Damn, they sounded good. I don't remember ever being as happy as I was that night, unless it was the time Jesse found me in Las Vegas.

I opened the front door and there was Frank on the couch, beer in hand, tapping his foot and smiling; Jack, Jess, Tennie and Dave playing music and Jess' voice echoing through the house. Frank sat us down on the couch, went to the ice box and brought two bottles of beer. It tasted like heaven.

I was without alcohol for five months and I won't ever drink as much as I used to. I smoked in jail, but being at Charlie's house I think I'll give it up. She doesn't smoke and her house is so clean, so pretty I wouldn't want to make it smell bad. But for now, I did take a cigarette from Jack and Frank lit it for me. His arm was around my shoulders again and he kissed my cheek. It felt good being with him.

"Come on up here and sing us a tune, Belle." Jess grabbed my hand and pulled me up. "Do you still remember 'San Antonio Rose'?"

"Sure do. Bring it on."

It was like I had never left. We were in sync, on tune, absolutely perfect. I saw Frank watching me with a big grin on his face.

When it was finished, Jess looked at me and punched my shoulder. "Damn, Belle, that's great. How about coming in with the band? I already talked with the guys and they said yes." Yeah, they all echoed.

"Well, sure, but where will we work? I'll need some practice, too."

"We'll be finished in two weeks at the Horse and Buggy. Jack and I will be scouting for the next gig tomorrow. We'll just have to charge a bit more so we can pay you."

"I can pick you up and bring you over tomorrow night for practice," Frank said.

"Okay. It's a deal."

Great. I'm just out of jail and I have a job and a place to stay already.

The guys went back to playing. I took Frank's hand and led him outside. We sat on the porch swing and rocked a little. It was chilly and I snuggled into his arms.

"Thanks for everything you've done for me, Frank. I don't know how I could ever repay you. But I feel bad that you lost all these months of work because of me."

"I wanted to do it, Belle. And I don't regret it one bit." He held me and kissed me, soft and gentle, on the mouth. I kissed him back. I felt safe in his arms and I didn't want him to let me go.

But he got up and paced in front of me. "Belle, I took a six month leave of absence and I'm staying on for awhile. I have enough savings and I really want to do it. I hope we can see a lot of each other while I'm here."

He stopped in front of me and took my hand, pulling me up to him. He put his arms around me and laid his chin on the top of my head. "I don't want you to feel obligated in any way, but I've grown to care a lot about you. I'd like to give us a chance, if it's all right with you."

I put my arms around his neck and kissed his mouth. "You don't think I'd let you go, do you? You are the sweetest man I've ever known."

"And you're the bravest and most beautiful woman I've ever known." He kissed me again.

Just then Jess and Charlie opened the front door. "Uh, excuse us. We're just going for a walk." Jess said. They headed down the path, Jess's hand on her elbow guiding her, and the moon shining on her hair. They were talking low and I could see their breath in the cold night air but I couldn't hear what they were saying.

"Charlie, I'm happy to see you again." Jess put his arm around Charlie's waist.

She pulled free. "Nothing has changed, Jess. I don't want to encourage you to think it has." She thought that maybe it had been a mistake to come out with him.

"Damn, girl! Don't you know I'm crazy about you?

Come on; tell me again why you don't want to marry me."

She stopped in the path and looked at him. "Marry? That's the first time I've heard that word come out of your mouth."

"It won't be the last time, either. I'll keep trying."

"Jess, we've been over this before. I don't want to live like a gypsy. I don't want to worry about where the next paycheck is coming from. And I don't think I'd like life on the road, either." She kept on walking, just a little ahead of him.

"I wouldn't ask you to live the way I'm living now, that's for sure." He caught up with her.

"I know all about married musicians and their girlfriends." She hadn't forgotten her conversation with Dave in Las Vegas. She wasn't about to get into another bad relationship. The moon shone bright on the path before them. Their breath came out in little puffs of steam.

"You might think you know about musicians, but you don't know about me, Charlie. I would never hurt you. Do you remember what I told you way back at the hot springs? And I still mean it."

She turned and looked at his face, pale in the moonlight. She felt weak. God, he was so handsome. He reached for her again, held her shoulders in his hands. His touch thrilled her. And she knew that she still loved him.

"Sweetheart, I want to marry you, and I'll ask you proper as soon as I have a steady income." He kissed her, softly, on the mouth. She kissed him back.

Abruptly, she pulled away and took his hands. "Don't, Jess. It's just no good. This only makes it harder for me."

He gave a heavy sigh. "Okay, Charlie. But you haven't seen the last of me, my girl."

She was already on her way back to the cabin.

Chapter 28

A bluster of cold winter wind pushed Jack through the cabin's front door. Jesse looked up from his chair and shivered. It was dusk and ice seemed palpable in the air.

"Damn, I'm frozen to the bone." Jack shed his heavy coat and pulled off a stocking cap, gloves and heavy boots.

"Dave is out getting some water to make coffee. That'll warm you up." Jesse got up and walked to the kitchen cupboard, returning with a bottle of Jack Daniels.

"Yeah, and throw in a shot of that Daniels. That ought to do the trick," Jack said.

"That's for sure..."

"Where's Tennie? As soon as my fingers thaw out. I want to go over that new George Jones number, 'Why, Baby, Why.'" He stood in front of the fire, stomped his feet and rubbed his hands together.

"He's stretched out on his bed, but I think he's awake." Jess said.

"Jess, did you have any luck today?" Jack poured a shot of Daniels and tossed it down his throat, not waiting for the coffee.

"Naw. Seems like everyone is staying indoors on Saturday nights what with this weather. How about you; any luck?" Jess couldn't help but think they would have a gig by now if he could have offered something besides country music. Maybe he'd better go out on his own. Arguing with Jack was getting old.

"Nope. Not a bite. I even offered one night free if they would book us for a six nighter."

"Hell, Jack, don't be giving us away. It's bad enough that we had to cut our price."

"Fuck you, Jesse; anytime you think you can do better for us, well, you just go ahead, okay?" Jack slammed his fist on the table.

"Maybe I will, Jackass. Anytime you want to step outside, I'll be right after you."

Jack went to the table and sat down. "That'll be the day."

"That day might come a lot sooner than you think, Jack."

"Then that'll be the day I whip your ass." Jack poured another shot of Daniels.

Jesse could smell the coffee and headed for the kitchen. *Got to get away for a minute before I punch him out.*

Jess was back in a few minutes with two cups, one for him, one for his cousin. "Here, Asshole, don't say I never did anything for you."

"Hey, thanks, Man." Jack came close to smiling. "This smells good."

"Okay, let's head out again tomorrow. We'll come up with something. If there's no job by the end of the week, then I'll look around in town for some other kind of work."

Jess cringed at the thought. He didn't want to do any other work. Now with Belle in the group, they were sounding even better than before. He knew that a good-looking female singer with a great voice was a draw for any group. Dave came in with a cup of coffee in his hand and sat down beside Jess. "How's everything, Bud?"

"Aw, hanging in there. Are you guys ready for some picking?"

"Sure. Hey, Tennie," he shouted, "come on out."

"Dave, are you still off the booze?" Jack asked.

"You bet." He smiled. "Not that it's easy, especially with the Daniels on the table. But I made up my mind. I want to keep my liver."

"Oh, sorry." Jess picked up the bottle and took it back to the cupboard.

"Hey, just because I quit doesn't mean you guys have to walk on eggs around me. Or hide bottles, either."

Jack looked up and patted Dave's shoulder. "I'm proud of you, guy. I was sure getting worried about the drinking. It was starting to affect your playing, you know."

"Yeah, and I thank you for pointing that out when you did. It helped." He stood up and reached for his bass. Tennessee sauntered out to the parlor, shuffling his feet and scratching his head.

"How the hell can we practice if Belle's not here?" He sat down next to Jess

Jack looked at him. "Just like we always did before she came along. She can catch up later. Besides, she'll probably be here after supper."

"Jack, how about learning that new Johnny Cash, 'Cry, Cry, Cry'?" Tennie said.

Jack emptied his cup. "Yeah, I heard it the other day. It's really good."

Tennie grinned and said, "That boom-chicka-boom

sound he does is out of sight."

Jess looked around the table. "Guys, see what you think of this. I want everyone to learn harmony. Lots of the groups are doing back-up like that, and I think it sounds great. How about it?"

Jack smiled and punched his shoulder. "Sure, Cuz, okay with me. You know I always go along with whatever you say."

Jess frowned and looked at him sideways. "Yeah, right."

It was noon straight up when Jess pushed through the door of Morry's Bar and Grill. In spite of the smoke that assaulted his nose, he was grateful for the rush of warm air that engulfed him. He waited for his eyes to adjust to the dark interior before drifting to the bar and ordering a whiskey.

At the end of the bar a 50ish blond sat perched on a bar stool with legs crossed. A cigarette smoked in her right hand. In her left hand she held a short drink. She wore a silky red blouse with a plunging neckline and a short black skirt, red high heels. She smiled and pushed her zebra striped purse to the side of the bar when Jesse looked her way.

There was no one else there but the bartender. He was a man of sixty or so with grey-speckled mutton-chop sideburns, balding on top.

"Is the manager around?" Jess took a sip of his double shot.

"You're looking at him. Sean Morrarity. But most folks call me Morry." He stuck out a hand in Jess's direction. "I double as the owner."

"I'm Jess Williams." Jess took his hand and shook it. "My band's available after the end of next week, if you have a need for some top entertainment."

"What's the name of your group?"

"One Night Stand."

"For real?"

"Yeah. I guess we settled on it just because we've done a lot of those over the last five years."

"What do you play?"

"Country."

"That all?"

"What did you have in mind?"

"Well, Jess, I tell you true. I just let a good country band go because we were losing customers. It got so dead in here that you could have rolled a bowling ball from the front door right to the bandstand without hitting a soul." He pulled up his stool across from Jess. "In the meantime, the Gables down the street was packing them in with a rock-abilly band."

"Maybe you just didn't have the right group, Morry." He bit his bottom lip. "We got a girl singer that would knock your socks off. And I sing pretty good, too. We have a top-notch lead guitar, bass, and drummer. We're thinking of adding a steel. And we all sing harmony."

"I don't doubt what you say one bit. But the crowds are asking for rockabilly like Elvis Presley stuff, along with country. Most country groups just don't do them." He wiped the bar in front of Jess and refilled his shot glass. "This one's on the house."

Jess took a deep breath. "Well, what makes you think we don't play some rockabilly?" He wanted to pick up his glass but his hand was shaking. He stuck it in his pocket and smiled.

"Do you?" Morry leaned across the bar, his eyes interested.

"We sure do play all that. We knew we'd have to if we

wanted to stay up with the times. Of course, our main focus is country." Jess picked up his glass and downed it all at once. "Thanks for the drink, Morry."

Morry narrowed his eyes and looked at Jess, a half smile on his face. "Well, sure the main focus is country. We're still a shit-kicking town here." He poured a whisky coke and carried it to the other end of the bar. He set it down in front of the blond and took her money.

Jess stood. He guessed there was no use staying any longer. He was getting hungry. He picked up his coat from the stool next to him.

Morry looked up from the cash register, closed the drawer and walked over to Jess.

"Tell you what, Jess. I like you. I'll take you on for a week with an option for a six month contract."

"Don't you want a tryout?"

"Nope. I'll take your word, one man to the other." Morry poured himself a shot of the whisky. He lifted it to Jess, then to his mouth, threw his head back and swallowed. "It's the way I've always done it and I'm too damn old to change my ways."

"That's good of you, Morry. You won't be sorry." He reached out his hand.

Morry shook it and clapped Jess on the shoulder. "So can you start a week from Friday?"

"You bet. We'll be here. Nine?"

"Nine it is. We'll wrap up about 1:30. We'll start with Friday, Saturday and Sunday afternoon. If all goes well, we can go six nights later. You got a contract?"

"I can get one if you don't." He bit his lip again. Now he'd put himself in a big mess. They had only ten days to learn new songs; songs that his brother didn't want to do and might even refuse to do. And eight of those days they were still obligated at the Horse and Buggy.

"Naw. I have one. Come on by tomorrow about three and we'll wrap it up." Morry scooped the glasses off the bar and dropped them into the sink.

Jess looked at the blond again. She smiled broadly showing a gap in her front teeth. She waved at Jess with the cigarette hand, leaving a thin trail of smoke that widened in the warm air. Jess nodded to her and pulling his collar up around his neck, walked out the door into the cold wind.

"Good news, guys! We've got a gig, starting week from Friday as soon as we're done at the Buggy."

They were all there, sitting at the table eating stew that Tennie had made earlier in the day. He said he let the beef simmer for hours until it was tender enough to fall apart on their forks. Then he added turnips, potatoes and carrots and his own secret seasoning. Jess' stomach rumbled at the aroma. He had missed lunch.

They rose from their chairs and cheered. Dave and Tennessee; even Belle and Frank whooped. Charlie was there too, clapping her hands. Only Jack sat serious, lifting another fork of stew to his mouth.

"What's the story, Jess?" He chewed slowly, raising his eyes to Jesse's face.

"Truth is, Jack, I had to promise we'd do some rock-abilly, Elvis Presley stuff, too. So that means lots of practice time for sure."

Jack swallowed and stood, scraping his chair on the bare floor. "What the hell did you do a dumb-ass thing like that for?" He pointed his fork at Jess.

"Because we'll be eating stew with nothing but a few left-over turnips in it next week, if we don't get work."

"I don't know who you think is going to play lead. It sure as hell won't be me." He threw his fork onto the table.

Dave said, "Come on, Jack, give it a try. At least we'll

have some work. We can still keep on looking for something else if we don't want to stay with it."

Tennie stood, too. "Hey, I'm with you Jack, you know that. But shit-fire, I'm getting desperate for money. I'm willing to try something different, if it means food on the table." He dropped his fork, too. "It's better than splitting up the group, isn't it?"

"To hell with you all." Jack pushed the chair again with the back of his legs and it fell over and skittered across the floor.

Jess pulled off a wet boot and threw it on the floor hard. "You know what, Jack? I'm going to play the kind of music the public wants, not what I think they should like. Now if that means quitting the group, okay, that's what I'm doing. And anyone who wants to come with me is welcome." He threw his other boot on the floor and walked over to Jack. "Feel free to quit if you want. I imagine I can find another lead somewhere."

Jack pushed his face into Jess'. "You bastard. After all I've done for you."

"And after all I've done for you." Jess pushed forward until he was almost chest to chest with his cousin. "Name your poison because I'm done fighting about this."

Everyone else stood immobile, watching.

Then Belle pushed her way between them. "Jesse, back off and go sit down."

She turned to face Jack. "Jack, get down from your mighty high-horse and stop acting the fool. We need work. It's not going to kill you to compromise a bit, for the group. Let's just get busy and learn some new stuff." She put her arm around his shoulder. "Please, for me?"

She always could get to him. When Jack was ten he was going to run away. He had a fight his mother and came to stay all night at Belle and Jesse's house. The next morning, he packed up a sandwich and headed down the path, saying he would never come back. Belle, just five, ran after him. She screamed and pulled on his shirt until he turned around and came back.

Jack sighed, the anger suddenly gone out of him. "I guess I'm outvoted."

"Thanks, Jack. You'll see; it'll be all right." Belle kissed his cheek.

"I'm not going to like it. Not at all." He lowered his head.

"That's okay. You don't have to." Belle sat down and picked up her fork. Everyone else did the same.

Chapter 29

Belle

Last night Frank asked me to marry him. I said I wanted to think about it. But that was a lie. I already know what I'm going to say.

Now I've been talking to myself and wondering what kind of fool I am. Here is this sweet guy who wants to take care of me and I'm going to say no. The problem is; I really don't want to hurt him. The bigger problem is; I want to be on the stage, singing and carrying on with the guys.

Frank and I get along just great. He's the nicest man I've ever known. And damn, if the sex isn't as good as it gets. I think.

Charlie and Jess are seeing each other again. She says only as a friend, but my hopes are up. She still won't say that she'll marry him and he keeps asking.

But I have to admit that when Charlie talks about Jess, I'm full of envy. I want what those two have. When she talks about Jess, her eyes get all misty. In Las Vegas, she talked about how handsome he is, how he looks so terrific on the stage. She said when he sings "Stay a Little Longer" she thinks she could just die right there. I know that I don't feel that way about Frank.

The first night Frank and I were together we were alone at Charlie's. Charlie and Jess went to a movie and we decided to stay in. Frank built a fire and brought me a whisky and coke and we just sat there, talking. Then his arms were around me and the next thing I knew, he carried me into my bedroom. Amazing, how his hand warmed my face and at the same time sent chills through my body. He whispered how he loved me and I told him I loved him too. And I meant it, I really did.

Afterwards, he got up and went into the bathroom. I heard water running into the tub. When he came back and picked me up again, I threw my arms around his neck. He was stronger than I thought. He carried me to the tub and dropped me gently into the sweet-smelling warm water. He climbed in, too. That was when he took both my hands asked me to marry him. And I said I'd think about it.

Then he reached over and put his hand on the back of my neck. I felt a chill cold as ice course down my spine. I startled and pulled away, reminded of when I was nine and my Ma dragged me to the prayer meeting. I remembered Black Bart and his hand on my neck.

He gave me a surprised look and frowned. "I'm sorry," I said. "I didn't mean anything by that." I got out of the tub, though. He climbed out, too, and got dressed. Soon he hugged and kissed me, and then went back to the cabin. I was glad that he didn't ask to stay all night.

That was a month ago and I still haven't got the nerve to give him my answer. But I'll have to soon. One Night Stand is going on the road.

We've been packing them in at Morry's Bar and Grill. It's standing room only six nights a week. Morry even gave us a raise and offered a contract, but Jack said no. Instead, we cut a record and our new agent sent it off to a bunch of DJs. It's pretty exciting to turn on the radio and hear ourselves playing and singing.

Charlie has been there almost every night, clapping and cheering. She dances with whoever asks her, but she always comes home alone. I saw her once, sitting at the table by the bandstand and staring at Jess. He was singing, "I'm so Lonesome I Could Cry" He looked down at her and I could see her eyes glistening in the dim light.

It was at the bar that Bill Jefferson found us. He was there all week, he said later, just listening to us. At the end of the week on a Sunday, he sat huddled at a table with Jack during first break. When they got up, the agent walked out the door and Jack was grinning like I never saw before. We climbed back on the bandstand and Jack was still grinning. We looked at each other, then at him.

"Okay, let's do 'Take Me Back to Tulsa'. Then you can all congratulate me on my superior negotiating skills."

We had to wait until next break before he told us. The next day he'd sign the contract with Bill Hawkins Agency. The following day we'd cut our first record, with Sam Phillips of Sun Records in Memphis. Sam Phillips! Sun Records!

Six weeks later we'd be on the road, living up to our name One Night Stand. And there was more money involved every month than we'd seen in a lifetime. It was all we could do to finish out the night.

The day we got to Memphis and found Sun Records, it was hinting of spring. It was still cool but the sun was on our backs as we got out of the car and walked to the entry.

The birds were singing as if they were celebrating with us.

I recognized him right away from the Grand Ole Opry. He was all in black. He looked like a panther, with his black hair and dark hooded eyes. I loved the stealthy way he walked.

"Hi, Johnny." I knew I sounded excited; my voice quivered. Johnny Cash. He looked like the bad boy he was reputed to be.

"Hello, Missy. You guys gonna cut a record?"

"We sure are. How about you?" Jess was grinning, too. Jack reached out his hand.

Johnny said, "I tell you something funny. I just signed a contract for tons of money. But I've only got fifteen cents in my pocket and there's no paycheck in sight yet." He gave his one-sided grin and I noticed how his eyes laughed, too.

He dug into his pocket, turned around and walked back to a panhandler leaning against the building. Then he dropped two coins into the panhandler's cup.

"I'd need twenty cents for a pack of cigarettes and twenty cents for a loaf of bread, so that fifteen cents won't be doing me any good at all." He laughed, waved his hand and walked on down the street.

It was a great session. The studio hired a steel guitar and fiddle and they made us sound even better. After, Jack was huddled in a corner with Elton Jackson, the steel guitar player. Once, he reared back and said, "You play fiddle, too? Great!" Next thing we knew, we had ourselves a steel man.

Chapter 30

It was after midnight a week later. Frank had just left and I was deep in thought, staring at the fire he'd made in Charlie's fireplace.

Frank had been moody. "So, Belle, if you're leaving in three weeks to go on the road, then what's going to happen to us?"

"Honestly Frank, I don't know. I just know that I can't get married yet." I was sitting beside him, my arm draped loose around his shoulders. I laid my head on his shoulder.

"How the hell am I supposed to deal with that? Go back to Vegas and wait for you to change your mind? Or just forget the whole thing." His face was dark, turned away from me.

I raised my head. "I wish I could answer that. All I know is, I love you but I can't settle down yet. I need to be on the stage, singing. If I could have my way, you'd be on the road with me."

"And what would I do on the road? Be kept by you? No, that wouldn't work for me. I'll go back to work, and we can see what happens."

"You are one hell of a guy and I'll probably regret it for the rest of my life if I don't marry you." I couldn't tell him how scared I was that he would find someone else. I really needed him, wanted him. "We'll be spending some of our time in Vegas, you know. And there's no reason that you can't join me on your days off, wherever we're playing."

"Sure. We can do that." His voice was flat. "Okay, Belle, see you later." He kissed my cheek, got up and left closing the front door behind him.

I heard a key turn in the lock.

"You still up?" Charlie dropped her keys on the table by the door.

"Yeah. I'm not sleepy yet."

I went to the kitchen and mixed a whiskey and Coke.

"Want a drink, Charlie?" I called to the other room.

"Sure. I'll have one. I'm going to get undressed while you make it."

We settled in front of the fire, both of us somber in our pajamas. I saw that Charlie had something on her mind, too. I knew that she was one to keep her emotions in check, but I've been around her enough to know when something is out of whack.

"So Charlie, what's up with you?"

"What do you mean?" She swallowed half her drink.

"Something's eating you, I can tell." I stared at her, willing her to speak.

"You might as well know. I'm not going to see Jess again." She emptied her glass and went to the kitchen to fix another drink.

I followed her in. "What? Now I'm really upset. Did he do something wrong?"

"Not really. But we've been sitting in the truck talking for an hour." She took her drink into the sitting room.

I followed her to the couch and sat beside her.

She got up and moved closer to the fire. She stared at it for a long time, not saying anything. I just sat and waited.

Charlie sat down again. She dropped her head in her hands. I could see her shoulders jerking.

I sat down next to her and hugged her. "Tell me what's wrong, Charlie."

She looked up at me and reached for a Kleenex. "We went to the club for a drink after the movie. Jess said he wanted to hear the band that was playing." Tears rolled down her cheeks again.

"Belle, we had a big argument that started in the club and continued in the truck on the way home. He yelled at me and said he was tired of me putting him off."

This was not going well. I was worried that Charlie would change her mind about taking the job of road manager that Jack had offered her.

"I guess he was just acting stupid, Charlie, but I know how much he loves you."

"I know. We talked about it for a long time and he apologized over and over. He said he was feeling frustrated but he wouldn't hurt me for the world. But it did hurt. I can't decide to marry him when I really don't know him that well. I'm not going to jump into anything, after my experience with Oliver."

"See? He didn't mean to hurt you, did he?"

"That's not the point. Is this what I would be looking forward to on the road; his constant pushing and me trying to defend myself?" She tossed her Kleenex into the fire "I don't need this shit, Belle. And I won't put up with it. Besides, I really need to stay independent. This just confirms it."

"Even if you don't get back with Jess, we'll still be friends forever. You're like a sister to me." I know I sounded scared, but I didn't want her to leave me. "Please take the job and go on the road with us. It would be great for you. What would you do in Nashville, anyhow?"

"Thanks, Belle. I'll sure think about it. And if I decide to go, it will be because of you, not Jess."

"I was thinking of how good you were to me when I was in jail. When I told you all the bad things I had done, you were okay with it. You stuck with me. Maybe you could forgive Jess, too."

Her eyes were red and her nose was dripping. "But you're a good person, Belle. That just shines through on you."

"I think Jess is a good person, too. What if you never took a chance with him? Will you always regret it?"

Charlie smiled at Belle. "You are so brave, Belle. You have the courage to follow your heart and try new things. I'd love to be more like you. We'll always be friends, you and me."

"Well, as your friend and sister, I say 'follow your heart' and you won't go wrong."

We sat silent for the longest time, both of us just staring at the fire.

Then I said, "Charlie, I'll tell you something. I'm not going to marry Frank. It wouldn't work; him in Las Vegas, me on the road. And I won't give up my music." I had finally put it into words.

She stood and put her arms around me. "Belle, I'm so sorry."

Will I regret not marrying Frank? If I change my mind, would he still be waiting? I don't think so, really. He's a great catch and someone will pick him up.

"It's okay. I've given it a lot of thought and it's the only way I can go." I said.

"I hope you made the best decision. He's a good man."

I knew she was right.

Chapter 31

Belle climbed the stairs and felt the last one give a little. She stumbled onto the porch, looking down at the shabby boards under her feet. They were sagging and splintered. Paint was peeling off the side of the building. Something that looked like egg yolk was splattered on the front door. A lone basket with a tired looking plant cascading down the side hung from the porch roof. Otherwise, nothing had changed, really.

Maybe she shouldn't have come. Frank, who was the only one who talked to Nadine recently, described her as "a little demented." But it was important to Belle to find out if her mother knew that Bart abused her. Did her mother turn away from the knowledge, or did he fool her, too, as he had so many others in the community. Would her mother be lucid enough for Belle to know the answer to her questions?

It was ten years since they had seen each other. Belle thought about visiting but until this day, she didn't trust herself to confront her mother with the question that haunted her all these years. Now, the day before she was to leave town again something was drawing Belle to her childhood home.

Or, perhaps she just needed to know if her mother really cared about her.

So she came, even though time was short. One Night Stand was leaving in their new tour bus the next day and she still had to pack. Frank was waiting for her to say goodbye before driving back to Las Vegas.

She knocked and waited, knocked again harder. From the corner of her eye she thought she saw the curtain in the front window move.

"Ma?" Belle shouted. "Ma, open up, it's Belle." She pounded on the door, hard.

Finally the door opened just a crack. Belle couldn't see who was there, but she guessed it was her mother. The door opened wider and a thin disheveled woman with a frightened look in her eyes, said," Belle?"

"Yes, Mama, it's me. Can I come in?"

"Oh, Belle, I'm so happy to see you. It's been such a long time." Her hands waved aimlessly in the air around her.

"Yes, Ma, it has, hasn't it?" Belle wondered if she should hug her. But Nadine turned and pushed a path ahead threading her way through stacks of magazines, boxes, and old radio and television sets. Belle followed behind through what looked like the back room of a Goodwill donor center.

"Come in, come in. I'll make some tea."

Belle saw that the door was shut to her old bedroom. She shivered though the house was hot. She didn't want to look inside that room. It held too many bad memories. She thought of her last day in this house, before she ran away. So much had happened since then. Sometimes her life before that day seemed like a bad dream, a nightmare.

In the kitchen, Nadine put a kettle of water on the stove. She searched the cupboards until she found two cups and two teabags. She sat down across from Belle at the metal kitchen table, running her fingers through her hair. It was mostly gray now, thin and stringy. Her lips pinched into a little bow. Her skin was wrinkled and sallow; a yellowish-gray.

It was disappointing. Belle had hoped for a warmer welcome.

Belle looked around the kitchen. It was the same, except the counters were cluttered, and dishes were piled in the sink. Her mother had always been so neat, even obsessive about having a clean house.

Nadine raised her eyes to the counter where a yellow and white cat was sniffing through the dishes in the sink.

"Rosie, get down!" Nadine swiped at the cat and Rosie bolted from the room.

The kitchen was hot but Nadine pulled on a sweater. "I just can't seem to get warm today. But the tea will help."

"Ma, how are you?" Belle searched her face. Nadine's eyes darted around the room.

"Oh, I'm fine, Belle." She glanced at the ceiling, then back at Belle. "You didn't tell me, how is school? Or have you graduated?"

"I never went away to school, Ma. What gave you that idea anyhow?"

"Someone told me that a long time ago." She stared at Belle and frowned, her eyes intent. "I can't remember who. My memory isn't so good any more."

"Well, I never went away to school. I ran away so I wouldn't get arrested. The Sheriff thought I killed Bart."

"Are you sure? That doesn't sound like Horace McMahan." She took the tea bag from her empty cup and laid it on the table.

"It's true, Ma. I just got out of jail."

"You were in jail? The detective from Las Vegas told me that but I didn't believe it."

"Yes, I was in jail. But everything is cleared up now. Everything is fine, Ma."

Nadine rose and stood behind her chair, leaning on the back of it.

"I just don't know what to do. I'm out of tea now and Joe won't be here to get groceries until tomorrow. I don't know what to do." Her fingers flitted over her mouth.

"I'll bring you some more tea, okay, Ma? But I want to talk to you about something. Do you remember when I ran away?"

"Oh, yes. You went away to school, didn't you? What was it you were studying, I forget?" Her fingers tapped across her mouth again.

"No, Ma, I ran away because they thought I killed Bart." All of a sudden Belle wanted to be out of there. *This was going nowhere*, she thought.

Nadine sat down and dropped the tea bag back into her cup. Her eyes circled the room again. Belle didn't know who this woman was, but it wasn't her mother.

Belle found it hard to breathe in the hot stuffy kitchen. She fanned herself with a paper that was lying on the table.

"The Reverend is in heaven now, God rest his soul. He was such a holy man." Nadine sat down again and rocked slowly in her chair, arms folded across her chest.

"I don't know where he is but I hope he's burning in hell." Belle's voice was angry.

Nadine stopped rocking. "Don't talk evil about the dead, Belle. I raised you better than that."

"Bart was raping me ever since I was nine years old. Did you know that, Ma? Sometimes I thought you did, and

I really hated you for that, for letting him do it. Did you know?" Belle tried to catch Nadine's eyes but she was staring at the table top.

The kettle whistled. Nadine pushed her chair back, making a little screech on the bare floor. She rushed to the stove.

"Oh, dear, the kettle's boiling. I'll just be a minute, dear."

Nadine dropped the kettle onto the table and sat down again.

"Ma, this is important to me. Could you see what was happening? And if you did, why didn't you stop him? I understand if you were afraid of him, too."

"Me afraid of the Reverend? No, I wasn't afraid of him."

"But he raped me!" Her voice was loud and angry.

"He always said he loved you, Belle, and he raised you like his own."

"For years, Ma, he raped me, and no one stopped him. He said it was God's will, and he forced me. I couldn't stop him." Belle's face was flushed and she fought back tears." I was a child!" Again it washed over her, engulfed her; the terror, the anger, the helplessness of a child.

Belle leaned across the table.

"I wanted to tell you but he said it would kill you if I did. I even told the Sheriff once and he didn't do anything about it either." Belle wiped tears from her face.

Nadine stared at Belle; eyes wide, mouth open Then she brushed away crumbs from the table in front of her.

"Oh, dear, could you be mistaken? Maybe you were dreaming." She lifted the kettle and poured hot water into their cups. Her hands shook and a little water spilled on the table. She wiped it away with a towel.

Belle thought of the day she poured tea for her dolls,

the day her Daddy shot himself. She could see Sarah and Janie waiting in their chairs. Janie was smiling, showing two little teeth, white and square as Chiclets.

It was all in the past. It had nothing to do with her today. She wouldn't let it come back. She wouldn't let it be a part of her life again.

Nadine reached over and patted Belle's arm, twice. Belle looked up at her mother. Two tears were tracing a path down Nadine's cheeks. Her eyes met Belle's.

"Oh, that's too bad. That's just too bad."

Belle sat back, stunned. She felt drained. She looked at her mother's face.

Then she drew her eyes away and stared at the cupboard under the sink.

Many years ago, so many that it almost seemed like it had never happened, Belle watched as her mother reached into the cupboard under the sink and brought out the box with the skull and crossbones on the front. Nadine opened it and sprinkled the white powder under the ice box.

"Don't get any on your hands, Belle. It's poison. The rats will eat this and die. It takes a couple of weeks, but it works really well." At night you could hear the rats scurrying around, their claws scratching the kitchen floor. Later, Belle watched her mother pick up their dead bodies with a broom and dustpan.

One night after Bart left Belle's room, she lay awake listening for her mother to come home. And she thought of the box of white powder.

Then one evening, just as she had imagined it many times, Belle took the box from under the cupboard. She took a teaspoon from the drawer, drew out a tiny amount of the white powder. Such a small amount surely couldn't be tasted. She swirled it into the mashed potatoes on Bart's plate of food. Then she quickly put the box back under the sink, exactly where she found it. She covered the potatoes with milk gravy that she had made from the pork chop grease, then carried it to the dining room table and placed it on the table in front of Bart.

After carefully washing her hands and the spoon, she fixed a plate of pork chops, gravy, mashed potatoes and green beans for her mother and carried it to the table. Returning to the kitchen once more, she fixed her own plate.

The next night, she added a bit more poison to Bart's plate. And the next, even more.

Sometimes Bart would bend over the sink, hold his stomach and retch bloody mucous. Nadine urged her husband to call the doctor, but he wouldn't. "I'll be fine. I just have a sensitive stomach," he would say.

Belle added more and more of the white powder to Bart's food. One evening, the night before he was killed, he stopped eating in the middle of supper and raised his head. He held his fork in midair, and stared at Belle. She lowered her eyes. He pushed his plate away, still staring at her. He asked her if she wanted the rest of his food. She shook her head, excused herself, and went to her room. Bart scraped his food into the trash. Nadine asked, *what was wrong*, but he said nothing.

This is what Belle told Oliver Force that day in jail when he asked her for the truth. He had stared at the floor for a few minutes, and then looked up at her,

When he spoke, his voice was low, almost a whisper. "Belle, I'm glad you told me this. Now listen carefully. Don't ever tell it to another soul. No one, you hear? Ever. You already have all the trouble you need. The poison did not cause Bart's death. You did not kill him. He was hit on the head with a rock."

She spent nine years believing that she killed Bart. Nine

years running and punishing herself. She collapsed with relief, falling onto the jail bunk and sobbing. Oliver awkwardly patted her shoulder, then got up and called the jailer. "Remember; tell no one." And she never had.

Then it hit Belle. Here in this muggy kitchen with the sink full of dirty dishes and Rosie jumping up on the counter again, it jolted her like a clap of thunder. Black Bart was gone and he couldn't ever hurt her again. But if she let him reach out from the grave and muddy up her life, then he still had control of her. She wouldn't forget what he had done, but she wouldn't let him invade her thoughts or spur her anger. She wouldn't let him make her bitter.

Belle stared out the smudged up kitchen window and smiled.

Nadine looked at her, cocked her head to one side and she smiled, too. "Belle, are you going to get my tea now?" She wiped her face with both hands.

Belle pulled her eyes from the window and looked at her mother. Then she stood, walked over to her and put an arm around her bony shoulders. "I'll go right now." Nadine reached up and patted her arm again, twice. Belle kissed her cheek.

Then she moved towards the kitchen door.

"Wait a minute." Nadine jumped up from her chair and stepped in front of her. She turned and beckoned for Belle to follow. She paused at Belle's bedroom door, and then slowly pushed it open. Shaking, Belle followed her inside.

It was exactly the way Belle left it. Stuffed animals, and her dolls, Janie and Sarah, sat on the pink chenille bedspread. Pink curtains, dusty and criss-crossed with spider webs, still hung in the window. Her comb and hairbrush on the dresser were just where she left them. Belle, stunned, sat down on the bed.

Nadine crossed the room and opened the closet door. She reached inside and brought out a battered guitar and placed it in Belle's lap.

"Ma! The guitar my Daddy made for me. I can't believe you still have it." Belle stroked the guitar, watched her tears spill down on it. "You always hated the music we played."

Nadine smiled, her eyes soft, head turned with her chin slightly elevated, and gazed at Belle. Ma had looked at her like that when Belle, age five, had recited a Bible verse in church. She pronounced each word perfectly, with just the right inflection, and didn't forget a single one. Her voice was firm and confident. Then she bowed and curtsied at the audience.

Nadine's smile gradually faded, her mouth opened and her eyes, vacant and staring, looked about the room. She stood and Belle followed her out. Belle took one more look at her bed with the pink chenille spread before she closed the bedroom door behind her.

"Don't forget my tea, now." Nadine, head bent, turned and slowly walked her way towards the kitchen.

Belle slung the guitar strap over her shoulder and made her way through the Goodwill room and out the front door. She stepped off the porch and looked back at the peeling paint, the sagging porch steps. *I'll have to get someone to fix up the house,* she thought, *now that I have enough money.*

A spring breeze cooled the back of her neck, damp from the stifling heat inside. She climbed into Jess' truck and turned the key in the ignition. She paused and looked at the guitar on the seat beside her and smiled.

She backed out of the driveway and pulled into the street.

Ahead, the road was clear.

Printed in the United States
203565BV00002B/577-606/P

9 781432 724788